PARADISE FOUND

MACY BUTLER

PARADISE PRESS

For my favorite race car driver. You know who you are and why this one's for you.

CHAPTER 1

*S*oft wet sand squishes between my toes. My fleeting footprints are washed away in the waves that tickle my ankles. Boomer bounds along beside me, weaving in and out of the surf, growling as he bites at the whitecaps of the breaking waves. The horizon explodes in color: orange, yellow, and peach fade into the bluest blue. The powdery white beach stretches to infinity ahead. The warm, salty air fills me so much I might burst. It is sunrise and I'm happy to be alive.

The cheery song of my phone's alarm dragged me from my dream. I squinted through one eye, dreading the light, but only a dim grey penetrated the sheer curtains covering my big bay window. June in San Francisco. I hit snooze and pulled a pillow over my head, wishing I could go back to that dream full of color and hope, resisting the grey reality of my life falling apart around me. I was surprised it wasn't the drowning dream that woke me like it so often had in the past months. If ever there was a day I felt like I was drowning, it was today.

Boomer's wet snout on my foot coaxed me from my despair and the bed. That dog has literally been my reason for getting out of bed in the morning for the past six months. His enthusiasm and unconditional love made up for so much I'd lacked since Chuck left. Many days Boomer was the sole source of my smiles. Except for Elliot. He's good for a grin, too. Especially after a cocktail or two.

The bathroom tile was freezing under my feet as I made my way to the toilet. Why did summer sometimes feel even colder than winter in the Bay Area? The fog, I knew, but I still hadn't gotten used to it even after seventeen years.

My phone vibrated on the counter beside me while I held my feet up off the cold tile as I peed. A reminder. SIGN PAPERS. As if I needed reminding. I turned the phone over and tried to forget.

I knew this day was coming, but knowing can't prepare you for the rug being yanked out from under your life. The floor seemed to shift under me when the phone buzzed with the vibration of a silent ring. Elliot. He'd be worried about me on this momentous day.

I wiped my tears as if he might see them when I answered. "Hey."

"Good morning, sunshine!"

"Oh yeah, great morning indeed." My sarcasm was as thick as the morning fog. Summer in the Bay Area was anything but summery. Today at least it seemed fitting for the grey circumstances.

Undeterred by my pessimism, Elliot continued excitedly, "It's the first day of the rest of your life. It *is* a great morning, you'll see."

I rolled my teary red eyes as I wiped my nose with the back of my hand. "Wow, you're overly chipper today."

"I thought you'd need cheering up. I'm on my way over."

"Over? You mean to my house? Why?" I smoothed tinted moisturizer over my face and neck to hide the splotches that always appear like a reddened raccoon when I cry.

"I have almond croissants from Boudins. After breakfast, I'll take you to sign the papers."

"Oh, that's sweet. But Leila is picking me up on her way in." I ran a brush through my brown locks that looked as dull as I felt.

"Wow, that's service."

It was true. Leila was going above and beyond her lawyer duties. But she had also become a friend during this whole ugly process.

I held the phone with my shoulder and leaned into the mirror to paint my lashes with mascara. Waterproof, of course. "Yeah, I think she was afraid I might not show up."

"Rightfully so. You haven't exactly been enthusiastic about the process," Elliot chided. He had nudged me along every stage of the divorce. "But you sound like you're doing well. So if you really don't want me to come over, then I guess I'll see you later?"

"Yeah, sure. Let's talk this afternoon." I didn't want to see anyone or do anything. I wanted to bury myself back under the covers and pretend this day wasn't finally happening. Did it really sound like I was doing okay? It sure didn't feel like it.

I gave myself a once-over in the floor length mirror after putting on a designer pantsuit. After six months practice, I was good at looking put together even when I was falling apart.

Boomer dragged me by his leash on a quick six-block walk through the foggy hills of Pacific Heights. Thank goodness we bought there a couple of years after moving to the west coast when the market had tanked. We were broke after buying, so it took us years to remodel and convert the downstairs into a high-rent apartment that had pretty much paid for the remodeling in the five years it had been renting.

At least I got to keep the top half of the house in the divorce. And Boomer. The two things I loved most in life. It could have been much worse.

The passenger door of Leila's Prius flung open as she rolled to a stop in front of my house. Her smile was infectious. "Hop in, chica." I love that she calls me chica, owing to her maternal Colombian roots. Something about it makes me feel young and vibrant instead of worn out and worn down.

The seatbelt tightened around me as we accelerated. "Thanks for picking me up."

"No problem." She was all business when she handed me a folder. "Here is the final draft of the settlement. It includes all the changes we discussed. If you want to browse through it now, it may be easier for you than when we're there."

I pressed my forearms down into my thighs to steady my shaking hands as I opened the folder. The blood left my face and sank into the pit of my stomach. There it was in black and white. Our names on two lines separated by a small space that somehow fit nearly twenty years lost. Charles Edward Bright and Teresa Marie Taylor Bright. Dissolution of Marriage. All the other words blurred.

It was us, dissolving. If I'd been anywhere other than in Leila's Prius, I would have vomited.

I blinked through the tears and smoothed the paper with my palms. Leila studied me while trying to focus on the road, her hand finding mine. "Hey now, you've got this. It's exactly like we discussed. All spelled out. Go to page three. That's where the real details start."

I turned the page and blinked three times, attempting to make sense of the legal jargon, but I couldn't focus on the words. I gave up and closed the folder. "If you say it's how we discussed, I trust you. I can't read it right now. It's making me kind of car sick." A lie, but a good one.

"Yes, it's exactly as we discussed. Pretty much everything split down the middle. The house is being divided on the deed into two apartments. He pays you for half the value of his car since you only had one. You maintain 50% partnership in the business, unless you've changed your mind on Chuck's offer. You may want to reconsider."

"No, definitely not. I'm staying."

"I hear you. But it's a lot of money. You could do something totally different, something that could be your own."

My heart raced and my face flamed in fury. "Fuck him. I worked my ass off for fifteen years building that business. Harder than he ever did. I made it what it is. There is no way in hell I'd sell out. He can start over if anyone does. I'm keeping what's mine."

Leila grasped my hand with the confidence of a friend. "I know, I know. You know how I feel about it. If you'd let me, I'd be pressing to get you more out of this deal. You're being far too kind, considering."

Considering that Chuck had made me the biggest fucking cliché ever when he left me for his doe-eyed secretary fourteen years his junior. He'd made a mockery of our whole existence, and for that, he should pay. I didn't see it that way though. I was too hurt and dejected. I just wanted to get it all over with. I couldn't stop him from leaving, but I wasn't about to let him take my life with him on the way out.

Leila eyed me as she continued, "But I can see why you want to stay in the business. And buying Chuck out may not be entirely out of the question. Even though he refused when you countered with the same offer that he made you, they did request that we include a clause that either of you has two years to request a buy out from the other at a similar price."

I squinted and wrinkled my brow. "My first instinct is to say no, but I'm trying to understand, why the caveat?"

"I guess it gives you both an out if the partnership is not going well, and a set price so you can't try to gouge or shortchange one another if one is desperate to get out. As it's written, it can't be forced upon either of you, but it's available as an option at your request. And of course, you are not obligated to accept. Think of it as a parachute. Not a bad idea to have one if you're flying high and potentially into a storm."

"Yeah, a shit storm." At least I could make myself laugh. "What's the specified price?"

"It's basically 90% of the offered settlement, so just under two million. Of course, if the company increases in value then it's to your disadvantage to have the set price. It's not likely to decrease in value, with your track record. Bottom line, it's a fair deal for the short term."

Two million sounded like a ton of money, but I was not the least bit tempted by it. I'd happily find a way to come up with it myself if Chuck would take it and get out of my life. Seeing him nearly every day for the six months since he left had been difficult at best, and torturous at worst. At least the slutty secretary had quit as soon as news of the affair broke. But still.

"Alright, sounds fair enough. Hopefully, he'll be the one to pull the cord." I imagined Chuck falling from the roof of a building, grasping and tugging at the ripcord in a panic. Some things still made me smile.

He was already seated at the conference table when we entered. His attorney and the mediator stood but Chuck didn't even bother. He kept his focus down toward the table when everyone else exchanged handshakes. Fucking coward. For some reason his shame or nervousness, or whatever it was, empowered me. I tugged at the hem of my blazer and lifted my chin before choosing the seat directly across from him. His attorney spoke first, to Leila.

"I take it you've reviewed the few minor changes made to the settlement with your client?"

"Yes, we have. Ms. Taylor accepts all of the proposed changes." Hearing my maiden name caught me off guard almost as much as the new prefix. Fifteen years as Mrs. Bright. Now I was Ms. Taylor again. How strange. I crossed my arms to squash the goosebumps that rose to the surface, a lame attempt to hold in the confidence I had gained from

Chuck's cowardice. It was seeping from my pores. Leila knew I wanted to change my legal name as soon as the divorce was final, but I wasn't sure I was ready to call myself Tessa Taylor again.

"If all parties are in agreement, then please proceed with signing the documents. Ms. Taylor?"

I pressed my hand flat into the paper that the mediator pushed toward me to mask the trembling. The invisible cracks in my shell had leaked the confidence like a sieve. I felt faint as a knot rose to my throat. I cleared my throat and kept my eyes fixed on the paper, trying hard to get my shit together. I squeezed the pen tight and focused all my concentration on signing my name on the line Leila pointed out for me. I placed the pen softly on the paper and pushed it to the center of the table when I finished. Only then did I exhale. Chuck took the paper and signed it quickly, without apparent difficulty. His lawyer passed it to the mediator to sign, and just like that, it was done. Legal. Dissolved.

Leila stood to shake the mediator's hand. I didn't think I could move, but somehow, I felt myself stand and extend my hand to him as well. My feet felt like someone else's as they carried me down the hall to the elevator. Leila's firm hand on my shoulder brought me back into my body as we waited.

"You did it."

The smile I feigned felt awkward. "Yay, me. I survived." I tugged at my blazer hem again. "Piece of cake."

"That's right. And now you can move on. Keep looking forward, Tessa. This is behind you. Congratulations!"

Forward seemed impossible now that my whole life was

behind me. Everything I had built. There was little appeal in anything that may lie ahead. I just wanted my bed.

I hugged Leila before the elevator doors opened to the lobby. "Thanks for everything. You've been wonderful."

"It's been a pleasure, Tessa. You know you can call me anytime. I've got your back."

"Yeah, I know. Let's have dinner in a couple of weeks, after the divorce dust settles."

Leila patted me on the back as we exited the turning doorway to the street. "Sounds great. Want me to give you a ride to the office?"

"No, thanks. I think I'll walk. I can use the fresh air."

Elliot sat on the edge of the giant planter at the top of the steps outside the building. His smile lit up when our eyes met.

I punched him lightly in the shoulder. "Hey, what are you doing here?"

"Moral support. And almond croissants." He held up a crumpled brown paper bag stained with buttery grease spots.

I laced my arm through Elliot's when he stood and walked with him. "You're a real sweetheart. But I'm okay. And I really have to get to the office. There's a lot going on today and I'm already late."

"Come on, can't you take ten minutes for a coffee? Did I mention almond croissants?" He shook the bag in front of me, knowing they were my favorite.

I squeezed his forearm. "Honestly, I can't right now. How about later?" The thought of food turned my stomach.

"Okay, dinner after work then?"

"Okay, maybe. Let's see how it's going."

"No, no maybe. You'll try to back out. Come on, I'll pick up Chinese and a bottle of wine and be at your place at six-thirty?"

I didn't want to be sociable, but booze did sound appealing. I could already use a drink. "Alright, alright."

"Okay. Don't stand me up." Elliot kissed me on the cheek.

"I would never." I squeezed his trim waist in a hug before I left him at the BART station and continued toward my office. Elliot was a persistent friend. More than once, he had shown up to force me out of bed, if only to snuggle beside me and watch Netflix on the couch all day. He had seen the ugliest parts of my struggle and somehow managed to pull me up from the lowest points—usually with crass jokes and insults. He would often say that no man was ever going to want me if I kept dressing in yoga pants and sweatshirts. Or how did I expect to find another man if I never washed my hair or left the house on weekends?

Elliot knew that getting a date was not even on the bottom of my priority list, but he liked to encourage it. And he was quite the expert, a Bay Area playboy of sorts. Between the plethora of bars that he frequents in the Castro and the gay hookup apps, picking up a guy is as easy as buying fresh bread for Elliot. I sometimes begged him to spare me the details, but he bragged often of his prowess. He claimed that getting laid would snap me out of the post-break-up funk.

"You need one big D to make you forget about Chuck. Just one, and poof, he will vanish from your consciousness," he told me over wine one night. I laughed, but what I thought was: *Yeah, one big D to erase a lifetime of memories... I don't think so*. Besides, I didn't want another D. Chuck's was only the fourth I had seen in my life and only the third I'd had inside me. The thought of opening myself up like that to someone new did not appeal. I was fragile and raw and not the least bit horny.

CHAPTER 2

*M*y quads quivered with each step up to the entrance of my office building. I was an equal partner and had done more than my share of the work in building our business, but the first day as a divorcee, no longer Chuck's wife, was annoyingly intimidating. Chuck was often regarded as the owner of our firm, and I his wife. Even in a progressive place like San Francisco, the boys club still ruled at the higher levels. Of course, I noticed. Of course, I was bitter. But I held my own by working twice as hard and ruthlessly negotiating better deals for us than Chuck ever could. I let others believe that he was in charge, I let him believe it. But I knew that I was the one calling the shots most of the time while Chuck was schmoozing the old white guys.

The sight of the sign on the door made my stomach drop. Bright Solutions. A nice little play on words when your last name is Bright. A gut-punch when it's not. I puffed up my chest with a deep breath and pushed into the reception area with feigned confidence. "Good morning, Rachel." I nodded as I passed the receptionist.

"Good morning, Mrs. Bright."

I stopped, almost corrected her, but instead smiled and carried on. In limbo between names, between states. I was a divorced woman. I was Tessa Taylor. I just wasn't ready to accept it yet. It was too surreal. I strode past the cubicles in the center and veered left to my office, stopping first at the desk outside my door. I picked up the stack of papers in the top tray on the corner of Marjorie's desk.

"Morning, Marjorie."

"Good morning, Tessa. Everything okay?" She looked over her glasses at me, trying to read my feelings, I could tell.

"Everything's fine." I shifted my gaze to avoid hers. She knew me well after twelve years of organizing my life, so she could probably tell that I didn't want to talk about it, but I closed my office door behind me just in case. I thumbed through the stack of mail, every last piece of it addressed to my former self. My palms itched with moisture and my stomach rolled over. I threw the mail onto the desk and leaned back in my chair and rubbed my eyes, trying to find clarity or perhaps to hold back the tears that threatened to spring forth. I didn't think I could do it, any of it. I wanted my bed and Boomer licking my face.

I went to my private bathroom and splashed water on my face, then gave myself a stern talking to in the mirror. "You've been doing this for six months already. It's no different now. Get your shit together and get to work."

I opened my laptop and pulled up my schedule. It was clear. That was strange. I was sure I had an eleven-thirty call scheduled with Milligan Software. I called Marjorie on the intercom.

"Marjorie, did they call to reschedule the Milligan call?"

"I moved it to Brad. I wasn't sure you'd be back in time. And since he's been working that account with you, I thought he could cover in case."

"Oh. Okay. Good idea. But I can take it. Please let Brad know. Or, never mind. I'll tell him to join me here for the call."

"Yes, Mrs... Um, alright, Tessa. No problem. Shall I let the Milligan group know?"

"You *told* them I wouldn't be on the call?"

She paused for long enough to make me think she was gauging my annoyance level. Her response was calm and even-keeled, as always. "Yes, when I confirmed the appointment yesterday afternoon I mentioned that Brad might be the one on the call, since you had another appointment out of the office that possibly could run long."

"Okay, no problem. Let Brad know to join me here for the call." I punched the button harder than I needed to disconnect the intercom. Damn her. I wasn't sure if I was more pissed that she had doubted whether I would have my shit together enough to handle the call, or that she was right in doubting me. Luckily I am motivated by anger. I was going to keep my shit together just to show her.

I pulled up the Milligan file and reviewed the details of the contract. Marjorie was right, Brad was a major player on that account. He had done most of the work after I negotiated the deal and made the proposal. He totally could have handled it on his own. But it was my deal. And I was calling the shots. Goddammit.

After the Milligan call, I ate pretzels from the vending machine for lunch and opened my schedule to plan for the rest of the week. The next day was clear. Nothing. I knew there had been a morning meeting with my design team on the Milligan account, and a call to Brumley's in the afternoon. I opened Monday of next week, and found it cleared too, as was the rest of the week. What the hell? Surely Marjorie hadn't taken it upon herself to rearrange my schedule for a week. This was going too far.

I punched hard at the intercom button again. "Marjorie, come in please."

She closed the door behind her when she entered without my asking. Highly unusual. She knew something was up. I narrowed my eyes at her when she sat across from me. "Can you please explain why my schedule is clear for all of next week?"

Marjorie folded her hands in her lap. "Yes, I cleared your schedule. I know it was presumptuous. And I apologize."

I blinked at her with an open mouth. "Why would you do that?"

"I have been extremely concerned for you. You have thrown yourself into your work and for all these months it's seemed to be your reason for living. You've been here twelve hours a day most days. I hope you don't take this the wrong way, but I feel like you need someone to say it. You are not taking care of yourself, Tessa. Your clothes are hanging off your body. You have dark circles under your eyes. And your focus is not what it normally is."

I took a deep breath and tried to visualize the color blue, a technique I had learned years ago while building our business to calm my hot head before speaking to people who weren't hearing me. If I weren't convinced of Marjorie's sincerity, I'd fire her on the spot. The blue trick wasn't working. I saw red. I stood and slapped the desk with both hands, making her jump. I immediately felt guilty for startling her but persisted in my rant. "Alright, it is one thing to be told I look like shit. But another entirely to imply I am not doing my job."

Marjorie stared up at me from across the desk with sad eyes. "Tessa, please don't take it personally. I was, I am, trying to look after you, because, quite frankly, no one else is."

I was insulted, but Marjorie's compassionate gaze dissipated my anger. She was right. I was running myself into the ground. Marjorie was playing mom, which was exactly what I needed. When I thought about the two thousand miles between me and my own mom... I bit my lip to try to stop it from trembling, but it was no use. I sat back down and covered my face with my hands. The tears I'd held back flowed like a river.

Marjorie came around the desk and laid a hand on my shoulder to comfort me without a word as I sobbed. When my sobs slowed, she squatted beside me. I swiveled my chair to face her.

She gently placed her hands on my knees. "Tessa, I've been with you almost thirteen years. You are like family to me. I want what is best for you. And right now, I think you need to get some rest and perspective. That's why I cleared your schedule for two weeks."

Two weeks? Was she crazy? No way could I be away from the office for two weeks. There was way too much work. What would I do with myself anyway? She was right, all I did was work. But I loved my work. I needed it to keep me grounded.

I needed it to make me get dressed and get out of the house every day.

I rested my hands on Marjorie's shoulders. "Thank you. You know you're like family to me, too. I know you are trying to look after me. And you're probably right, some time off would do me good. But I can't be away for that long. There is too much going on here." Although it might be nice to go back east to visit family, three days would be plenty of time for that. Maybe I would do that sometime soon.

Her warm smile reminded me of my mother's as she squeezed the tops of my knees before standing. "I'll be right back." Marjorie returned with a folder and sat across from me.

"Here's what you had on the schedule for the next two weeks. Primarily it was the coordination of the Milligan and Brumley accounts. Brad has been working on both of those with you, and neither of those projects are in the early stages. There are no new clients scheduled. I easily shifted the meetings to Brad. You don't *need* to be here."

She had no idea how much I needed to be there. While spending fifteen straight days in my bed seemed like a dream, I knew that was a dark hole I'd better not fall into. It was hard enough to crawl out of it on Monday mornings. Two weeks alone with my thoughts might put me over the edge to Cuckoo Land.

"Marjorie, I appreciate you. But I really do need to be here. It's good for me to focus on work. It keeps me going right now. Please shift everything back to my schedule starting next week. I'll take tomorrow off. I need a pedicure and I'll get a massage to recharge. I'll be back on Monday good as new."

Marjorie pushed another paper across the desk to me. I blinked as I read it, trying to make sense of the words. Flight itinerary? SFO to GCM—a redeye leaving Saturday night, the day after tomorrow. GCM? Where was that? I read the fine print. Owen Roberts International Airport. Never heard of that either. Passenger details. Teresa Marie Taylor Bright. What the hell?

"What is this? You booked me a flight? To where?"

"Yes. As I said, I know it was presumptuous. But I knew if I asked you'd say no. And you're not likely to book a holiday for yourself right now, even though it's exactly what you need."

Heat rose to my face. "Ha! Wow, this is really something. Where are you trying to send me exactly?"

"Grand Cayman. I booked you into an all-inclusive five-star resort as well." She handed me another paper from the folder.

An angry fire burned in my belly but I was also on the verge of laughter at the ridiculousness of it all. "Oh, did you now?"

"Yes, I booked the ticket and the resort with company miles and points."

I leaned back in my chair and inhaled deeply to keep my cool. "Thank you, Marjorie, but that is impossible. Please cancel it immediately. I hope you can get a refund. It would be a shame to waste all those miles on this mistake."

"It's fully refundable until tomorrow night. Will you at least think about it? I am sorry if I overstepped. But honestly, I think it would do you some good."

"I'll consider a vacation soon but this is not the right time."

The finality in my tone left nothing further to discuss. Marjorie nodded as she gathered the papers and stood to leave.

She was almost to the door when it occurred to me to ask. "Why Grand Cayman?"

"I went for a day on a cruise a couple of years ago. It was gorgeous. Beaches that stretched for miles and the bluest water I've ever seen. It seemed the perfect spot to get away from it all. I thought you'd like it." The endearing sweetness of her voice oozed sincerity and cooled my annoyance.

"Maybe I will someday."

I spent the rest of the afternoon organizing my schedule for the next week. I hated to admit it, but Marjorie was right. Everything was under control. My workaholic tendencies were good for more than just distraction, it seemed. Work was the thing I felt like I was doing right. The only thing. Letting go of that right now, even for a vacation, didn't seem good for me.

CHAPTER 3

*E*lliot juggled two bags of Chinese food in one hand and two bottles of wine in the other while Boomer wagged his whole butt. "Hey, buddy. Did you miss me?"

I laughed. "You're his favorite visitor."

"I'm your *only* visitor, Tessa."

"Oh shut up. Did you work late?"

"Yeah, it's been a little crazy."

He reached behind me to retrieve the wine tool from the drawer while I unpacked the paper boxes of food. "I didn't get to ask you this morning, you were in such a hurry. Did everything go as planned? I mean, no surprises?"

I had to smile. Elliot didn't trust Chuck any further than he could throw him. "No, no surprises— No wait, there was one that caught me off guard, but I think it is beneficial for us both so we let them have it."

Elliot cocked his head. "A last-minute change that was in *your* interest? What might that be?"

"A clause allowing either of us to request a buyout in the next two years, for a specified amount, but no obligation to accept."

Elliot nodded and poured two generous glasses of a Sonoma cabernet that we both loved. "Hmmm, I guess that could be good if you get sick of him and want to sell out. So then he can't try to cheat you."

"I was thinking of it the other way around, that hopefully he'll want to sell and won't be able to gouge me knowing that I'd love for him to go the hell away."

"Yeah, I think you both feel that way. It's so funny you both fought to stay in it together but neither of you really wants to be there with the other."

I rolled my eyes and took a big sip of wine. "Yeah, that's hilarious."

"Oh, you know what I mean. And I get it. Neither of you would dare let the other have it. You're equally stubborn. So, the future is precarious."

"It will be fine. We've been doing it for six months already. The one thing we were good at together was business. We're adults. We can do what needs to be done."

"I know you can do it. I know you will do it. But I wonder if you can be happy doing it. It's good that you have a built-in out."

"Yeah, Leila called it a parachute. I wish he'd pull the cord already and get out of my life."

"He's as stubborn as you are, so that's not likely. But how are you taking it? Did you feel any different?"

I laughed and handed him a plate of Szechuan chicken. "You ask as if getting divorced is like losing my virginity. And in both cases, no, I didn't feel any different. Not really."

"I felt totally different after I lost my virginity. Both times."

Elliot was always good for a laugh. "Both times?"

"Yeah, the first time was in high school, with a girl. I felt way different after that one. I was pretty sure before, but having sex with Molly McMadden made me 100% certain I was gay."

I giggled while chewing a bite of scrumptious chicken. I didn't realize how hungry I was. "Ha! Well, I guess that was life changing."

"How about yours? Who was your first?"

"Brandon Reynolds. The dreamy quarterback I had dated for over six months senior year. It was okay. But not life changing."

"Sex with the dreamy quarterback was just okay? I'd expect much more, Tessa."

"Yeah, well, I did, too. He was kind of a jerk. I finally gave in to his persistent pressure and just did it. It wasn't terrible, but it wasn't what I had imagined." How many times have I had that same thought since in my life? Maybe my expectations set me up for let-downs. Or maybe I keep betting on the wrong horse. "Anyway, back to the original question. No, I don't feel different. It's been a long time coming. Signing the paper doesn't change anything."

Elliot threw his hands up. "Um, yes it does. It changes everything. You are free!"

Then why did I feel like I was drowning? I looked down at the wine I swirled in my glass and chuckled. "I don't feel free yet. Maybe it hasn't sunk in."

"Well you are free, and you should start acting like it."

"Free to do what?"

"Free to do whatever the hell you want. Free to go where you want, be who you want, sleep with who you want!" The excitement level in his voice rose with each proclamation.

"But I've been free to do all those things for six months already, hence my feeling that nothing's any different now."

"Well, you sure as hell haven't *done* any of those things in the last six months. Maybe making it legal will allow you to actually move on."

Ouch. It was all true, but it wasn't easy to hear. "Yeah, maybe. But, to be honest, I am living the life I want to live. I mean, I know I work a lot, but I love my work. As far as going places and sleeping with other people, those things are just not on my mind right now."

Elliot pushed his glass to the side and reached across the table to take both my hands in his. "But, Sweet T, those are things that *should* be on your mind right now. All you do is work. And hang out with me when I make you. You really do need to get a *new* life."

I reached across the table to squeeze his hand and smiled. "You and Boomer are all I need right now. Thanks for bringing dinner."

"Someone's got to feed you. You've skipped too many dinners lately, my dear." He grinned. "Your booty is disappearing.

Those yoga pants are supposed to be snug. How are you going to find a man with your hip bones sticking out like that? This isn't LA, Tess. Men up here like a little meat on the bones."

"I know you know what men like more than I do, but you shouldn't worry about me. You guys act like I'm wasting away here, wallowing in misery. I'm really fine. Just fine."

"You guys? Who else is worrying over you? I thought it was only me."

I washed down a bite of food with a sip of wine. "Oh no, Marjorie too. She tried playing Mother Hen today before I put her in her place."

Elliot's eyes grew wide. "How so?"

"She thought I needed to take some time off, so she took it upon herself to clear my schedule for the next *two weeks*."

Elliot's eyes widened. "Wow, that was pretty bold. But, honestly, it probably wouldn't be a bad idea, Tessa. I mean, you could use a break."

I laughed, hard. He couldn't be serious. "Yeah, right. After fighting so hard to stay in the company, I'm going to take a two-week vacation right after the divorce is final? No fucking way. I am not the weakling."

"Taking care of yourself does not make you weak, my dear. It makes you strong."

"What the fuck ever. No way is that happening right now. And especially if it's not my idea. I mean, imagine, she went and *booked a trip* for me. Airfare. All-inclusive resort. The whole nine yards. And somehow, she thought I might actually go for it. Ridiculous!"

Elliot looked amused. His dark brows raised. "Get out! The whole trip booked? To where?"

"Grand Cayman." I said it like she was sending me to the moon. Or Nebraska. "I've never thought once about going there. Never heard a single thing about it. And, poof, I'm supposed to disappear Saturday night for two weeks on a whim, on *her* whim. Um, no."

"Whoa. She did that? *Marjorie* did that?" He knew meek little Marjorie.

"Yeah, I was pretty shocked, too. I mean, really, does she not know me? As if." I huffed at the ridiculousness of it all.

He pushed the box of Szechuan chicken toward me. "Clearly she knows you well. She knows you need to get away from your work and your ex-husband and take some time for yourself. She probably knew the chances you'd do it were slim to none, but at least she tried."

"What? You don't think it was way out of line? I mean, that's nuts!" I waved off his attempt to get me to eat seconds.

"I think it is pretty far out there but not out of line. She's looking after you, Tessa. Someone has to."

I glowered at him. Was the world turning against me? "Seriously? That's exactly what Marjorie said. What the fuck is that supposed to mean? I can look after myself!"

My angry overreaction rolled off Elliot like water off a duck's back. "Listen, honey. Drop the defensive BS. The two people who spend the most time with you are trying to look out for you. Be glad that you have us. We only do it because we care."

He knew how to put me in my place without being

offensive, and how to show me he loved me without having to say it. I wish Chuck had figured that out. "I know." I did know.

"So, you're not going to Grand Cayman, I take it?"

"Of course not," I scoffed.

"Well, I think you should."

"Well, that's not happening." I tried to shut down the discussion but Elliot was not easily deterred.

"And why not? I mean, don't you deserve a vacation after all you've been through? You've kept it all together through the separation and the negotiations. Aren't you allowed to blow off some steam and just relax?" Elliot washed down the food he was chewing with a gulp of wine. "If anyone deserves a vacation right now, it's you."

"I appreciate your concern, I really do. And Marjorie's too. But now is not the time. There is too much going on."

"Oh, come on, Tessa, there is always too much going on. When was the last time you and Chuck took a real vacation?"

Fuck. It had been nearly seven years. I was too embarrassed to answer. "We couldn't take a vacation. It was our company. We couldn't both leave." I made the excuse that we'd always made but I couldn't help but wonder if that was a cause or a symptom of our demise.

"Exactly. But now?"

I started to understand what he meant by being free. Elliot was right. Marjorie, too. There was no reason I couldn't leave now. Chuck was there to run the company which pretty much ran itself thanks to me. But still. I wasn't convinced. "So I should go sit on a beach in the middle of nowhere, all alone? How is that going to help things? I mean, what the hell am I supposed to *do* for two weeks?"

"Well, you can relax. You can read. You could try new things. Parasailing. Snorkeling. I hear the water is beautiful in Grand Cayman. And the beaches are supposed to be phenomenal. Imagine morning walks along the shore with the waves at your feet."

I remembered my dream from early that morning. That endless beach.

"But all alone. How pathetic is that? I can't go there by myself."

"It's not pathetic at all. Lots of people travel alone. You can do anything, Tessa. Vacationing on your own is a piece of cake. In fact, I prefer to travel alone so I can do what I want and not have to worry about anyone else."

"You mean you prefer to travel alone so you can hook up with different guys when you want." I'd heard his vacation stories.

"That may be partially true. But so what? Maybe you should try it now that you're single? You know, it wouldn't hurt you to get laid, Tess."

"Yeah right. I don't think I'm quite ready for that. Sex is the last thing on my mind. I don't want to hook up with random guys and I don't want to go on a tropical vacation by myself, Elliot. It just feels sad and lonely."

"You deserve to have some fun. And a good dose of D would work wonders for you. Trust me. But, whatever, you don't have to fuck anyone, but be open, Tessa. Just go, let loose, and have some fun." I wasn't sure I remembered how to do any of those things.

He pulled out his phone and scrolled for a minute. "I have stuff I can't move Monday and Wednesday but I could join you, say, Thursday next week."

My jaw dropped. "You're serious? You'd come to Grand Cayman with me?"

"Um, hell yes. I'm guessing Marjorie didn't book you into some three-star B&B. I know it will be awesome. I'm there in a heartbeat, honey."

"Oh no, it's a five-star all-inclusive resort." I put on my most posh-sounding voice to say the name. "The Palms. As you'd expect when Marjorie is spending my money. Well, the company's money." Part of me wanted to go because Chuck would be paying half. Was I actually considering this now? "Wow, if you're serious, that may change everything."

"I'd hope so! You say the word and I'll put in the vacation request."

The strange sensation of a spontaneous smile surprised me. "Alright then. Let's do it."

"Seriously?" Elliot looked apprehensive.

"Seriously."

He blinked slowly in disbelief before lifting his glass. "To Grand Cayman."

CHAPTER 4

y head hurt from too much wine the night before when Boomer licked me awake. I went through the motions of the morning walk in a daze. Was I really doing this? If so, I had so much to do. First off, I had to tell Marjorie not to cancel the booking. I sent her a text. *Don't cancel Cayman. I've reconsidered.* My phone rang five minutes later.

"Hi, Marjorie."

"Hello, Tessa. Did I understand correctly that you're planning to take the trip to Grand Cayman?" She sounded cautious.

"Yes, I decided that you were right." I winced when I said it but the admission was easier than I expected. "Did I catch you in time?"

"Yes, you did. It's still booked. Shall I send you the itinerary? And book your car for the airport for tomorrow night?" I could tell she was smiling when she spoke.

"Yes, please do. And while you're at it, book a ticket for Elliot

Neilsen to join me on Thursday for the rest of the trip. I'll have him send you his date of birth and passport number. First-class on company miles." Chuck could half-fund my vacation with my gay boyfriend. Fuck Chuck. I was sure I'd be footing the bill for his escapades with the slutty secretary. I probably already had.

And just like that, I was going to Grand Cayman.

I thought and overthought everything I might need to do before I left. With the day off work, there was plenty of time to prepare. Marjorie had covered most of it. I only needed to take care of the things she couldn't—namely myself. I headed to the salon for a pedicure and added a much-needed bikini wax. If I was going to be on the beach, I needed a bikini, too, so I went shopping.

I hadn't tried on swimsuits in years. It was way more fun now that I was at my skinniest since college. I chose a simple black string bikini and a racy red one that showed far more of my backside than I was accustomed to. It was totally out of character but I was trying to follow Elliot's advice and be open. I found a few sundresses and some shorts to flesh out my scant summer wardrobe. I packed in no time and was set to go by six o'clock.

Which meant I had a whole day to doubt my decision. Boomer led me to his favorite dog park a few blocks from our house on our evening walk. I pretended not to watch while he sniffed every canine butt he could get his snout near. I stared blankly into the leaves on the tree above and hardly noticed when someone sat beside me.

"Is he a labradoodle?"

I smiled at the handsome man nodding toward Boomer and replied. "Um, yeah. He is."

"Great dogs. I always wanted one myself."

I eyed his Jack Russell terrier. "Why didn't you get one?"

"My ex-wife liked small dogs. And I guess it made more sense, living in the city and hardly ever being home."

"Yeah, sometimes I think Boomer has a very sad life home all day on his own. He gets a midday walk from a service, but that's it. Sometimes I feel guilty. I think he just sleeps all day."

"Sleeping all day sounds kind of nice." The man's mouth curled into a smile as he nodded toward our dogs. "He seems like a very sociable dog."

My hands covered my mouth while I gasped at the sight of Boomer awkwardly trying to hump the small terrier. I ran over to break up the party. "Boomer, stop that!" I had to physically pull him away from the bouncy little dog, who didn't seem to mind the attention. "Go play with someone your own size. You'll hurt that little girl."

I turned back to the owner who grinned as I apologized. "Sorry about that. He's overly affectionate sometimes."

"It's okay. Jill didn't object. And who could blame him? She's a cutie." He smiled.

"A Jack Russell named Jill? That's clever." *Or cheesy.*

"You think so? My ex-wife named her. I always thought it was kind of cheesy. But it's been her name for five years now, so what can you do?"

"Ha. I guess you could change it. Might confuse her though."

"I think it would confuse me even more. Anyway, it grew on me over the years. I think it suits her now."

Jill chased a shitzu in circles. I stood to try and spot Boomer who had wandered out of sight. It was time to head back. "She's cute no matter what you call her. You guys have fun."

I was confused by the sensation of something catching my hand as I walked away. His hand was on mine, tugging me toward him gently. "You're leaving so soon? I didn't even catch your name?" My gaze moved from his hand to his face. Anxious eyes that might be kind met mine.

"Oh, right, sorry. I'm Tessa. And you are?" His other hand slid under mine so it was sandwiched between his. "I'm Ben."

I wiggled my hand free while I studied his face. Something was not quite right. He was probably just lonely, but it felt kind of creepy. "Nice to meet you, Ben. We've got to get going. Bye now." I fought the urge to look back but I felt his sad eyes following me. I pulled Boomer close on his leash to keep any other creeps away, and walked as fast as I could across the wide-open field to get out of his sight. I am the queen of overthinking, so it's no surprise that by the time I reached home my thoughts had led me to a dark place. My throat closed up when I saw my suitcase packed and ready to go inside the front door.

I envisioned myself the lonely divorcee on the beach, sipping cocktails and avoiding contact with others. What the fuck was I thinking? No fucking way.

Elliot was out on a date. I texted him anyway.

I know you're busy, but I was thinking...

Maybe I should wait and go with you? I don't want to be there on my own.

He replied five seconds later. *Go.*

I don't know

Go.

I'm not sure

Go.

I don't think I can

My phone rang. I bit my lip as I forced a pleasantry to procrastinate broaching the subject at hand. "Hi, Elliot. How are you?"

I strained to hear his voice over the sound of a crowded room. "I'm fine, dear. How are you? A little uncertain it seems. Why all this back and forth?"

A tightening in my throat made it hard to answer. "I was ready to go, packed and ready. I got a pedicure and a bikini wax. I even bought bikinis and sundresses."

"That's great. I hope they're sexy!"

The tears came and my voice broke. "I just can't, Elliot. I can't be around anyone else right now. I can't be alone."

His voice lowered. I could picture him turning away from people to speak to me through somewhat gritted teeth. The annoyance in his voice bled through the forced empathy. "You can't be with anyone or you can't be alone? Which is it, Tess? You're talking crazy. What happened?"

He was right. I did sound crazy. My explanation sounded even worse. "I was at the dog park with Boomer and this creepy guy tried to hit on me."

"What do you mean? Did he try to force himself on you?" The sudden compassion in his voice comforted me. "Jeez, I'm sorry, Tess. Are you okay?"

"Oh no, no, nothing like that. He was actually quite nice, and

35

pretty handsome. But he seemed sad and lonely. Pathetic, really. I started thinking about myself alone on the beach and felt just as pathetic. I'm not ready for this."

Elliot sighed. "Thank God it's nothing serious. Tessa, listen to me. You have to go. What else are you going to do? Just go. I'm a little busy right now with a really hot guy from Uruguay. So please, get yourself together."

"But Boomer."

"Boomer is staying with me until I go, then Emilio is taking care of him at your house, like we planned. He'll stay there at night and take him out twice a day. Boomer will be fine. And so will you. Did you download a few good books like I told you?"

I sniffled and wiped the tears from my cheek with the back of my hand. "Yeah."

"Good, then you're all set. Just go and stop thinking about it. Really, Tessa, now is the time to stop thinking and just do." I understood the finality in his voice. Not only did he not want to hear any more of it, he didn't want me wasting my time on doubt.

He was right. And resistance was futile. "Okay, then. See you in Grand Cayman." I wasn't sure I could make myself go, but I was sure I had to try.

"Thatta girl. Talk to you tomorrow."

CHAPTER 5

I distracted myself with work emails, then senseless YouTube videos, all morning Saturday. Resisting the many urges to call Elliot again and find a way to back out, I called my mom instead. Once I told her I was going, I was going for sure. No turning back. Mom thought it was a great idea, just what I needed. Get away from it all.

What she, nor Marjorie, nor Elliot seemed to get was that "it all" was what had kept me sane. I wasn't sure I was ready to be alone with myself and my feelings. I didn't know what I might find, but I was pretty sure there was a lot of pain buried there. But I forced myself into the Uber to the airport and didn't look back.

Despite the two glasses of red wine, I watched two movies on the way to Miami, meaning I didn't sleep a wink. After landing, I went to the first-class lounge in a daze and ordered a mimosa at half-past five in the morning, no more convinced I was doing the right thing than I had been twenty-four hours earlier, but I was committed.

"Early flight?" the bright-eyed elderly bartender asked, his white mustache curling up at the corners of his rosy lips.

"Yeah, following a late one. I just landed from San Francisco."

His mouth turned upward. "Oh, that's a brutal redeye. Sleep much?"

"Not a minute."

"Careful not to miss your flight, dear. Which one is yours?

"Grand Cayman. It leaves in an hour and a half. Surely I can stay awake that long."

He wiped the bar around my champagne flute. "Alcohol can have a profoundly relaxing effect after a sleepless night. Don't worry, though. I'll look after you."

Everyone was looking after me.

I managed to stay awake through two more mimosas in the lounge and one more on the plane before take-off. I forced down a few bites of my first-class breakfast, surprisingly good for airplane food, then curled up with my blanket and fluffy pillow for an hour or so of sleep. The flight attendant woke me to put my seat upright shortly before landing.

I pushed open the window shade and squinted down at white sailboats that looked like toys in the crystal blue harbor. The aquamarine water met a wide pink-white beach that stretched for miles. We dropped fast and passed over buildings and trees a little too closely for my comfort, then touched down and braked fast. Short runway plus big jet equals slightly uncomfortable landing, but it wasn't too bad.

The hour sleep was enough to sober me up, mostly, but not enough to make me feel rested. I was in an exhausted daze when I climbed into the back of a taxi and gave the driver my resort name.

"Oh, nice place," the driver said with an unusual accent that was neither Caribbean nor British, but something in between. "First time on the island?"

"Yeah, first time."

"We'll take the scenic route to show you around."

"No, that's very kind, but I need to rest. We should go straight to the hotel."

"Oh don't you worry. There's only one route. And it's all scenic." I hoped we were on the fastest path because I was rapidly melting into the car seat. I needed a bed. Twenty minutes later, we pulled up to the hotel. At least he didn't take me for a ride. It was more than I could say for my ex. What a bullshit ride these last six months had been.

Thinking seething thoughts about Chuck and then navigating the check-in process made me realize that I hadn't completely sobered up. Thankfully my room was ready. A handsome young man led me through a beautifully landscaped tropical garden down a white brick path to my bungalow. We entered through the back door of the cottage into a small kitchen area with a wet bar and coffee maker. The bellboy flipped the light switch to the bathroom off to the left. Blue glass tiles accented the white porcelain and marble. I lingered, admiring the fringe of candles around a huge jetted tub that took up half the room.

I followed the bellboy into the large open room, filled with light. A king-sized bed clad in white linens was on the right, and a long light blue sofa sat facing the wall of windows that looked out to the sea. The bellboy parted the flowing sheer white curtain to reveal the view and opened the French doors to the private terrace that stepped down directly onto the white sand beach. He motioned for me to walk ahead of him.

The calm sea the color of the glass bathroom tiles was breathtaking. The warm ocean breeze carried a sweet hint of jasmine. I drew in a deep breath and held it. I couldn't wait for Elliot to get there to have someone to share it with.

When I blinked my eyes open, I realized I must have zoned out for a few seconds because the bellboy was staring expectantly and awkwardly waiting for a tip. "The sea is gorgeous, isn't it? Remember that scuba diving and snorkeling are included in your package here, in case you want to explore all that our island has to offer underwater as well."

"That's interesting. I haven't scuba-dived in years." Nearly fifteen years, to be exact. Not since our honeymoon. I loved it. Chuck hated it. We never did it again. Scuba was the last thing on my mind. I needed sleep, and the best way to make that happen was one more drink. "Is the restaurant open for breakfast?" Where could I get the next mimosa before my nap? That's what I needed to know.

"The beach restaurant serves the breakfast buffet as well as a la carte options. It's right down there." He gestured toward the large palm-thatch roof a couple hundred yards down the beach.

I wandered past the hostess to the bar and perched myself on an empty stool. The pretty, young dark-skinned bartender smiled as she placed a napkin on the bar in front of me. "Good morning, madame. How can I help you?" I chuckled at the formality, considering the crassness of my morning mission to get a buzz before my nap.

"A mimosa, please."

"One mimosa." She sat the bubbly beverage on the napkin in front of me. "The buffet is open if you wish to dine."

"Thank you. I'm fine for now." That wasn't the least bit true. I sucked down the juicy drink in less than a minute, and slid off the barstool, a little wobbly on my feet, to wander back to my room and the bed that beckoned.

I undressed in front of the vanity and left my clothes in a pile on the bathroom floor. The warm water on my face washed away the residual grime of the trip but I couldn't remove the filthy feeling from the divorce becoming final. I studied myself in the mirror while I brushed my teeth. I was a mess. Hair in knots, bags under bloodshot eyes. That's what six drinks and a sleepless night will give you. Nothing a good day's sleep couldn't cure. The fluffy white bed looked like a cloud. If I couldn't sleep here, I couldn't sleep anywhere.

I settled under the lightweight down comforter and pulled my satin eye mask over my eyes to block out the sunshine flooding the room. It felt like I had been asleep for days when the ringing telephone on the bedside table startled me awake. My heart nearly jumped out of my chest when I pushed the mask up to my forehead in a panic and searched the strange room for something recognizable. That split second of waking in a new place after so many years of the same, when you wonder where the hell you are and how you got there, was unsettling. I squinted to focus and find the source of the noise, then fumbled to reach the receiver.

"Hello?" I hardly recognized my raspy voice.

"Tessa! Oh my God, did I wake you?" Elliot sounded anxious but relieved.

I cleared my throat. "Um, yeah. But it's okay. Hi, Elliot. What time is it anyway?"

"It's nearly five o'clock here, so almost eight there. I've been texting you all day. I was worried you hadn't gotten on the plane."

"Oh really?" I fumbled for my cell phone beside the bed. No service. "I guess my cell doesn't work here. And I didn't log into the WIFI before I went to sleep. Sorry to concern you, but there's no reason to worry, I didn't chicken out."

"Thank goodness. After your little panic session, I wondered. Thankfully I remembered the resort name so I could call. Anyway, I'm glad you made it. What did you do before your nap?"

"Checked in, chugged a mimosa, and nothing else. I think I was in bed by ten this morning."

"Wow, you must feel great now. Ten hours of sleep."

"I feel like I could sleep ten more. But I better get up and eat something."

"Good plan. Are you awake? You sound like you're still half asleep."

I sat up on the edge of the bed and pulled the mask off my forehead, forcing my eyes open wide. "Yes. I'm awake."

"Okay, good. Go get yourself some dinner and promise me that you are going to have a good time."

"I promise."

CHAPTER 6

The double shower in the room made me more aware of my solitude. Jesus, was I in the fucking honeymoon suite? When Elliot arrived we wouldn't be using that together, but it would sure be nice to have his company. I pulled on one of my new sundresses—the black one with red flowers that looked like a short and sexy version of a flamenco dress. I could have worn a bra with it, but the straps would have shown, and what was the point anyway? My tits looked fabulous under the dress in the bathroom mirror.

My own voice echoed my mother's approving words as I told myself in the mirror, "Go out and have yourself some fun, Teresa Marie." It was now or never, and a girl had to eat. Nevertheless, my heart knotted up in my throat as I approached the full dining room alone.

"Table for one?" I felt the jab like a knife to the gut. Did you really have to put it that way, cute young skinny hostess lady?

I gulped down the tears that rose. "I would prefer to sit at the bar if that's okay?"

Her full lips spread into a broad smile. "Of course, right this way."

She led me to the same stool where I'd drank my morning mimosa. The bartender was a handsome black man. "Good evening, madame, can I offer you a drink before dinner?"

I just wanted to get dinner over with so I can get back to my bed. I didn't have the energy for this. "Black label on the rocks, make it a double, and a menu please."

"No problem, miss," he replied in the same ambiguous Caribbean British accent I had noticed on the taxi driver earlier in the day. The booze and long sleep had left me so disoriented that it felt like several days had passed since check-in. How would I survive until Thursday?

The flowery descriptions on the menu confused me. I was in no condition to try and decode them. "I'll have a skirt steak and an arugula salad?"

"Oh, yes, of course." He filled a high ball glass, first with ice, then with whiskey, in front of me.

I looked around as I sipped my drink, alone at the bar. The first sip was more like a gulp, and it was as harsh as the reality that slapped me as I scanned the dining room. Happy couples exchanging stories and smiles. I gripped the highball glass with both hands and wished I could be somewhere else. By the end of that drink, I was drowning in my sorrows and was sure I had made the biggest mistake of my life by coming to this remote Caribbean island to "get away from it all." All I had managed to get away from were the distractions from my loneliness. I was a mess. A cute dress and red lipstick couldn't change that.

Just as I was ready to forget about my food order and make a run for it, my salad arrived. I ate all the meat immediately then set in on the greens. I needed the food to counteract the glass of whiskey that had gone straight to my head, so I ate it like it was my job. I was oblivious to the man who'd sat across the bar until I honed in on his voice when he spoke to the bartender.

"Hey, Carlos. How's your night going? Can I have a tequila when you get a chance, please?" A deep voice with a distinctly Irish accent that matched his messy head of strawberry blonde waves more than it did his Caribbean demeanor, perplexed me.

I swallowed hard and averted my gaze from the piercing green eyes that lit up with his smile when they met mine from across the bar.

Carlos replaced my empty drink with a full one. I pushed the greens around on my plate with my fork and strained my ears to listen to their conversation. They seemed to be speaking in a different dialect of English, and with a potpourri of accents that further masked the words when Carlos asked about someone named Melissa.

"I haven't seen her for a while." I looked up to steal a glimpse of his broad shoulders in a fitted blue linen button-down. I tried not to stare but my eyes were drawn to the smooth tanned skin that peeked from beneath his rolled-up sleeves.

Carlos chuckled. "I guess she wasn't the one?"

"I don't know if I believe in 'the one'—in my experience,

there's only been the *last one*. Melissa was the last one. And the next will be the *next* last one."

I could only imagine his smug smile because I kept my eyes down to keep my chuckle under my breath. What a player! Who could blame him? He was young and hot. But it was so blatant it was comical.

He shrugged as he continued. "That's the way it goes, Carlos."

"Someday that will change, but until then, enjoy the next last one."

"I always do."

I looked up to his boyish grin. His airy way was sexy as fuck but his smugness left a bad taste in my mouth. It was probably from feeling *played* for over a decade with Chuck.

The plate of greens was no longer appealing. I pushed it away and placed my napkin on it, then held the high ball glass in both hands. The cool glass felt good. I wasn't used to this heat and humidity, especially at night. The whiskey warmed me even more with each sip as I continued to eavesdrop on the conversation between the bartender and the sexy young man. The warm liquor tingled all the way down to my crotch when I let my eyes wander to his chest. I uncrossed my legs and shifted on the stool before crossing them again. The booze was getting to me. I suddenly felt flush. I set down the glass and rested my cool hands on my neck for a second, then picked up my ice water and chugged it down fast. I felt both men's eyes on me when I finished the water.

The young player got up to go to the bathroom. The perfect time for a hasty exit. I waved to Carlos for the check. I was off my stool and pivoting for the exit when I nearly ran into a broad chest clad in light blue linen. All the whiskey hit me at once and my knees wobbled under me. His hands caught my elbow as I took a slightly stumbling step backward.

"Leaving so soon? I was hoping I could buy you a drink."

My cheeks warmed with embarrassment. I figured he was just being kind but his offer to buy me a drink took me by surprise. "Yeah, no, I have to get some rest. I didn't sleep a wink on the redeye to Miami last night." Never mind that I'd slept nearly all day after the flight.

"Another time then, I hope."

I smiled. "Time I have plenty of, it seems. I'm here for two weeks."

"Oh, is that so? Lucky me." The Irishman's eyes lit up an even brighter green with his pearly smile.

It was hard to tell if he was flirting or merely humoring the lonely older woman. Either way, it was to be expected from a player. I laughed as I started off. "Okay, I'll let you buy me a drink sometime. You're in luck, my drinks are free."

He flashed a cheeky grin. "That's why I offered."

"Ah, smart man."

He reached for my hand. "I'm Gavin, Gavin Scott."

I stared down at my hand held between his, the same way the man from the dog park had done. But this time instead of feeling creepy it felt all kinds of right. "I'm Tessa. Nice to meet you." I shook his hands to try to shake the current his touch sent through me.

"Nice to meet you, Tessa." His eyes held mine long enough for me to make out orangish-brown specks in the light green iris. I was left wanting when his grip on my hand loosened. What had gotten into me? I let my hand float down to my side.

I managed to squeak out a reply. "I'll see you around."

"I'll be looking for you."

I smiled and looked back to the bartender. "Thanks, Carlos. You guys take care." I focused hard on walking a semi-straight line out of the bar. Once I was a few yards down the beach I looked back over my shoulder. Gavin smiled and waved. Yep, he was watching. The rest of the way to my room I imagined him concocting an excuse to follow me to my door. I looked back to the lights of the restaurant down the beach as I unlocked the door before entering alone.

I studied myself in the mirror as I brushed my teeth. Not half bad. Better than earlier. Something was different. My eyes were more alive, brighter, happier. I was smiling. That was it —I was smiling. I giggled as I rinsed my mouth then washed my face. Of course, the first guy I find attractive in like a million years would be a twenty-year-old player. Of course, he would. That's what Chuck was when I met him, too.

I climbed under the fluffy comforter and flipped through the channels of the big screen TV. I stopped on an unsolved murder mysteries forensics show. I loved those. Chuck once joked that he worried that I was studying up on how to get away with murder because I watched them so often. Now it seemed more like a fantasy than a joke. I imagined hiring a hitman to take him out while I was on a Caribbean island vacation. Make it look like an accident. Maybe hit by a bus or falling down an elevator shaft. How tragic. I laughed out loud at my sinister thoughts. Of course, I didn't *really* want

Chuck dead. But I wouldn't mind if I never had to see him again. Ever.

I pulled the covers up under my chin and smiled as I realized that I didn't have to see his smug face for two whole weeks that I'd be in Grand Cayman. I hadn't gone more than two days without seeing him in nearly twenty years.

I turned the TV off after the last mystery was solved and attempted to replace my morbid fantasies of Chuck's demise with more pleasant thoughts. I tried to call upon Gavin's image when I closed my eyes, but I couldn't quite remember the details of his face. Was his jawline square or narrow? I recalled the fullness of his lips but wasn't sure about their shape. The only thing I saw clearly were those pale green eyes with orange and brown specks. That was all I was sure of, those colors swirling in the kaleidoscope of my pre-sleep daze.

CHAPTER 7

*T*he cheerful melody on my phone's alarm woke me at a quarter to seven. I had forgotten to disable it. I rolled over after I turned it off, and put a pillow over my head to block out the light and try to go back to sleep. It was no use. My mind kicked into gear and would not let up. Monday morning. I should be getting up to walk Boomer and go to work.

I spotted the fancy coffee machine on the countertop beside a carved wooden box containing different flavored coffee pods. I hated those machines for the environment but I loved their practicality. I made myself a salted caramel cappuccino. I lifted the piping hot mug to my nose, resisting the urge to email Brad about the Brumley meeting. The sweet scent of the cappuccino filled the room as I walked through to the porch overlooking the beach.

Standing at the top of the stairs, I looked right then left at the beach that stretched as far as I could see in both directions. The sky was lit from a reflection of the recently risen sun in a soft light that made the blue of the cloudless sky blend with the blue of the sea in a blurred line on the horizon. I looked back to the side-by-side Adirondack chairs but opted instead to sit on the edge of the wooden steps to listen to the waves lapping the shore. I was tempted to call Elliot to check on Boomer, but it was only six o'clock back home, and he would not appreciate the wake-up call.

I missed Boomer but I could walk without him. I changed into shorts and a tank top and carried my flip flops as I set off down the beach. The warm breeze grazed my face while the foam of the waves on the shore tickled my feet. With no cell phone service, I had only the few songs that were downloaded to my phone to get me in the walking groove. The first was Gloria Gaynor's "I Will Survive" which ended up playing four times on that walk. I sang the words to myself as I undressed to shower. I was learning how to get along, and I would survive.

I looked around the room while I towel dried my hair after the shower, not sure what to do with myself. I might as well soak up some rays. Parts of me hadn't seen the sun in years. Hell, most of me hadn't. I donned one of my two new bikinis and lathered up with sunscreen. I pulled on a new sundress and headed to the restaurant for a quick bite before I staked a claim on one of the two beach chairs underneath an empty umbrella. Everything was set up for couples. Everything reminded me that I was no longer a part of one.

I pushed aside thoughts of Chuck and his new couple as I settled in and opened one of the books I downloaded before I left. It was a World War Two novel written from the perspective of Death. Not exactly uplifting, but it was critically acclaimed, and Elliot had recommended it months ago. Within ten minutes, I was sucked into the story of an orphaned teenage girl whose foster family was hiding a

Jewish boy in their basement. My problems seemed small by comparison. I spent the next hours immersed in the story, only stopping to take a dip in the ocean to cool off. Around two in the afternoon hunger rumbled in my stomach so I wandered back to the room to change. I made my way back to the restaurant bar where I didn't feel so obviously alone to order lunch. The same bartender from the morning met me with a warm smile as I perched myself on the stool I'd occupied on my previous two visits.

"Are you having lunch or a drink?"

I smiled into her happy eyes. "Both, I think. What's your most tropical cocktail?"

Well, if you haven't had one yet, I'd recommend a Cayman Sunset."

Sounds perfect. And can I get a lobster bisque, and a salad with grilled fish for lunch, too, please?"

"Yes, of course."

She disappeared to punch my food order into the computer before going to the blender to make my drink. I watched her pour from several bottles before mixing. Uh oh, I could be in trouble. "What's in it? I didn't even ask."

"Three types of rum, two juices, brandy, and grenadine." Whoa, that sounded strong. She set the colorful beverage in front of me on the bar and poked a paper straw into the icy mixture. Just what I needed.

I sipped the fruity concoction, licking my lips as I savored the swirl of tangy-sweet flavors. "It's delicious."

"Good, I'm glad you like it."

"And I'm glad you're using paper straws. That's impressive."

"Yes, it is, 'specially since the man who owns most of this here island got rich making plastic cups. He come here with all his plastic money, buying up our homes. I think I'm anti-plastic just to spite 'im." Her thick Caribbean accent punctuated the strong sentiment.

"Oh really? That's fascinating. Who is he?"

The bartender looked around before she leaned across the bar to answer in a whisper. "I'm not supposed to talk about him. But you can google it."

I looked around too, as if someone was watching us, and lowered my voice. "Okay, I will. For the record, I hate plastic, too."

The juices masked any flavor of the several types of alcohol in the drink. The fruity frozen drink went down easy, too easy. I started to feel it on the last sip, when my soup appeared. "Would you like another drink?"

"It's a long time until sunset, but, yes, I think I can have one more."

"Dis drink is made for drinking all day. Don't you worry."

I wasn't worried. Worst case, I'd take a nap before dinner. Hell, what was a vacation supposed to be if not cocktails at inappropriate hours and afternoon naps? I returned to the beach after I finished my salad and I waded into the waves to swim before I planted my ass in the chair where I planned to spend the next three days waiting for Elliot. I got back into the war story, but I may have been dozing off when a voice jarred me back to reality. I sat up from my reclined position when I realized a man was standing over me. I clutched my tablet and blinked behind my dark glasses.

"I'm sorry. What did you say?"

"I said, that must be a good book you're reading."

I looked down at the tablet in my hands and then up to the silhouette of a muscular young man in a polo shirt with the resort logo before me. I struggled to make out his face in the shade, backlit from the bright sun reflecting off the sand and waves behind him—Gavin.

Something stirred in my stomach, nervousness or excitement—or both. Seeing him made me forget who I was and what I was doing there. I stumbled for words.

"Oh, yes, it's a really good book, actually."

"I guess so. I waved from over there a few times and you didn't even look up." He motioned down the beach. His Irish accent seemed even more out of place on him than it had the night before. His boyish grin made me wish I could see the green eyes hidden behind his sunglasses. They'd surely be sparkling with his smile.

I straightened up. "Oh I'm sorry, I didn't see you."

"That's okay. It's Tessa, right?"

I nodded as I stammered. "Yes, good memory. Nice to see you again, Gavin." A smile spread across my face faster than the heat that spread up from my neck.

"At your service." His grin ignited a spark in my stomach. I liked the sound of that. "Are you enjoying your day?"

I smiled nervously and nodded. "Yes, very much. It's been a long time since I relaxed on a beach with a good book."

"Maybe it's something you should do more often, then. Suits you. I'll let you get back to it." He started to wander off.

"So you work here?" I called to draw him back. He turned

back and looked down to where I'd glanced at the logo on his shirt.

"Yeah, I run the dive shop. Are you a diver?" He smiled like he hoped I'd say yes.

"Yes, well, sort of. I only did it once, a long time ago."

His smile faded. "Aw, what happened? You didn't like it?"

I answered without thinking. The afternoon booze had hindered my filter and my response sounded bitter. "Actually I loved it. It was my ex-husband who didn't, so I never did it again."

"That's a real shame, Tessa. You should never give up something you love because someone else doesn't like it."

His words pierced my soul. He had no idea how much of myself I had given up because Chuck didn't like it. "Sometimes that's just how goes."

"Doesn't have to be. Why don't you give it a try again?"

I shook my head emphatically. "Oh, I don't think so. It's been so long. I've forgotten it all now."

He flashed a grin. "Well, we happen to specialize in teaching people how to dive."

"Oh thank you, but it seems kind of silly to learn it all over. I'll probably never do it again."

"You said you're here for two weeks, right?"

He pushed his sunglasses up to his head so I could see his green eyes, which distracted me so much I could barely answer. "Yes, that's right."

He smiled. "It only takes a day to do a refresher course, then you're good to go. You should do it."

I squinted, considering his suggestion. He was a good businessman. "Thanks for the offer, but I think I'll stick to the beach and my book."

"Alright, then. But you don't know what you're missing." Gavin grinned and studied me with a lingering gaze. "So what's your story, Tessa?"

"My story?" I strained a smile as I looked him in the eye. Goddammit, he was cute.

"What's a lovely lass like you doing here on her own? There must be a story."

I chuckled at his description of me. "There is, but it's a long one."

Gavin checked his dive watch. "I've got plenty of time."

I smiled at his persistence. "It's not really that long, or that interesting. My company sent me on this trip and my friend who is joining me couldn't come until Thursday, so here I am, alone."

"Ah, I see. And your friend who is coming Thursday, is that a man friend?"

"Man friend?" I had to laugh. "Well, yes. He's a man."

"I figured it was too good to be true. A pretty lady like you, single."

I studied his face through narrowed eyes while his twinkled playfully. He was a practiced ladies' man. I had to give him that. "Thank you."

"You're welcome. Think about the diving. I'd love to get you in the pool tomorrow."

The way he said it sent a wave tingling through me. "I may take you up on that."

"You only live once. What've you got to lose?"

A flash of my drowning dream crossed my mind. "My life, for one."

He chuckled. "We'll be in a *pool*. I won't let you drown, I promise. It will be fun."

Elliot's advice echoed in my mind. *Let loose and have fun. Be open.* I took a deep breath and said it out loud to take the leap. "Alright, I'll try."

"Excellent. Meet me at the dive shop at nine tomorrow. It's just down the beach." He pointed in the direction beyond the restaurant.

"I'll be there."

Gavin grinned and flipped his sunglasses down over his green eyes. "I can't wait. See you then."

A warm rush returned to my crotch as I watched him stroll down the beach. He was sexy and charming. And a fun kind of flirty. But of course, he was. He was a player by nature and was just doing his job, drumming up business. Oh, to be young again. I shook my head at the preposterous thought and turned on my tablet to return to my story.

CHAPTER 8

a current buzzed through me when the alarm sounded Tuesday morning. I wasn't sure if I was more nervous or excited about getting into the pool with Gavin. I threw on a bikini and a cover-up and headed to the restaurant.

A different pretty young hostess smiled as I approached her station. "Table for one?"

I felt a whisper of hesitation but I was ready. "Yes, table for one, please."

After coffee and a bagel, nervousness fluttered in my stomach as I made my way to the dive shop.

"Hello, Tessa." Gavin leaned on the counter in his resort polo and navy-blue swim trunks and flashed a flirty grin, handing me a clipboard. "The resort requires you to sign all these waivers. I hope you don't mind."

"Of course not. No problem." I scanned and signed the bottoms of the forms and handed the clipboard back to him.

"Alright then, are you ready to go breathe underwater?" He drummed the countertop excitedly.

Thinking of it like that scared me a little. "Uh, sure. I guess so." It had been a long time. Maybe I was too old for this.

"Let's get you geared up." He led me to a rack in the back of the room behind the counter where several vests hung. "First, let's fit you with a BCD. Remember these?" He held up a vest.

"Sort of, a buoyancy control device?"

He handed me the one he held. "That's it. Try this one."

I slipped my arms into the vest and fumbled to untangle the bulky hose that had flipped under the shoulder strap.

"Let me help you." Gavin leaned in and reached around my waist to free the two velcro ends of the cummerbund that were folded back behind me. Heat radiated from his cheek less than an inch from mine and his breath tickled my neck as he struggled to find the end of one strap. My nipples grew hard under my bikini and warmth spread between my legs and down to my knees, making my legs shaky. I steadied myself with a hand on his shoulder, causing Gavin to lift his eyes to mine, which were the size of saucers. I felt short of breath.

"How you doing there? Alright?" He pulled away from me just enough to be able to cinch the cummerbund tight around my waist, and then smoothed the front of the velcro closure with his hand. "Perfect. Looks like that fits perfect." The pressure of his palm on my belly stirred the excitement in my stomach. His gaze held mine as he smiled. I blinked hard and took the deepest breath I could manage, pressing my hands into the sides of my thighs to quell the overwhelming urge to grab him. I hadn't felt so flustered by a man in, well, maybe ever.

"Go ahead and take it off so we can set up the gear on the tanks." He handed me a regulator. "You remember what you do with this thing?"

"Yes, of course. You breathe with it." I could use some help breathing about now.

"That's right. Set up on the pink tank there." He pointed to a neon-colored tank near the back door.

I fumbled with the BCD strap but remembered how to tighten it around the tank after a minute or so. I removed the dust cap from the tank valve and studied the regulator to figure out which way it hooked to the tank.

"You need help?" Gavin asked gently.

"Yeah, maybe. Are the regulators on the left or right?"

"The second-stage goes on the right. Snorkel on left, reg on right."

"Ah, right." I flipped the regulator around and screwed it into place. "Is that right?"

"The best way to check is to turn the air on. But hook the air to your inflator hose first."

"Oh yeah, I forgot about that one." I pulled back the metal sleeve of the connector and snapped the hose into place.

Gavin turned the knob on the tank and air hissed into the hoses. "Good, no leaks." He turned the air off again. "Now you need a weight belt and we're ready for the pool. Grab one of the shorter ones off the wall there and string it up." He handed me two three-pound weights. "That should do it." I threaded the belt through the slots on the rubber-coated weights. I held it up on both ends. "Like that?"

"Yep, just like that." He took the belt and held it by the loose end. "Well done. You passed the gear test."

"That was a test?"

His full lips spread into a grin. "Aye."

I snickered at his pirate expression. "I'm glad you didn't tell me, so I didn't get nervous."

"Nothing to be nervous about. If you get it wrong, you get to do it again. You get as many do-overs as you need to get it right."

"Thank you. That actually helps." I'd like a do-over for the past eighteen years, please.

"Good. Follow me." He carried my gear out the back door of the shop and placed it in a wheelbarrow cart, where there was already a tank set up, along with two sets of mask and fins.

I made small talk as we made our way down the paved path to the pool. "How long have you been teaching scuba diving?"

"I got my dive master as soon as I was allowed at eighteen and then did my instructor training the same year. So, a long, long time."

"What, like five years?"

His playful green eyes level on me. "More like ten. I'm twenty-eight, I'll have you know."

"Oh, well, twenty-eight. You're positively over the hill."

Gavin chuckled. "What the hell are you even talking about? You can't be much older than twenty-eight yourself."

I didn't even try to contain my laughter at that compliment. He was a player, alright. "Gavin, you are too kind. While I wish it were true, I'm afraid that lately I'm looking even older than I am, which, by the way, is a lot older than twenty-eight."

"My mum always said never to ask a lady's age, so I won't. She also said to guess five years younger than you think if ever asked to guess. So, maybe I was exaggerating a little. In all honesty, I thought you were maybe thirty-three or thirty-four."

"I don't mind if you ask my age. I'm forty-one." He didn't need to know I would be forty-two next month.

"Believe me when I say you look closer to thirty than forty. Not that forty is old, anyway."

Gavin pushed the cart of gear under the shade of an umbrella by the pool. "Do you plan to swim in that?" He eyed my dress.

I took a deep breath to banish the bashfulness and pulled the white slip dress over my head, tossing it onto the lounge chair.

Gavin paused while unloading the gear and smiled. "Nice suit."

I fought the urge to wrap my arms around myself to cover all the bits left exposed by the tiny bikini. "Thanks." I looked down at the tank he set on the side of the pool.

"If you sit on the first step, it's easy to slip your arms right in. Put your weight belt on first."

I did as he instructed while Gavin looked down from the edge of the pool. "Good, now rinse this before you put it on." I took the bright yellow mask from him.

"Should I spit in it first? I seem to remember something like that."

Gavin grinned. "Saliva is a great anti-fog agent. If it doesn't gross you out, then go for it."

I spit into the inside of the mask and rubbed it in. "It's my saliva; why would it gross me out?"

"You'd be surprised. Some people are easily offended." He handed me two yellow fins. "Here, sit back down and put these on." I did so while he got his gear out of the cart and threw it over his shoulder. He walked down the steps holding his mask and fins then stood at the edge of the pool to adjust his BCD and mask. "Is your BCD tight?"

"Yeah, I think so." I tugged at the rings on the shoulder straps.

He waded into the waist-deep water and before I knew it his hands were at my waist again, opening the velcro closure. "You have to pull the cummerbund snug, otherwise it will flop around when there's air in it." He tightened the belt then pressed it flat against my belly, letting his hand linger there for a second, watching me through his mask. "Are you ready?"

I wasn't ready for the quickening of my pulse or the flutter in my belly, but I nodded anyway.

"Good. First find your regulator. Remember reg on right. So you can lean to the right and pull your elbow back close to your body, then extend your arm out back behind you and sweep your arm forward. You should run into the hoses."

I mimicked the movement he showed me to find the regulator and brought it to my mouth. I took a deep breath but felt resistance, so I took the reg out and examined it for a clue. "Something's wrong."

"Did you turn your air on?"

"Oh, I don't think so. That could be it." I fumbled over my shoulder to feel for the knob.

"Don't worry, I got it." Gavin leaned in to reach the tank valve behind my head, placing his chiseled chest inches from my nose. I hadn't realized how tall he was before, or how muscular. I held my breath and bit my lip to stop myself from running my hands over his smooth pecs. My heart raced faster than my dirty thoughts, which must have been evident on my face, judging by the wry smile that spread across Gavin's when he finished. My air wasn't the only thing he turned on.

Gavin handed me the regulator. "Try again."

I could breathe easily but felt breathless from his stare when he asked, "All good?"

I nodded my head and gave him the thumbs-up sign.

Gavin shook his head while he made a circle with his thumb and index finger and the other three fingers splayed upright. "You mean this?"

I nodded as I mumbled into my regulator. "Ah, um-hum."

"This is the okay sign, not to be confused with this," he pointed his thumb upward, "which means you're going up, or it's time to go up. Got it?"

I nodded and mumbled into my regulator again. "Um-hum."

His green eyes lit up with his smile as he removed the regulator from my mouth. "As you can see, it's hard to communicate with a reg in your mouth. But communication is vital to safe diving, and pretty much everything, so we rely on hand signals. You've got the okay sign and the ascent sign." He made the signs again to be sure. "Let's review a few more of the important ones. If I point at my gauge, I want you to tell me how much air you have, in fives." He made a fist then opened his hand and spread out all five fingers. "Five fingers for every 500 psi in your tank. So 2000 psi would be…"

I showed him five fingers four times.

"Good job. Now, if I point to my ear, I'm either reminding you to equalize the pressure in your ears as we descend, or I'm asking how your ears are feeling. So if your ears are okay, be sure to use the okay sign, not the ascend sign. If they feel a little weird, you can give me the weird feeling sign." He held his hand out flat, palm down, and wiggled it. If you do that, I'll probably give you the ascend sign and we'll go up a few feet together to let you clear your ears. Yeah?"

I loved how he assumed a commanding role yet remained calm and supportive. A good instructor makes you aspire to be a good student. "Got it."

"Okay, good. Do you remember the most important rule in scuba diving?"

My brow wrinkled in thought. "Um, I'm not sure. Always dive with a buddy?"

"That's important… but that's not it. It's *never ever* hold your breath."

More important than not being alone was remembering to

breathe. I could relate. I nodded as he continued. "That's especially true for the ascent. You remember why?"

"Is that the bends?"

"No, that's different. The bends has to do with nitrogen in your blood. This is about the air in your lungs expanding as you ascend, which can cause lung injury."

It had been so long, how could I expect to remember all the ways I could die diving? Maybe I should have done the whole class again. Or maybe I shouldn't be here at all.

The worry must have shown on my face. Gavin squeezed my shoulder. "As long as you breathe continuously there is no risk of that whatsoever. Just breathe."

I inhaled through my nose and nodded. How many times had I told myself to "just breathe" in the last six months? Too many. "Okay."

"Now put some air in your BCD and let's swim to the deep end. After we get there, we'll descend together and sit on the bottom so you can get used to breathing underwater again."

Air hissed into the vest when I pushed the button, tightening around me to keep me afloat. I swam beside Gavin to the other end of the pool where we floated on the surface.

He locked my eyes while he commanded. "Regulator in. Inflator hose up. Ready to go down?"

His suggestion of going down made me giggle into my regulator. Even with heightened nerves, Gavin provoked dirty thoughts I hadn't had in years. I took a deep breath through the regulator to try to focus. My stomach knotted, but I gave the okay sign anyway. Gavin loosely held the shoulder strap of my vest and gave me the thumbs-down sign to descend. I looked through my mask into his eyes while I held the inflator hose up and pressed the deflate button, sinking fast when the air left my vest. His eyes stayed fixed on mine as we sank together to kneel on the bottom.

Anxiety constricted my chest on the first breath. My throat closed. I had a strong urge to bolt to the surface—which looked to be twenty feet overhead—when in fact it was only six. Gavin tightened his grip on my shoulder strap and stared through his mask into mine with a question in his eyes. I couldn't inhale, or exhale. I was breaking the number one rule already and holding my breath.

I looked up again, too afraid to surface for fear of bursting a lung, but on the verge of a full-blown panic. Gavin squeezed my shoulder, his touch drawing my eyes back to his.

I tried to breathe in but only tiny sips of air entered, almost like a hiccup. Gavin pulled me closer to him, eyes locked on mine. He wasn't going to let me get away. I sighed into my regulator, surrendered. The gurgling sound of the bubbles as they danced to the surface calmed me as I finally exhaled. Each breath became easier than the one before. The panic passed.

I gave the okay sign back in response to his. I was okay.

After several more calming breaths, Gavin loosened his grip on my BCD and gave me the thumbs-down sign to stay down. We kneeled on the bottom for a couple of minutes before he gave the thumbs-up sign. I kicked on the surface to keep myself afloat while the weight belt tried to drag me down.

Breaking the surface, Gavin instructed, "Put some air in your BCD. It's much easier to swim with flotation."

I felt around my left shoulder to inflate the vest and bobbed on the surface.

"You did great. How did you feel?"

I removed the reg from my mouth and held it. "At first I felt like I was going to drown, but once I realized I could breathe I liked it."

"That is what is so magical about scuba. You can breathe. You must. Life is very short underwater if you don't," he said with a genuine smile.

I laughed even though the last thing I wanted to think about was how short my life might be if I panicked on the bottom of the pool again.

"Okay, now that you remembered how to breathe, let's work on buoyancy control. Let's go down again and try to get neutral. Neutral is the balance between positive and negative. With a weight belt dragging you down, you are negatively buoyant, which means you sink. Adding air makes you positively buoyant, so you'll float. The goal is neutral buoyancy, but you have to experience the feeling of both positive and negative so you can play between them to achieve it. Make sense?"

"Sure." It sounded simple enough. But even though I had become somewhat of an expert on bouncing between positive and negative in all things in life, I had yet to find the balance between the two.

"Once we're on the bottom, you'll add air to your BCD a little at a time until you start to rise off the bottom. If you put too much, you'll have to dump some to avoid rising too fast. I'll hold you, so don't worry. Just remember that if you're too negative, you'll sink but at least you can breathe. And if you're too positive, you'll float away but that's easily controlled by letting a little air out of your vest."

"Okay. Got it." I trusted him. He wouldn't let me die.

Gavin held my BCD and gave the down sign. We sank together again to sit cross-legged on the bottom. He let me go to demonstrate inflating his BCD until he was hovering about a foot off the floor of the pool like a buddha. He deflated his vest to end the demonstration, then held his hand out to signal that it was my turn. I pressed the inflator hose button for too long and rose alarmingly fast. He let me go up so I could feel that I was out of control for a second before he tugged me down. I dumped the air to start over. The next time, I hit the button only briefly. Nothing happened, so I did it again, and again, waiting after each burst shot into the vest, until I started to slowly rise off the bottom.

I floated up to just above the level he'd reached in his demo. When I started to go higher, I dumped air to sink back down a bit, then leveled out a foot or so off the bottom. The sensation of weightless equilibrium was intoxicating.

Gavin gave me the okay sign, which I returned. I was more than okay. I was euphoric. He made a fluttering sign with his fingers to signify a kick and pointed in the direction of the shallow end of the pool. He took my hand in his and guided me to swim alongside him for a small loop that brought us back to the deep end. After kneeling on the bottom for several seconds we surfaced.

Gavin had to remind me again to inflate my BCD once we were up. "You're a natural."

Hardly, but I'd take the compliment. And I understood the point of the exercise. "Thanks. It wasn't too bad once I understood that the key is to go slow and wait for the adjustments to happen."

"That's why you're a natural. When we go out on the reef, you will use that same technique to get neutral and keep doing it throughout the dive to stay neutral. And the reef will thank you. If you stay off the reef, it stays alive." Gavin paused to make sure I was following him. I nodded eagerly for him to continue. "So you have to always be aware of where you are in the water and what's happening with your buoyancy, and make adjustments as needed to stay at the same depth. Sometimes it's tricky because you get distracted by a pretty fish or a nice patch of coral. But if you are always feeling where you are, you'll be able to do it."

His faith in my ability to know where I was at all was greater than my own. I knew he was trying to teach me that I would be self-sufficient in my skills if I found myself floating away, but I liked to think that he'd be the one to ground me if I needed it. "Well *if* we go out to the reef, I hope you'll be holding onto me in case I float away."

Gavin squeezed my shoulder again, and a heat throbbed under his touch through the cool droplets on my skin. "Don't worry. I've got you."

He took me down again to review a few skills. After I successfully demonstrated mask clearing and removing and recovering my regulator, Gavin gave me the thumb-up sign to surface.

"Well done, Tessa. You passed with flying colors. I deem you ready to dive to the depths with me."

"We'll see about that." Fear lingered but the excitement of the pool dive—and the flirting—made me want to try.

After showering off and lugging all the gear back to the shop in the cart, Gavin invited me to lunch. "It's nearly one, I'm famished. How about you?"

As had become usual, food was the last thing on my mind, but I didn't want to decline. I craved his company more than a meal. "Sure. Want to grab a bite at the restaurant?"

Gavin's face twisted in distaste. "Not particularly. I eat here far more than I care to. Let's go out."

"Sure, what'd you have in mind?"

"There's a great little spot down the road. Their burgers are fantastic."

I hadn't had a burger in years. "With a recommendation like that, what have I got to lose?"

CHAPTER 9

I hoisted myself up into Gavin's old Land Rover. The motor's rumble reminded me of my dad's old farm truck. The warm breeze wafted through the open windows and whipped my hair around as we turned onto the main road. I pulled it back and held it with my hand behind my neck for a minute, then let it free. Not much point in worrying about how my hair looked since the rest of me looked like I'd been in the pool all morning.

I admired the lines between the muscles of his arm that gripped the wheel. "Now it's your turn. What's your story?"

"My story?" Gavin grinned as my eyes wandered from his biceps up to meet his as he continued playfully. "What makes you think I have a story?"

"That thick Irish accent that you can switch to a convincing Caribbean creole on demand, for starters. Do you come from Ireland?"

His accent was purposefully thicker when he responded with a smile. "Aye. From Belfast."

"How or why did you end up here? Just being a scuba bum?"

He laughed, his eyes flitting to mine before returning to the road. "No, not exactly. I came because my father was sick. I stayed because he needed me to take over the business."

"Oh, your dad owns the dive shop?"

"Yes. A few of them. He's from here."

"How did you end up in Ireland, then?"

"I was born there. My mum's Irish. "

"So you grew up there?"

"There and here. We lived between the two, about half and half, until I started secondary school, what you guys call high school. Mum wanted me to study in Ireland, which was probably a good idea. I don't know. After boarding school, I stayed for uni and then got a corporate job, because that's what you do." The corners of his mouth turned down as he shrugged but then broke into another grin as he continued. "Luckily Dad got sick and made me come back home, though."

He hurried to add, "Just kidding, of course. It was a blessing, though, to get away from that bullshit corporate lifestyle. I never want to do that again, I'll tell you."

I laughed out loud, probably a little too loud. One of our biggest challenges at the office was finding young people with drive and good work ethic. They all seem to want the full benefits of a career without the commitment and hard work required to build one. Gavin seemed to fit the millennial mold. After a taste of the real world, he came running back to Mom and Pop. Lucky for him that his father had a place for him.

There was a flash of confusion in his eyes. "Is that funny?"

I straightened in my seat when I realized I may have offended him. "Sorry, it is. But only because I've been in that corporate life for nearly twenty years now. I kind of like it."

Gavin grinned. "As long as you're happy."

Ouch. I knew I wasn't happy, but that wasn't work's fault. I stared out the window without words to reply.

Palm trees and colorful buildings lined the road that snaked along the coast. "It's a cute little town."

"Yeah, a damn sight nicer than Belfast, I'll say. But little is right."

"Do you miss the big city?"

"Not much. But I do miss the pubs."

"Isn't there an Irish pub here that makes you feel like home?"

"There are a couple, but they're mostly for tourists. Nothing like back home."

"It must have been hard to leave a bustling city to come live on a tiny island." I couldn't wait to leave my small farm town and get out into the world. He'd done that and then had to come back. I couldn't imagine.

"Not so much. The city life wasn't for me. And it was like coming home. Leaving home to come home." Gavin chuckled. "How about you? You never even told me where you live."

I smiled coyly. "You never asked."

He met my gaze with a flirtatious grin. "I'm asking now."

"California. San Francisco."

"The City by the Bay. Never been, but would love to see it. You like it?"

"Yes. I love it. Though the weather is much better here."

"Have you always been a city girl?"

"Oh no. I grew up in a farm town in Iowa."

"America's heartland."

I appreciated his attempt to acknowledge my homeland, but I had to interject a little reality to counter his idealism. "Also known as the most boring place to grow up in you can imagine."

"I can relate." From the sincerity in his smile, I knew he could. "When did you leave Iowa?"

"I left home to go to college in the big city of Des Moines when I was eighteen. It wasn't a big city at all, but it felt like it compared to the town I grew up in."

"Did you fall in love with city life?"

"No, I fell in love with Chuck and followed him to California. It was his dream, not mine." My brow wrinkled as I paused, realizing how bitter I sounded. "Actually, I wouldn't say that. I wanted to leave. I was ready for bigger and better, and the promise of opportunity."

Gavin nodded. "Then what?"

"I joined the evil corporate world." My eyes narrowed and my voice lowered ominously with the last words, drawing a chuckle from Gavin. "Then I started working for a marketing agency. After a couple of years, I started my own company, with my ex-husband."

"It's not really the corporate world when it's your own

business. There's a big difference between successful entrepreneur and corporate slave."

I laughed. "The corporate slave usually earns more and works less."

"That may be true, but the entrepreneur has the one thing the slave never has... freedom." His smile when he held my gaze drove home his point.

"I suppose you're right. The problem is that you're too busy trying to succeed to enjoy any of that freedom."

We turned into a gravel lot to face a tiny yellow shack with a tin roof. "Here we are. Welcome to Morgan's. Best kept secret on the island."

"Is that so?" I swung the heavy door of the Land Rover open and slid off the seat.

"Yeah, not many tourists find this place."

"I can see why." The screen door creaked open into a room no larger than my living room back home. I pushed my sunglasses up onto my forehead and blinked to help my eyes adjust to the darkness. The wood floors creaked under my feet as I followed Gavin to the only open table.

"It's not much to look at, but they have great burgers."

I sat on the wooden bench across from Gavin. "The little hole-in-the-wall places are often the best, no matter where you go."

Gavin leaned onto the table, raising his brows. "What's your favorite hole-in-the-wall in the big city?"

"I have a few. For drinks, I like Louie's. For sushi, Kai. But my all-time favorite is a little restaurant in Chinatown, Sam Wu."

"What makes Sam Wu so special?"

I smiled, recalling the bizarre premise. "The waiter refuses to let you order. He chooses what he thinks you'll like. You'd be silly not to take his recommendations, and he makes sure you know it. It's a trip, and always delicious."

"Really? That seems strange. Why do they even have a menu then?"

"You're always free to order what you want, but the whole premise is that you trust them to give you the thing that you will like best."

A waiter appeared at our table. "Hello, folks. What can I get you today?"

Gavin shot me a smile as he asked, "What do you recommend?"

The waiter's brow wrinkled; his face said *seriously?* "We've got the burger you always order, or the chicken burger, or the fish burger. Three flavors of burger. What are you in the mood for?"

"I'll have the regular burger and a beer."

The waiter rolled his eyes. "The usual, then. And you, pretty lady?"

I loved the familiarity, but I felt myself blush at the unexpected compliment. "Sounds great. I'll have the same."

"See how easy that was?" The waiter chided as he shot Gavin an annoyed glance, but his smile showed he was equally amused. "Two burgers."

Gavin watched the waiter walk away. "So, not like that, I gather?

"No. The service is the right level of surly but more like 'Oh, you like burgers, you should try the pork surprise.' And then you're a fool not to take his advice."

He smiled. "I gotta admit, I'd have to know what was in that pork surprise."

I grinned. "Of course you would. That's why it works."

His brow furrowed. "Fascinating, but I'm not sure I like the idea of being told what I'll like. I think I've had enough of that in my life."

"I can relate to that. But that's the beauty of it, I suppose. Going against that need to control and just surrendering. It makes the reward of the surprise even sweeter."

Gavin stroked the stubble on his chin. "I could see that."

We settled into a comfortable silence as my eyes roamed over the other patrons—mostly locals, mostly male. Caribbean British accents hummed all around while the greasy scent of burgers frying mixed with the fresh sea air.

The gruff waiter sat two mugs of beer on the table and disappeared without a word. The cold glass felt heavenly in my warm hands, and the beer tasted divine. I held up the mug after the sip. "Oh, sorry, cheers to you for helping me rediscover scuba diving this morning. It was good fun."

"Cheers to you for taking my advice and going for it. Sometimes all it takes is someone else's suggestion to encounter something you like. Like Sam Wu, right?"

I licked the foam off my upper lip after another big sip of beer. "Right."

"I'm glad you liked the pool, but that was just the beginning. Come out to the reef with me. You will love it."

He didn't need to convince me, which was what scared me. As determined as I was not to be played, I seemed to want to play right into his hand. "I'll think about it."

His whole face lit up like he'd gotten a brilliant idea. "You know what you should do? You should come with me on a trip over to Cayman Brac tomorrow. There's pristine diving that no one else sees, and I'm going on a mega yacht, so you can't beat that."

"That sounds amazing, but my friend will be here Thursday." And there was no way I was going away on a yacht with this man. I couldn't trust myself.

"Don't worry, I'll have you home before your boyfriend comes."

I swallowed hard to try to untangle the knot that formed in my throat. Heat rose up my neck, setting my ears and face ablaze. "He's not my boyfriend. He's my best friend. My *gay* best friend."

Gavin's brows raised over wide eyes and his mouth twisted into a mischievous smirk. "Oh, is that so? Why did you say he was your boyfriend before?"

I huffed out a smart assed reply. "I didn't. I said he was male. You just assumed."

Gavin's eyes were smiling when he shot back, "You let me think he was your boyfriend. Why is that? So I wouldn't hit on you?"

I loved the confidence of his challenge. The fire in my cheeks burned from pink to fuscia. His putting me on the spot had me all out of sorts. I swigged my beer to calm my nerves. "Hardly. I didn't think it was any of your business. Besides, even though you were chatting me up, and being nice, I wouldn't think that you were actually hitting on me, anyway." I shifted on the hard-wooden bench and gulped down my beer, hoping he'd bought my indignant act.

Gavin leaned across the table toward me. The corners of his mouth turned downward while his gaze narrowed, like he was trying to figure out what I meant. The more nervous I got, the more relaxed he seemed. "And why is that?"

His Irish accent was killing me. Could he possibly be any sexier? My knee bounced up and down in an anxious tic under the table. I could have easily puked right then and there. I smiled the biggest, fakest, most sarcastic grin I could to try and feign confidence. "Oh, I don't know. Maybe because I'm old enough to be your mother."

"Ha!" He laughed so loud it made me jump. "My mother was older than you when I was born. Age is just a number."

The waiter slung the burgers onto the table, in two wicker baskets lined with brown paper that was already splotchy from the grease oozing from between the buns. He asked gruffly, "Another beer?"

Gavin eyed his nearly empty mug. "Sure I'll have another. You?"

"Yes, please." I'd use my manners even if the service was barely civil. I pulled the nearest basket toward me. There were no utensils around so there was no way to eat it lady-like. I'd have looked and felt like a fool eating it with a knife and fork anyway. I got my hands around the bun and leaned over the table so it would drip into the basket. I could barely get my mouth around it, it was so thick. When my teeth sank into the juicy beef, I knew I would have it all over my face from the first bite. It was so delicious, I didn't even care. The mixture of the flavors made music in my mouth and escaped as moans as I chewed. Tender beef, red onion, crunchy lettuce, juicy tomato, pickles, and the buttered bun. Magnificent simplicity. Good God, how long had it been since I last ate a burger? Two, three years?

Gavin grinned. "I guess you like it then?"

I grunted and nodded affirmatively until I could swallow and answer. "Oh my God, yes. It's amazing." I wanted a drink of beer but was afraid to put the burger down since it was already falling apart in my hands. I placed it upside down in the basket and reached for a napkin to wipe the juices that had run down to my wrists.

"Messy, though, isn't it?" Gavin's eyes danced with his smile.

"Yeah, but worth it. I mean, seriously, that may be the best burger I've ever had. It has something, something different. What is it?"

"Coriander. It's the secret ingredient."

"Ah, that's it!" I chugged a quarter of my mug of beer and carefully picked up the burger again. I didn't even care how savage I might have looked devouring it. I finished before Gavin did because I never put it down again.

Gavin eyed my empty basket and grinned. "I guess you were hungry?"

"More so than I realized." I threw my napkin into the basket and exhaled. "God, that was good." I sipped my beer and studied him as he finished his burger. God, he was sexy. But while he wasn't the baby child I thought him to be, twenty-eight was still young. And he was a ladies' man. Definitely bad news. He was still fun to look at and to be around.

Hoisting myself up into the Rover was no easy task after two beers and a hardcore food buzz. The warm air in the truck made me want to melt into the seat. "Wow, I could use a nap after that. Thank you, it was nice to try something off the beaten path. I never would have found that without you."

"There's plenty more to see. If you come with me tomorrow you'll get to see things that most tourists don't."

I lifted my brows at the suggestive comment and smirked, "I bet I would."

"Don't get the wrong idea. I'm a gentleman."

It sounded like a line he'd used before. "I'm sure you are." I eyed him. "I assumed you'd have a girlfriend anyway." I figured from eavesdropping in the bar that he didn't, but I wanted to see what he'd say about it.

"Nope."

"I'm guessing that's by choice since I'm sure you'd have no trouble finding one."

"Finding a good one has proven impossible thus far. I don't think I'm cut out for it anyway."

I nodded. "Not marriage material?"

Gavin shook his head. "Yeah, no. After seeing my parents berate one another for my whole life, it's not the least bit appealing."

My eyes widened and my heart winced a little at his open admission. "Oh, I'm sorry."

"Don't be. I'd rather be alone anyway. It's bad enough having my dad to answer to now. The last thing I need is a wife telling me what to do."

I chuckled. "I guess that goes back to finding a good one."

"I won't be holding my breath for that."

I grinned. "Holding your breath is the most dangerous thing you can do."

His flirty green eyes sparkled. "You're a good student. But how about you? Are you still looking for a good one?"

"I'm not looking, and not holding my breath either."

"Have you had a string of bad ones, too?"

I should have known he'd ask me after I asked him, but I wasn't prepared to answer. I took a deep breath and did anyway. "Only one—well, one that lasted eighteen years."

Gavin's expression softened. "Oh, sorry. I didn't mean to pry."

"It's okay. I started it. It's no big deal. I just got divorced. Last week. That's how I ended up here. My secretary thought I needed a vacation and my best friend agreed, so they convinced me to come."

"Love always turns sour sooner or later, I suppose." A brief cynical frown was quickly replaced with a warm smile. "I'm glad you're here. Hopefully the vacation will help get your mind off things. I'd love to show you around—in and out of the water—if you'll let me."

I wasn't sure if he meant to be so suggestive or if it was just my dirty mind entertaining torrid thoughts. He could show me around, alright. "That would be amazing."

"Unfortunately I've got a lot of work this afternoon since I took the morning off, or I'd offer to take you diving on the reef right now."

"Took the morning off? You were working all morning, teaching me to scuba dive again."

"Well, that didn't feel like work. And it's not really my job. But I wanted to be the one to take you." Thankfully his eyes stayed on the road when he cocked his head to the side and grinned again, so he couldn't see me melt into the truck seat from his hotness.

I tried to up the ante on the flirt game that I still wasn't sure that we were playing by being coy. "Oh really? Why is that?"

He turned toward me to answer, locking my gaze, dead serious. "So that you'd feel safe. So you'd love it and want to go down with me again."

My stomach dropped straight into my crotch and stirred an excitement I hadn't felt in years. I wanted to go down, with him, on him. I was grateful he had to look back to the road so he couldn't see me bite my lip while I squeezed the handle on the armrest.

The turn signal clicked and the Rover slowed. "If you don't mind, I need to stop at one of our shops on the way. I need to sign some checks and pick up deposits for the bank. I'll only be a minute."

We stopped under an enormous rectangular sign, a dive flag, with its red background and white diagonal stripe, superimposed with the Jolly Roger pirate flag and Blackbeard's Dive Center in a vintage font. A pretty solid logo. Effective, immediately invoking curiosity about the history of pirates on the island. My designer eye approved.

"You can come in if you want, much cooler there. But if you prefer to stay here and admire the sign, feel free."

"As much as I do admire the sign, I'd rather stay cool, thanks."

I flung the door open then lifted my knees to peel my sweaty thighs off the seat before I could swing my legs out the door. A breeze wafted under my dress, cooling the wetness both behind and between my legs.

"Afternoon, Mr. Scott." The silhouette of a woman called cheerfully from behind the round counter in the center of the large store. Light reflecting off the water from the dock outside the wall of windows flooded the space.

"Afternoon, Agnes. Is Harlon upstairs? I need to sign the checks for him."

"Yes, he's been waiting." Her tone was mostly matronly but slightly scolding.

"I know, I had a busy morning." Gavin's green eyes sparkled as he glanced at me with a grin. "I'll be right down."

"Agnes, meet Tessa. She's joining me on the private charter tomorrow."

The grandmotherly woman looked up over the rims of her glasses with surprise. "Is that so? How exciting!"

I tried to shoot Gavin a look that said *What the fuck?*, but he was already halfway up the stairs and laughing to himself.

"Actually, I'm not so sure, but Gavin's been trying to convince me."

Agnes eyed me over the rim of her glasses. "He can be very persuasive." Her lips pursed in a knowing smirk.

"He certainly thinks he is."

On the way back to the resort, Gavin made light of his joking with Agnes. "I didn't mean to put you on the spot there. I was just kidding."

"I know. No worries."

"But I wasn't kidding that I'd love for you to come with me. I'm going over in a private yacht to pick up the owner's niece and nephew and bring them back. It's ridiculous to take that giant boat, but the wealthy are often ridiculous."

I cocked my head as I questioned him. "I don't understand. Why are you going to pick them up?"

"He hired me to certify them to dive a few months ago. Now he says he doesn't trust anyone else to dive with them." He shrugged. "I won't turn down a night on a three-hundred-million-dollar yacht and a hefty fee. You shouldn't either."

His persistence made me smile. "Three hundred million dollars? Christ, that must be some yacht."

"Positively ridiculous."

My stomach fluttered at the thought of a night on a billionaire's boat with a flirty young playboy. It was positively ridiculous that I was considering it. I wasn't ready for any of that. "While it sounds tempting, I have to pass."

Gavin turned to me with a serious face after we stopped in the parking lot. "I'm not going to beg. But if you change your mind I'll be on the dock at eight. Just ask the front desk to get you a taxi to where the *Caribbean Dream* is docked. You can't miss that boat."

I loved that he was trying so hard to get me to go. That's why I couldn't. "I'll see you when you get back. We can go diving after Elliot gets here. He might like to learn, too." Although Elliot would hardly discourage me from hooking up with the hot, young scuba instructor, I knew I was better off with a chaperone.

After a long bubble bath, I made myself a cocktail from the minibar and went out to the porch to watch the sunset. My arms felt heavy as I sank into the Adirondack chair. The day in the pool and the heavy lunch had worn me out. As the sky changed colors over the ocean, I imagined what the reef must be like in that crystal blue sea. Recalling the exhilaration of breathing underwater made me want to see for myself. Elliot would be game. He never said no to something new. And he would hold my hand if I lost my nerve.

I mused that he must have read my mind when my phone rang. We were connected like that.

"Hey, Elliot, I was just thinking about you."

"Imagine that, Sweet T, I was just thinking about you, too. Hence, the call." He was such a smart ass.

"Yeah, yeah. What are you up to?"

"Putting out fires left and right."

"Oh yeah? What's up?"

"Just a shit show at work. Nothing I can't handle though. I'm having to work overtime to take care of things before my trip."

I sipped my coconut rum with pineapple juice. "I can't wait for you to get here! This resort is incredible. You won't believe this room." I described the bungalow, right down to the west-facing porch perfect for sunset cocktails.

"Sounds heavenly. I can use a getaway after this week, and it's only Tuesday. One more day of hell. Have you managed to have any fun on your own? Please tell me you're not just sitting in your room."

"I went for a scuba refresher course today, I'll have you know. And then let my hot, young scuba instructor take me to lunch. I'm doing a lot," I insisted proudly.

"I'm impressed—mostly about lunch with the hottie. What's the story there? Any interest?"

"He's pretty to look at and as charming as can be, but you know I'm not looking for anything like that, especially with a guy fourteen years younger than me."

"Hey, don't knock it! A vacation fling with a hot, young scuba instructor may be *exactly* what you need right now. Did he hit on you?"

I chuckled before taking the last sip of my cocktail. "It's hard to say. He's flirty, but I have a feeling that's just how he is with everyone. He seems to be a player."

"There's nothing wrong with hooking up with a player, T. You're not looking for a husband. Don't overthink it."

"I'm not thinking about it at all." That wasn't exactly true, but I didn't want Elliot to know that I'd entertained dirty thoughts of Gavin all afternoon.

"Well, you should. Don't let an opportunity for the perfect rebound sex pass you by. You're long overdue. A lot less thinking and a little more fucking is what you need right now."

"I don't think I'm ready for that." I've never been one for superficial sex. I'd never had any kind of fling—ever.

"Sometimes you just have to fake it till you make it. If you don't get back on that horse soon it might forget how to leave the stable."

"My horse is perfectly happy in the stable. I won't be seeing him again before you're here. He's taking a three-hundred-million-dollar yacht over to another island tomorrow to pick up some kids for the billionaire owner and take them diving. He'll be back Thursday. Maybe you'll want to learn to dive? He's a great teacher."

"Oh, is he now? I got certified in Puerto Rico last year."

I didn't remember diving in the stories from the trip. "Really? I only remember hearing about your hookups in Puerto Rico."

"Those were better stories. But, yeah, I like diving. I'd go again for sure."

"Great! Then you can meet Gavin for yourself."

"He sounds sexy. Especially on a three-hundred-million-dollar yacht. Holy hell. Can you imagine?"

"I really can't. I was tempted to go with him just for the boat trip."

Elliot nearly shouted with surprise. "You mean he invited you?"

I winced, regretting I'd mentioned it. "Yeah, kind of. He offered to take me diving on the way over. I told him I'd wait until he comes back. That way you can go, too."

"Oh, honey. You can't pass this up. If you do, I may never forgive you. It's just too perfect."

"I know it sounds like a fairytale, but I wouldn't feel comfortable."

"Why the hell not? You don't have to sleep with him, Tessa. He invited you to go diving. Just go and see what happens. But don't pass up this opportunity. You may never have another one like it."

I bit my lip and shook the ice in my glass, wishing it wasn't empty. "I don't think I can, Elliot."

"Nonsense. Of course, you can. He's not a creep, is he? I mean, do you think he's *expecting* sex if you go?"

"No, I don't think so. He claimed that his intentions were innocent, that he was a gentleman. But isn't that exactly what a player would say? I don't know. He's probably not interested in me anyway."

"Well, if that's how he framed the invite, and you said he's a nice guy, then you should take it at face value. It doesn't have to be about him at all. Go for the boat ride. Go for the diving. Go for the fun. You deserve it!"

I appreciated his insistence, but I had to nip it in the bud like I'd done with the silly thoughts of Gavin. "That's crazy talk. I'm not going. Shut up and get back to work so you can leave Thursday."

"You're so stubborn. I won't waste my breath. Try and let loose, T. I'll see you Thursday."

I could picture him rolling his eyes at me. He was annoyed but at least he'd let it go. "Good luck with the fires. Text me when you're on the way."

I was exhausted. The thought of getting dressed for dinner did not appeal. Nor did dinner, for that matter. I mixed myself another drink and snuggled up with my laptop on the sofa. Curiosity got the better of me, and I googled the *Caribbean Dream*.

My eyes nearly popped out of my head as I scrolled through the images. Jesus. It had a helipad. And a pool. It looked like a cruise ship. I clicked a link to an article about the boat. It was a 248-foot vessel commissioned by Clifton Drake, the third richest man in the world, which had taken two years to build. It was the ninth-largest private yacht in the world. My jaw dropped. Holy shit. I wanted to text Elliot to tell him, but I knew he'd tell me what a fool I was for not going. He'd probably be right.

A quick search confirmed my suspicion that Clifton Drake was the Plastic King that the bartender had referred to ominously and with great disdain. That figured.

When I finished my cocktail, I put Sublime on the sound system and danced while mixing another drink. Last one. I didn't want a headache tomorrow. I curled up with my cocktail and found a diving documentary on Netflix. The focus on the environmental impact of diving was grim. The images of reefs that had been destroyed by tourists were shocking. The healthy virgin reefs they compared them to, full of color and teeming with fish, made me want to dive again, but the message of the film made me not want to be part of the problem. I was thoroughly depressed at the sharp contrast in highly-trafficked sites. Humans were a plague to nature.

Fortunately, the tone of the story changed to show how divers can contribute to protecting and restoring the fragile ecosystem. Remembering Gavin's passionate comments about staying offf the coral made me smile. He was part of the solution. Then I remembered what he said about seeing virgin reefs that no one else gets to dive. It would be a shame to miss it, he'd said. I was starting to think he was right.

Brazen with liquid courage, I decided that Gavin and Elliot

were both right by the time I finished my drink. It's not every day a girl gets the chance to go dive a pristine reef on a billionaire's boat. I wasn't going to let this opportunity pass me by. I'd done too much of that in my life. Fuck it, what did I have to lose?

I was drunk on more than the three cocktails as I flitted around the room packing my small backpack. The buzz of taking a chance and doing something wild and crazy made me feel like my old self again. I used to be spontaneous and adventurous—before succumbing to the evils of the corporate world. I giggled as I shoved both my bikinis in the bag. Gavin might be wiser than I gave him credit for. Even if he was a spoiled millennial, his philosophy may be a better one than mine. He lived well.

And tomorrow I'd be living well on a three-hundred-million-dollar yacht.

I fumbled clumsily to set the alarm for six-thirty to be sure I wouldn't miss the boat. I'd gotten more tipsy than I intended. At least sleep came easily.

CHAPTER 10

*L*ight blinded me as I blinked out of a deep sleep. I'd forgotten to draw the curtains. My head throbbed so I was slow to register just how bright the sun was at first—too bright for six-thirty. I rolled over and panicked at the sight of the clock. 7:18. Fuck! I checked my alarm, that was still set, to six-thirty *p.m.* Idiot. That's what I get for three cocktails and no dinner. I was going to miss the opportunity I'd finally decided I couldn't pass up.

I threw back the covers and rushed to get dressed. I called the front desk to order the taxi and rushed to the bathroom. I caught sight of myself in the mirror while I quickly brushed my teeth. I looked like shit but there was no time to worry about that. It didn't matter anyway. I wasn't trying to impress anyone. I threw my toiletries into my backpack and took off running.

The same taxi driver who'd dropped me at the resort three days earlier waited for me at the curb. He wouldn't be surprised at the sight of me, he'd already seen worse. "Well, hello. Nice to see you again." He smiled as he held the door open.

I practically dove into the back seat as I called out, "Nice to see you too."

He eyed me in the rearview mirror as I caught my breath. "In a hurry?"

"Yeah, I'm late. How long will it take to get to where the *Caribbean Dream* is docked?"

"Ten minutes. Don't worry I'm sure Mr. Drake will wait for you. He wouldn't leave a pretty lady waiting on the dock."

"I don't think he will be on the boat. Gavin from the dive shop is there." It was impertinent that he was not exactly expecting me.

"Ah, is that so?" He grinned into the mirror.

I realized I'd probably contributed to island gossip—Gavin taking a drunken and disheveled hotel guest out on the local billionaire's yacht.

"None of my business. But you're better off." The locals were obviously not impressed with Clifton no matter how flashy his wealth. Lucky me that I could take a trip on his yacht without having to meet him. If I could get to the damn boat. I wished the driver would just shut up and drive.

We pulled into the harbor lot at 7:57. "There she is." He stared up with eyes wide with wonder. Whether he liked the owner or not, this yacht was spectacular.

I gawked at the sleek modern structure that towered several stories above the water—a masterpiece of design. *Caribbean Dream* was right. "She's beautiful." I recognized the yacht from the photos but it was far more impressive than I could have imagined. It didn't seem real until Gavin surfaced through an opening to a railed gang plank. He glanced in my direction but then focused on the two tanks on the dock that he was heading for. He did a double-take and my being there finally registered. His eyes narrowed but his whole face lit up in a smile that made my stomach flutter.

"Did you decide to join me?" His wry smile made me weak in the knees, but this wasn't about him.

"I *decided* that I'd be an idiot to miss out on diving virgin reefs on an incredible yacht."

He stood with his hand on his hips studying me so hard it made me uneasy. I didn't realize I was holding my breath until I finally exhaled when he replied. "And you are clearly no idiot. I'm glad you changed your mind. Now grab a tank."

I started to pick up the tank but a voice behind me interrupted in a European accent I couldn't place.

"Don't worry, I'll get it." A bubbly blonde girl in a cut-off tank top with the dive shop logo over red spandex shorts grinned broadly at Gavin. She had the body of a model and a smile that could blind. Gavin raised a brow when she brushed up against his chest as she reached for the tank he had planned to carry. Their relationship seemed far more familiar than coworkers. Was this Melissa? Or was she the next last one? Either way, I suddenly felt like the third wheel. If knowing that Gavin was a Casanova wasn't enough of a deterrent, seeing him in action would put the last nail in that coffin. Who was I kidding, though? With the distraction of the European supermodel, I wouldn't even be on his radar— and that was a good thing.

He wrapped his fingers around her wrist. "We've got it. These are the last two."

She looked at his hand and smiled even wider before she lifted her eyes to his. "I don't mind."

"I know. Thanks, but my student needs to learn to take care of herself."

"You have a *student*?" From her incredulous tone, I guessed he was serious about not teaching much anymore. She finally addressed me, in a huff. "Lucky you. I begged to go on this trip and *someone* wouldn't take me." Relief flashed through me that she wasn't joining us.

Gavin smirked. "*Someone* has to work in the shop. Speaking of which, you have students arriving about now. You'd better get going."

Her smile faded. "Alright. Have fun out there. I'll see you tomorrow night." She squeezed his hand as she kissed him three times on alternating cheeks and then waved quickly in my direction. "Enjoy the diving."

"Thanks," I answered weakly. It didn't matter. She'd already turned a cold shoulder and was on her way.

Gavin nodded at the tanks. "Shall we?"

I lifted one tank by the valve and followed him up the gangway into a dark corridor. It took a few seconds for my eyes to adjust to the light before I could appreciate the lavish interior of the yacht. Wood-paneled walls and brass rails were illuminated with a soft yellow light that gave the space a warm, cozy feel. I put the tank down and looked around to take it all in. "Wow, this is amazing."

Gavin grinned and grabbed the tank I'd dropped. "And this is only the service quarters. Wait until you see the rest."

Whatever doubt I still held about going was left on the dock. "I can't wait!"

He stowed the tanks in the storage area. "Lucky for you, I brought extra tanks. We can do a couple of dives on the way over. There's an awesome wall, probably one of the nicest dives in the world."

I followed him down a narrow hallway past several wooden doors that I imagined opened to crew cabins. A boat like this would have a sizable staff. He hung a left to the landing of a grand staircase.

"Lucky me. That's why I decided I had to come. I watched a documentary last night about the impact of diving on the reef. I realized the opportunity to dive reefs that no one ever sees might never come again. I couldn't pass it up."

"Well, I'm glad the sea could lure you even if I couldn't." Gavin chuckled. "But you made the right decision. It's incredible. I'm still blown away by it every time."

He seemed bristly, which was slightly amusing since he was the reason I wasn't going to go in the first place. His ego was bruised. Poor little thing. But I was here for the trip, and it was better we establish that from the get-go. "I literally can't wait! When will we be there?"

"We'll be there by noon if we get off the dock by nine. I'll show you to your cabin."

My mouth hung open as we topped the stairs into a large living space. Floor-to-ceiling windows lined both sides of the room. Five sleek ivory sofas surrounded an enormous coffee table, two on either side and one on the end nearest the wall. The other end opened toward a bar constructed entirely of backlit natural quartz, opposite which sat a baby grand piano. *Fuck.*

Gavin paused to let me admire the piano for a couple of seconds, smiling. "I'm afraid the entertainer isn't with us, but I can play you a song later if you like."

My eyes narrowed before meeting his. "You play the piano?"

His face lit up. "Aye. And the guitar. And the mandolin. And the fiddle." He winked. "Very Irish."

I gawked as he exited through the other end of the salon. He was full of surprises for a millennial scuba bum.

He led me to a door and swung it open. "You can take this cabin. I'm staying in the master cabin down there at the end." He pointed in the direction of the back of the boat. I entered the door he held to a stateroom every bit as nice as my five-star bungalow.

I stepped into a sitting area with a sofa and an upholstered armchair, beyond which was a king-sized bed that looked out a wall of windows. The other walls were made of exquisite wood with a rich grain that gave a cozy feel to the expansive room. "How many rooms does this boat have?" I had read that there were a dozen, but I couldn't believe that eleven more rooms this size could fit.

"Twelve staterooms, including the master, plus the captain's quarters and fourteen more crew cabins. She's quite the ship."

"I'll say." I took a last look around the room. "Can I get the rest of the tour?"

"Sure thing. We're almost ready to push off. Have you eaten? We can have breakfast after we get underway."

"I just woke up, so breakfast would be lovely."

"You definitely need to eat before diving the wall."

His mention of our diving destination worried me. "How deep is this wall?"

The top of the wall is at about ten meters but it drops off into the abyss. Don't worry though, I won't take you deeper than twenty meters."

Sixty feet? Six feet of water above me in the pool seemed like a lot. Would I make it to the surface if something went wrong from that depth? My palms got clammy. "I've never been that deep before."

"It's okay. The water is so clear it won't feel that deep. You'll do great, I'm sure. You're a natural."

I didn't want to refute his confidence in me, but I was pretty sure it was misplaced. I was so sure, in fact, that I briefly entertained the fantasy of making a run for it. We hadn't left the dock yet. Maybe this was all a huge mistake. It wouldn't be the first I'd made after too many cocktails on an empty stomach. But I pushed that doubt to the back of my mind, determined. I was here for the diving. I was going to at least try.

"I trust you." Saying it out loud made me realize how true my statement was. Trusting him was why I'd decided to come on the trip.

"Good." Gavin took my hand and pulled me toward the door of the cabin. "Let's go for that tour."

When he released my hand, I wished he hadn't. I followed him through another sitting room with a more traditional wooden bar at one end. Burgundy leather couches surrounded a gas fireplace that seemed out of place in the Caribbean. The lounge led to the dining room where an ornate chandelier loomed over an enormous wooden table that probably sat at least twenty. The mix of earthy, traditional decor in some rooms with the sleek modern feel of others could be a design faux pas unless it's very well done. They'd pulled it off with flying colors.

We ascended to the next deck—the pool deck. Once again, my jaw dropped as my gaze traveled to the large jacuzzi at the end of the rectangular pool. "Holy hell. You've got to be kidding me."

"I know, right? It just doesn't stop." He led me to a table under an umbrella already set for two.

"I need pictures of this." I set my backpack on the table and I fished through all the pockets in search of my phone—which was nowhere to be found. I remembered setting it on the bathroom counter while I frantically threw my toiletries in the backpack. Fuck.

My panic must have been apparent. "Something wrong?"

"I left my phone in my room." I blinked slowly, as surprised that it had taken me this long to realize I had left it.

"Don't worry, I can send someone to bring it from your cabin if you tell me where it is."

I shook my head in a shocked daze. "At the hotel."

Gavin's forehead creased with surprise but he quickly waved off my concern. "There's no service for most of the trip anyway."

My brow wrinkled. "I'm guessing there's WIFI on this boat."

"Good point. But it's probably for the best. Aren't you on

vacation? Maybe a night without your phone is a good thing."

It was too late to do anything about it now anyway. The boat was leaving the dock. "That would probably be good for everyone. It'll be fine."

"You can sit out by the pool after breakfast if you like. I have some work to do."

"That sounds divine." I took the seat at the table across from Gavin. By the time the waitress brought two large plates of fresh fruit, we were out of the harbor, surrounded by nothing but the blue of the ocean that was almost indiscernible from the blue of the sky. None of it felt real.

Gavin briefed me on the dive plan over breakfast. "We'll do the wall dive and then a half-hour surface interval before we do a shallower reef dive."

"Can't we do the shallow reef first?" It would sure make me feel better.

"It's better not to do a reverse profile, for the nitrogen loading. Besides, the wall is on the way. Don't worry, Tessa. You know I've got you." He smiled before popping a big chunk of pineapple into his mouth.

"I know." I was committed, so there was no point in letting worry in. I'd just have to trust him and hope for the best.

I changed into my bikini and lounged by the pool with my ebook. It seemed like I'd only been there a few minutes but it had been an hour and a half when Gavin came to find me. "You ready? We're almost there."

"As ready as I'll ever be."

Gavin already had all our gear out and assembled on the

enormous swim platform off the back of the boat. "I wanted you to put your rig together so you know it's done right."

"I'd be more confident if you did it, but that makes sense." I smiled as I cinched the tank strap of the BCD in place. "You wet it for me already?"

He flashed a grin that made my heart jump up into my throat as he spoke. "It works much better when it's wet."

"It certainly does." And he knew how to make it wet. My eyes darted toward the floor as my face flamed. Was I finding sexual innuendo in everything he said or was his mind as dirty as mine?

I took a deep breath and focused on connecting my regulator to the tank and BCD. I turned on the air to test the regulator and inflator hose. "No leaks. It's good to go."

"Alright, gear up. We're going to put air in the BCD to float and swim holding that line to that big orange ball out there. There's a down line from there. We'll descend, remembering to equalize as we go." He pinched his nose and pointed to his ear. "If you feel weird for any reason, ever, you just give me the sign." He waved his splayed hand. "I'll be there and we can deal with anything that comes up down there. There is no reason to bolt to the surface, ever. Even if you can't get air, I have an octopus for you." He pointed to the redundant second-stage regulator clipped to his vest.

His calm and commanding demeanor eased my anxiety. I put on my weight belt, mask and fins, then slipped into my gear that a crew member held up for me. I shuffled to the edge beside Gavin.

"Look out to the horizon and take a giant step." Gavin demonstrated and bobbed on the surface to wait.

I held my regular and mask in place and took a deep breath before stepping into nothingness. I kept my head out of the water as we swam to the line, and my heart pounded when I put my face in the water and looked down into the deep blue with no bottom in sight. I felt my chest constrict with my first instinct to hold my breath. I willed myself to inhale. I could breathe but I couldn't do this. No fucking way. The tightening around my torso was all I could feel and all I could think was that I had to get out of that gear or it might drown me. I kicked wildly to keep myself afloat—unnecessary with the air in my vest—and pushed my mask up onto my forehead.

Gavin calmly took my BCD strap in his fist and held my regulator in my mouth with his other hand. The serious look in his eye when he spoke brought me down from my hysteria. "Put your mask back on."

It was an order, and exactly what I needed. I obeyed.

"Take a few breaths—full, slow, deep breaths."

I kept still under his gaze and felt myself relax.

"Keep breathing and put your face in the water. Look at the down line. We're going to hold that line. The line will take us right to the wall. You can see it there if you look." I nodded and put my face in the water and lifted it again after I'd seen the coral beneath the line.

"When you're ready, you give me the okay-to-descend sign and we'll start down slowly. You've got this. And I've got you."

I took a deep breath and dumped the air out of my BCD, gripping the descent line for dear life. The deeper we sank, the more relaxed I felt. The bubbles of my breath were music to my ears. By the time we reached the reef, I was in an almost ecstatic Zen state. Every color in the rainbow speckled the top of the wall as soft corals swayed in the current. Fish of as many colors gathered in packs around giant barrel sponges. It was like swimming in an aquarium.

Gavin got my attention by tapping my hand that still gripped the line and asked if I was okay with the sign. I returned the signal and released the line. He held my BCD as we drifted slowly down the wall. I was so awestruck by the coral display that I didn't think to look at my gauges until Gavin pointed at his. Once we reached 60 feet, Gavin gave me the sign to stay. I put a puff of air in my BCD and felt myself level off, neutral.

After we'd swum along the wall for a couple of minutes, Gavin released my BCD. We stopped to examine a patch of coral. Gavin pointed out a tiny purple shrimp in the center of a sea anemone whose translucent tentacles waved in a slow rhythm. A little further along, Gavin spotted a giant grouper hiding in a hole in the wall. The next opening housed a small black and white spotted eel who seemed annoyed with our presence, darting his head out to flash his mouth full of teeth. I laughed into my regulator before becoming mesmerized with a fish that looked like it was wearing neon body paint, ready for a rave. I laughed harder, smiling so much that my mask seal leaked.

Gavin smiled almost as broadly when he took hold of my BCD and signaled for me to clear my mask. I did so easily and gave the okay sign, so he released me and we carried on. He stopped at an opening that went deep into the wall. I waited while he poked his head deeper into the cave. Even though only half his body was inside, suddenly I could no longer see Gavin when a cloud of sediment swirled around him. I didn't know what was happening until I saw a grey flash and felt the hard bump against my mask—just before it was ripped off my face.

I grasped wildly and blindly at the water hoping to catch the mask somehow but it was gone. In my panic, I sucked water in through my nose and had a coughing fit into my regulator. The salt water burned my eyes while I looked up, down, and all around, searching for the light of the surface. I had already started kicking when I felt a sharp tug on my BCD.

I could barely make out Gavin's form when he pulled me close to his chest. He held my regulator in my mouth—a smart move since my instinct was to spit it out and bolt for the surface, probably holding my breath the whole way and killing myself in the process. I wanted to scream and cry but Gavin's tight hold reminded me that I could still breathe. I closed my eyes and held my nose, focusing on letting air and not water in. Gavin dragged me through the water. I started to kick to help him swim when I realized he must be taking me back to the boat. I had no choice but to surrender and let him lead me blind.

The minutes we swam felt like hours. Gavin dumped air from my BCD, and I knew we were going up. Thank God. Getting to the surface seemed to take forever too. When the air hit my face I thought I'd cry, and when I saw the boat, I did. I sobbed into my regulator while Gavin inflated my BCD.

"It's okay, Tessa. You're okay. Look at me."

I blinked through tears and took my regular out, gasping for air. "I'm sorry. I panicked. What happened?"

"Let's just get you on the boat. Come on. I've got you." He laced his fingers through mine as we swam for the ladder. I gripped him tight and didn't want to let him go when the time came.

A crew member helped me out of my gear, and I staggered to sit on the deck, trembling. Gavin sat beside me and put his arm around my shoulders. I cried ugly tears until I didn't have any more while he told me it was okay, it was all going to be okay.

I finally calmed enough to lift my head and speak. "What happened?"

"I guess I spooked a big reef shark when I poked my head in his hole. He must have knocked your mask off on his way out."

"I'm sorry I panicked."

"Don't be ridiculous. I'm so sorry that happened to you, Tessa. In the twenty years I've been diving, I've never seen that happen."

Lucky me. One in a million chance. At least I wasn't a cliché. "Great. Just my luck."

"Well, maybe it's not such a bad thing. Now you know you can deal with anything. You did great."

"I was ready to bolt to the surface." He had saved me from myself.

"You stayed calm and let me help you. You did great."

I didn't feel great, but his arm around me did. His face was inches from mine and the still of the silence between our breaths drew my lips toward his, but I stopped myself. I couldn't let myself go there, even in a moment of weakness. I sat up and took a deep breath. As long as I could breathe, I was alright.

Gavin rubbed my shoulder. "You should relax. We can shower off on the pool deck and chill in the jacuzzi."

A shower and my bed sounded better. I couldn't trust myself with him in a hot tub. "I think I need to rest."

"Oh, right. Of course, you must be tired. No worries. Do what you need to do."

What I *needed* to do was keep myself from making a huge mistake, even if the mistake was exactly what I *wanted* to do.

I was almost afraid to shut my eyes for fear that the drowning dream might kill me this time, like hitting the ground in a falling dream. *Would you ever wake up?* Now that I knew firsthand the adrenaline rush that comes when you think you might die, the dream might be too real. Fortunately, there was nothing but black and I slept so hard it felt like the middle of the night when I woke to a knock at my cabin door. I checked the clock on the nightstand—a quarter to seven—before I wrapped my robe around me.

Gavin leaned into the doorway with one hand on the wall and a tender smile. "Hey. How are you feeling?"

"I'm okay. Good, actually. I must've slept for hours."

"Fantastic! You're up for dinner then?"

I looked down at my robe. "Um, sure. After I get dressed."

"Of course, take your time. We can either eat in the dining room or my room if you prefer, something a little less formal."

Less formal sounded good. I was still groggy so the thought of talking to people didn't appeal. "That sounds perfect."

"Alright, I'll order and see you there." He tapped the wall, his smiling eyes holding my gaze for a long second before he turned to walk away.

I felt the air leave me as he vanished down the hallway. I'd been holding my breath again. I never seemed to learn.

CHAPTER 11

I threw a T-shirt over cutoff shorts and brushed on a touch of mascara. Thank God I didn't have to dress for dinner or see anyone else. I purposely didn't get prettied up.

I reached the end of the hallway at the back of the ship and knocked on the sole door.

Gavin answered, dressed just as casually as I was in board shorts and a T-shirt. "Perfect timing. The food just arrived." He stepped aside and held out his arm to welcome me.

My mouth gaped open at how the room went on and on. It was the entire stern of the enormous boat. The whole back wall was windows. At least fifty feet of windows. A sitting area separated the dining area and the bedroom space. It was positively palatial.

A chess set atop a small table alongside the window caught my eye. It was carved of some sort of stone that was probably rare and expensive. "Do you play?"

"I do! Want to have a go after dinner?"

"I wish. I don't play, but I've always wanted to."

"I can teach you. It's easy."

I narrowed my eyes. "That's not what I've heard. I'd love to, but another time. I'm too wiped out to have to think."

"Okay, rain check then. Are you hungry?" Gavin tugged gently at my wrist to pull me toward the table.

He removed the silver covers to reveal two lobster tails stuffed with a creamy concoction. "I hope you like Lobster Thermidor."

My mouth watered. "I've never had it but I'm sure I'll love it."

The flavors mixed in my mouth in a symphony when I bit into the succulent meat. Aside from a few groans and affirmations that the food was incredible, we were so intent on devouring the feast and washing it down with nearly a full bottle of white wine that we barely spoke through the meal.

I put my napkin on the table and leaned back into my chair after I finished the last bite.

Gavin grinned. "I ordered a chocolate mousse to share. I hope you're not too full."

"I could never be too full for chocolate mousse."

"Good. I have a port to finish it off nicely."

More wine might finish me off but I wasn't going to turn down a port on a mega yacht. The bottle probably cost more than my airfare or a night in my five-star resort. "I won't say no."

We savored small spoonfuls of the rich mousse. "I have to admit I'm a little jealous. You have a nice life here."

"It's all relative. You take the good with the bad."

"What's bad about it?"

"This right here, nothing at all. This is damn near perfect. And we're out of cell phone range so my father can't even call me."

I nodded sympathetically. "Do you butt heads?"

"Only when I don't follow his orders. He's happy to let me do all the work as long as he gets to call all the shots. It's tiresome."

"Family business can be tough." And broken family businesses were even worse. I realized what a relief it had been to not think about work, or Chuck, for the better part of two days now.

"The funny thing is that I never wanted to run the family business. I took over while my dad was sick but he seemed to like the arrangement even after he recovered. I'd planned to leave, but anytime I mentioned it I got a guilt trip from him and my mom. It's the only thing they can seem to agree on." He chuckled and shook his head, resigned to it. "And it is a nice life, as you said, so I've been stuck here in this holding pattern for three years now."

I sipped my port and licked the chocolate from my lips. "Would you want to go back to Ireland?"

"Maybe... no, not really. I'm not a big fan of the weather, and I'd miss the diving. I'd probably lean toward Greece or Croatia if I were to go back to Europe. But I'd consider anywhere with nice water and sunshine."

"That's good criteria. I could probably use more of those in my life." The Bay Area didn't have much of either.

"You can always change your location." He shrugged with a smile.

That was easy for a twenty-something nomad to say. "In theory, yes. In practice, it would be complicated. My life is pretty well established there."

"Where there's a will there's a way."

My iron-will was what kept me there. I wasn't giving up my home and my business just because my marriage fell apart. I couldn't say that, and he wouldn't understand anyway. "We do make our own path."

"Easier said than done with my father at the reins." He motioned toward the last bite in the cup of mousse. "That's yours."

"I won't say no to that either." I smiled and picked it up to scrape every last bit onto my spoon. I moaned at the flavor on my tongue. My food buzz was as strong as my wine buzz. I was so content I'd have a hard time saying no to pretty much anything he might suggest. "This might be the best meal I've ever had."

"You deserve it after the day you had. I hope it makes up for it. I feel terrible."

"What? Why? You didn't do anything wrong."

"I'm glad you feel that way. And I'm glad you're okay."

"I'm great, especially after that meal. Thank you for inviting me. Even with all the excitement, it's amazing to be here."

"It's amazing to have you here. You can't imagine how

surprised I was to see you on the dock. I was shocked—happy-shocked."

A flutter in my stomach made me smile. "I'm happy-surprised that I came."

"Well if you're delaying your first chess lesson, then shall we watch a movie?" Gavin looked at me expectantly before he hurried to add, "Unless you're too tired."

I was exhausted but I didn't want to go. "I'd love to watch a movie." I wouldn't have to leave but I wouldn't have to talk much either.

"Have you seen *Walk the Line?*"

"The Johnny Cash story? No, I haven't, but I want to!"

We took the port to the sofa and settled back for the film. Sipping sweet wine while Johnny's story unfolded made me emotional. I'd always loved him. I didn't know why I hadn't ever seen the film. Oh, wait. Chuck didn't like Johnny Cash. That would be it. When he met June, it was magic from the start. He made her believe in herself and she became his rock. Nothing like my marriage. I was lucky to be free.

I tucked my feet up under me, shifting closer to Gavin. He leaned in so that our shoulders touched, and a heat grew in that spot where flesh longing to find flesh burned through the layers of cotton. I was free. I could let my body do what it craved if I wanted to. I knew I was in trouble when I thought I must be crazy for considering it but didn't pull away to break the spell of his touch. It made me feel alive, and after today I was happy to be alive.

Gavin was pensive when he asked, "Do you ever wonder if love like that exists in real life?"

I laughed. "This is a true story. It is real life."

He looked skeptical. "It's the Hollywood portrayal."

"By all accounts, theirs was love like no other, but it was real."

"Maybe it's one in a million."

I chuckled at his dubious comment. "I bet your odds are far better than that. You'll find love. I'm sure the girls line up for a chance." His odds were far better than mine.

"I'm not into that. Things just get complicated. The morning after makes a one-night stand not worth it. Every once in a while, there's one I think might have potential, but so far they've been empty shells."

"There's a whole world full of women, and you have all the time." I paused as his gaze locked mine. "The woman that steals your heart will be a lucky one."

His hand rested on my bare knee, sending a surge between my thighs when he answered. "I don't know about that."

Feeling his skin on mine was like having a single nibble off a chocolate bar—and the whole bar was right there for the taking. Resisting the urge to eat it all, no matter the consequences might require a self-control I wasn't sure I possessed. I glanced at his hand, secretly hoping it would move up my thigh. If he was going for it, I was game. One-night stands had never been my thing either, but maybe a lot less thinking and a little more fucking was what I needed. I'd had just enough wine that I didn't even try to refute the desire with logic.

Unfortunately for me, or fortunately perhaps, Gavin's hand didn't move until he tapped me at the end of the movie and stood up rather quickly. "Good, wasn't it?"

"Great is more like it." A great American love story. Johnny and June had their happy ending, but apparently, I wasn't going to get mine tonight.

I didn't have the nerve to make the first move. I couldn't bear the rejection if Gavin turned me down. I was probably reading into his flirty personality. Why would he be interested in a woman my age, anyway? I felt foolish for even thinking he might be. I took a deep breath as I swung my legs off the sofa and slipped my feet into my sandals.

"Can I offer you anything else?"

That was a loaded question if I'd ever heard one, and one I wasn't prepared to answer truthfully. "No, I'm good." I stood and stretched my arms overhead, pretending to yawn. "I'm beat."

"I bet. Sorry again for the excitement. I'll make it up to you tomorrow, I promise."

If I were bolder I would have told him he could make it up to me right now, but I wasn't. "You don't have anything to apologize for."

He walked me to the door. "Get some rest. We'll do a nice shallow dive with the kids tomorrow and I'll be sure not to scare any sharks."

I wasn't in any hurry to get back in the water. "I'll see how I feel."

"Oh, come on. You have to get back on the horse. Don't let the shark win."

"Doesn't the shark always win?"

"Only if you let him." He grinned and kissed me on the cheek. "Breakfast is at eight on the pool deck."

I'd tried to let the womanizing shark win, but he didn't take the bait.

I cursed myself as I brushed my teeth. Maybe knowing that Elliot was coming tomorrow let the tingling between my legs cloud my judgment and made me want to seize the opportunity. I'd let my guard down when Gavin showed me his sweet side and made me doubt my perception of him as a player. I was wrong alright, in all the wrong ways. I'd nearly made a complete fool of myself. At least Elliot being around would help ensure that wouldn't happen again.

I snuggled under the covers of the nicest linens that might have ever touched my skin. Turkish cotton, I imagined. The tension of the day left my body as I sank into the feather-top mattress, but my mind wouldn't stop. I could still see Gavin's chiseled chest and his pearly smile when I closed my eyes.

His boyish good looks and his hero antics made me want him. Damn him. Remembering his hand on my knee made my heart beat faster exactly as it had when he put it there. The electric current that Gavin had sparked returned to my core. My fingers were drawn to my flesh like a magnet as my lips had longed for his earlier. This time I didn't resist.

My fingers slipped under the waistband of my panties and between my warm lips. I hadn't touched myself in months, and even when I had it hadn't felt like this. Waves of pleasure spread from between my thighs when I grazed my swollen clit and my nipples grew hard under the soft fabric. I wished it was Gavin's hand there between my legs, or better yet, his tongue. Imagining his head between my thighs as he licked up the sides of my folds where my fingers moved made me moan. I tried to picture his cock—probably as perfect as the rest of him. The yearning for him inside me made me realize how empty I felt. I clenched around my fingers when they pushed into the emptiness. The wetness surprised me. I hadn't been that wet for Chuck in years.

My fingertips slid over my clit and all thoughts of Chuck left as quickly as they came. Gavin's green eyes peered into mine while his cock filled my depths in my mind. I imagined his soft lips on my mouth and could almost taste his sweet breath while my fingers explored my silky folds. My other hand moved to my nipple, which seemed to be directly connected to my crotch the way the sensation intensified. I groaned and squeezed my nipple hard while my fingers moved faster between my legs. I could feel Gavin's hands moving over my skin, his tongue in my mouth, his cock inside me, his lips over mine. My breath quickened with the pace of my fingers over my clit as the tingling waves spread through me. My hips writhed under my touch, wishing it was his as my body exploded in the fastest orgasm I'd ever achieved, self-induced or otherwise. I bit my lips to stifle the moans that escaped while my pussy clamped at the emptiness that needed to be filled.

I laid panting for air when the contractions inside me subsided. Gavin had awakened something in me that had been dormant for months—if not years—but I could finally sleep.

CHAPTER 12

*T*he alarm clock sounded so foreign that I wasn't sure why it was ringing when it woke me from a deep slumber. I must have crossed into full vacation mode. It seemed like weeks had passed since I last had to get up and go to work. I had finally disconnected. I had forty-five minutes before the Clifton's sister arrived.

Gavin stood at the railing on the pool deck, looking like a pirate in his white linen shirt fluttering in the warm breeze as he looked out across the blue water to an island in the distance. He smiled when I approached, and the way the morning light caught the shades of red in his golden hair blowing in the wind made my heart pound in my chest even before he spoke. "Good morning, dive goddess."

"Hardly." I smiled and shifted my gaze to the island in the distance. "Cayman Brac, I presume?"

"Indeed."

"Why are we so far away?"

"We can't get this monster boat any closer. The kids and their mom will be out in a tender shortly."

I sat across from him at the table set for five as a cute, young waitress appeared with a carafe of coffee. "Coffee?"

She smiled at Gavin bashfully and her cheeks blushed when he answered. "You know how I like it."

I cleared my throat to mask a chuckle. He was a class-A flirt and I was an idiot to think he'd been into me. The waitress poured his coffee and added milk. "And you, miss?"

"Yes, please, just black."

She poured my coffee and asked softly. "The chef is doing eggs Benedict with salmon, but you can order something different if you prefer."

"That sounds lovely." She nodded and paused to smile again at Gavin before she left.

He sipped his coffee. "God that's good."

I bit my lip as I took a deep breath. "I'm not so sure about the dive today. Maybe I'll sit this one out. You already have children to look after. You don't need to have me to save."

"You certainly don't need saving. But we're doing a shallow reef dive. It will be far less dramatic than our wall dive, I promise."

I tried to sound brave. "I'm not afraid. I just thought maybe it would be easier if you had one less student in the water."

"Having you there would be anything but a burden. It would be a pleasure." He flashed a grin before he turned serious again. "Don't back out, Tessa. You need to get back on the horse. If you let fear take hold, you'll never dive again. And that would mean that I failed miserably. Don't do that to me."

I had to laugh. Was it a male trait to make everything about them somehow? I'd spent so many years taking someone else's ego into account ahead of my own that it was an ordinary occurrence. "I wouldn't want you to look bad."

"I don't give a fuck how I look. I don't want to let you down. If you don't dive again after what happened, then I will have failed you miserably."

I didn't want to let him down. But—more importantly—I didn't want to give up. He gave me the courage to face my fears. "Okay, if you're sure, then I'll try."

"I'm positive."

I wished I could say the same. "Okay then."

A shrill voice called from behind me, "Gavin!" His lips spread into a broad grin as he stood to welcome the little girl who ran toward him with open arms.

"Hey, princess. You ready to go diving?"

She threw her arms around his neck. "I can't wait!"

I wished I shared her enthusiasm. I stood to meet the girl and the elegant woman who approached with a younger boy. I felt underdressed in shorts and a tank top compared with the mother's designer white suit as she hugged Gavin.

"Elizabeth, meet Tessa. She's visiting from San Francisco. We did a refresher course a couple of days ago. I hope you don't mind that I invited her along for the ride, and the dives."

"Of course not." She smiled and offered me her hand. "Well, aren't you a lucky lady? Nice to meet you, Tessa."

"I am." I wouldn't mention the bad luck of the shark incident. No one needed to be as freaked out as I was. "Thank you for the opportunity."

"Any friend of Gavin's is a friend of ours." Her smile was more than friendly, and told me she admired and held him in high esteem.

Gavin high fived then fist-bumped the little boy at her side. "This fine young man is Evan, he's ten. And Eleanor is eleven. They are my star students."

I grinned and extend my hand to Evan. "Maybe you can teach me a few things. I'm no star."

Evan shook his head as he timidly took my hand. "Gavin is the best teacher in the world."

He certainly had a way of making everyone admire him. I grinned at Evan. "That I can believe."

We sat for breakfast—the most delicious depiction of eggs Benedict I'd ever experienced. Elizabeth was as an attentive mother and as gracious a woman as I'd ever met. You'd never know that she had the world at her fingertips. It felt like we could have been best friends. I figured she had that gift—making everyone feel connected to her somehow. Maybe that was what Gavin had too. With both of them doting on me, asking questions, and seeming genuinely interested in the answers, I felt like the guest of honor in a fairy tale daydream.

"I'm counting on you to help Gavin look after my most prized possessions."

"I'll do my best to take care of myself so that Gavin can tend to them fully. That's pretty much all I can promise."

She leaned in and whispered before she kissed my cheek, "Enjoy yourself."

"I'm sure we will all enjoy ourselves. Gavin will see to that."

She leaned in to kiss his cheek. "I have no doubt in that."

Neither did I.

We said our goodbyes down on the platform at the stern of the boat where Elizabeth boarded the tender back to her home on the island. As soon as we'd waved her off, Gavin put us to work setting up our gear for the dive. "We'll be at the reef in half an hour. Get everything ready now so we can get to the fun stuff right away." The kids got right on task, no questions asked. I stood in silent awe for a second while Eleanor found her pink BCD and regulator and Evan took his to set up the tanks. They were obviously well trained, which shouldn't surprise me. But to see two kids so focused and efficient was shocking. It's a special talent, or a gift, to engage children to that extent. The level of respect Gavin invoked in them, and their mother, was impressive. If he was anything, he was impressive.

He checked all our gear before we went to change while the boat moved to our first dive site. Gavin waited on the platform and gave us the pre-dive briefing when I arrived behind the kids. "The ledge underneath us is at thirty feet. We're going to swim out to that buoy there and go down the line together. Afterward, we'll pair off in buddy teams. Eleanor, you'll be your brother's buddy. I'll stick with Tessa, but I'll be keeping my eye on you if you need me. You won't though, I know." Gavin winked before he helped her into her gear.

We gathered at the buoy and followed Gavin's signals to descend to the reef. I fumbled with my equipment at first but my stubborn determination to be self-sufficient made me focus. I gave Gavin the okay sign once we were all settled hovering over the sand beside a coral ledge teeming with colorful fish. My eyes followed the bubbles that left my regulator to the surface that seemed just above us and a whole world away.

Gavin signaled for the kids to swim along the ledge ahead of us and we filed in behind them. We stayed close, in a pack of four, and Gavin took my hand in his while we made our way along the ledge for twenty minutes or so. He stopped to point out fish and corals along the way. The kids seemed so much more confident than I was that I felt like the child of the group. But by the time Gavin signaled that it was time to turn around, I was ready to let go and be on my own. Gavin coaxed an eel out of its lair and roused a turtle out of hiding as we followed the ledge back to the boat. Thankfully, there was not a shark in sight.

I slipped out of the gear on the deck and helped Eleanor out of hers while a crew member helped her brother. Gavin smiled admiringly when he got his gear off. "Great job down there. And up here now. Look at you taking care of everyone."

I beamed with excitement from the dive. "That was incredible! The sea turtle might be my spirit animal."

"They're the grandfathers of the ocean. No matter how big or small, they seem like they know something that no one else does."

"Exactly." It was the wise eyes that struck me when the turtle left in an annoyed huff.

"I love the lobsters. I'll never eat a lobster again. They're so much better alive." Eleanor declared with quiet resolve.

"That's stupid. You eat fish like every day. They're smarter than lobsters, dummy," Evan scoffed.

"Maybe I won't eat fish either," she sneered.

Gavin interjected with a soothing tone to stop their bickering. "Well, that's your choice, princess. But that's a big sacrifice."

Eleanor put her hand on her hip and replied defiantly, "I don't care. I don't need lobsters or fish to survive."

"No, but you like them. If you like them so much that you don't want to do without them, then you'll find a way to make what you believe in and what you like work."

"Is that what you do?" Eleanor stared up with eyes that asked if he loved the lobsters as much as she did.

"Every day, princess." Gavin patted her shoulder. "But I still can't eat octopus"—he flashed a smile my way— "or turtle."

"I would never eat a shark," Evan chimed in.

"No one eats sharks." Eleanor rolled her eyes to emphasize how preposterous the idea was.

"Oh, but they do. The Japanese kill thousands of sharks every month."

Evan stared in shock. "Why?"

"Because lots of people eat them, especially the fins in a soup."

Eleanor's nose wrinkled. "That's gross."

"I agree. That's why I give money to an organization called Greenpeace that helps fight that practice."

I had to look away so as not to laugh out loud at his cunning conversion of the heirs to the plastic empire into conservationists. He might have just secured long-term funding for that project.

After nearly an hour of rest, I was as anxious as the kids were to get back in the water. Gavin led us down to another shallow reef where we slowly circled one large patch. We stopped to examine corals, and swam through a swarm of baitfish before Gavin found a sea cucumber and passed it around so we could feel it. Evan waved us over to a nurse shark which didn't appreciate the audience and took off. Maybe it was because it disappeared into the distance, but I didn't feel the least bit scared.

The diving was the reason I came, and it did not disappoint. As we rinsed the gear after the dive, I thanked Gavin. "This was amazing. Thank you so much for inviting me. I'll never forget this."

"You'd better not. But this is just the beginning. There's so much more for you to see."

"I hope so. I love diving and look forward to doing more of it. Thank you for that."

"It has been my pleasure." He leaned close to take my BCD from my hands, his proximity stirring something in me that I kept trying to ignore. A flashback of the pleasure he'd inspired me to give myself the night before made me look away.

I took a deep breath and forced a grin as I lifted my eyes back to his. "Then the pleasure is mutual."

Gavin looked at me intently with a suggestive smile. "As it always *should* be."

The fire that blazed between my thighs made it impossible to hold his gaze. "I should get in the shower."

"Me, too."

I was secretly hoping he would continue the flirty banter and proposition me to join him in the shower. I was clearly not in my right mind. He couldn't help himself but to flirt, but he had no real intention of going any further.

He winked a green eye that sparkled in the sunlight. "I'll meet you out by the pool."

We spent the rest of the day swimming with the kids and lounging by the pool. The sun was getting low when the yacht reached the port. Evan and Eleanor kissed us both goodbye before climbing into a brand new pearly white Range Rover with blacked-out windows.

I watched the car pull away. "They're remarkably grounded and well-behaved children. I hope they stay that way once they're no longer oblivious to their wealth."

Gavin took a deep breath and said with a sigh, "So do I." He watched as the car disappeared in the distance. "Shall we go for a sunset cocktail?"

I was tempted, but Elliot would be landing any minute. "I'd love to, but I'd better get back. Elliot will be here soon."

"Ah, right. Rain check, then?"

I grinned. "You got it." I climbed up into his old Rover.

My excitement that Elliot would be there within the hour grew on the short drive to the resort. "Thanks again for everything. It was incredible." I slid down out of the seat and closed the door with a thud. I looked back over my shoulder to be sure Gavin was out of sight before I skipped down the walkway the rest of the way to my room.

I ran straight to the bathroom to grab my phone to call Elliot. He would surely be on his way. I fumbled to try to dial him, stopping to stare at the screen when the words finally registered. Nineteen missed calls—From Elliot. And a whole slew of text messages that ranged from *Where the fuck are you?* to *I'm seriously going to call the police if you don't call me in the next five minutes.* That was yesterday. I opened the first of four voicemails. He needed to talk to me. Call him ASAP. The next was more urgent, like his texts. In the third, he finally dropped the bomb. He'd done his best but he was stuck dealing with an emergency at work. He just couldn't get away.

I stared at the phone for several seconds as it sunk in. He wasn't coming. I stumbled back two steps to lean on the glass shower door and slid down to the floor. My head dropped back and I stared blankly up at the wooden beams of the ceiling. "Goddammit," I called out to anyone who cared, knowing no one would hear.

This couldn't be happening. But of course, it was. The only reason I'd agreed to come on the trip at all was now null and void—like everything else in my life. All the elation from the dive trip left me like air from a balloon.

I knew I had to call Elliot, but I needed a drink for that. I pushed myself up off the floor and staggered to the minibar. I poured two tiny bottles of whiskey into a glass and downed it in one swig. I took another glass of whiskey to the sofa looking out on a splendid sunset. Goddammit. No Elliot and no Gavin. No one to enjoy this with.

Elliot answered after three rings, yelling in a whisper, "Tessa! Thank fucking God. Are you okay?"

"I'm fine. I left my phone. I went on the yacht." I'd been so excited to tell him about my adventure but the words were stale and empty when they tumbled off my tongue.

He continued to speak in an anxious whisper. "I heard. The hotel tracked you through the taxi they'd arranged when I threatened to call the police."

"I'm sorry. I didn't mean to worry you. Are you busy?"

"Yes, very. It's a shit show. I'm sorry, Sweet T. I really tried."

"I know you did." Elliot wouldn't leave me hanging if he had the choice. But he wasn't here. The one person I could count on had let me down—through no fault of his own—but it still felt like a punch in the gut. There was no need to make Elliot feel any worse than he already did though. There was nothing more to be done. "I'll be alright. Don't worry about me. Go take care of business. I'll catch up with you later."

"You sure you're okay?"

"I'm sure." It was the biggest lie I'd told all year, and there'd been a few, mostly to myself.

I put Adele on the sound system and took yet another glass of whiskey to the tub. I tried to drown my sorrows and wash away the despair until the album had played through twice. I stepped out of the tepid water and toweled off my pruned skin.

There was no escaping the grim reality. I was alone. Whether Elliot came or not, that was still my reality. I was officially divorced. Officially alone.

I caught sight of myself in the mirror as I tied the plush robe around my waist. I was a drunken mess again. I should eat but the thought of food made me nauseous. I brushed my teeth instead. Fuck it. I was giving up on this day.

CHAPTER 13

The rumble of my empty stomach woke me. I threw on a sundress and ran a brush through my hair. I didn't even bother to look in the mirror. What was the point?

The smiling skinny young hostess annoyed me, so I preempted her question. "Table for one please."

I might as well get used to it.

Remembering Eleanor's insistence that she would never eat lobster again made me feel a little guilty as I wolfed down an enormous lobster omelet.

I wandered down to the beach and spread out my towel on the chair I'd claimed as my own. I tried to read, but concentrating was difficult. I just couldn't be bothered thinking at all because all I could think was what the hell was I going to do for eight more days? I was tempted to have a cocktail but thought better of it. Drinking myself further into this pit of despair was probably not the smartest option.

Unable to focus on my book, my gaze kept straying to scan the length of the beach, hoping to catch sight of Gavin.

I must have drifted into a deep sleep because a beach attendant woke me when the sun was already low on the horizon. "I'm sorry to disturb you, miss. I just wanted to be sure you're okay."

I wasn't, but it was nothing he could help with. I sat up, embarrassed. "Oh, thank you. Yes, I'm fine. I must've fallen asleep. Thank you for waking me."

"No problem. Good afternoon." He clasped his hands behind his back and bowed slightly before he walked away.

I made my groggy way back to the bungalow and sank into the fluffy white bedding as I unwrapped the chocolate they'd left on the pillow. It wasn't a bad place to be stuck. The rich sweetness of the chocolate removed the bitter taste in my mouth. Feeling sorry for myself seemed absurd.

I showered and slipped into a sleeveless cotton shirt dress. A little makeup made me feel more put together for dinner. I smiled at the hostess and walked straight to the bar. No more table for one. Carlos greeted me with a broad grin. "Good evening, Tessa. What can I get you?"

"How about a rum and coke, and a fat, juicy burger." I'd been craving another one since I'd indulged at Morgan's.

"Medium?"

I contemplated. "Medium rare."

"Good choice. Fries or salad?"

"Fries." Fuck it, I was on vacation.

I was on my second rum and coke and had just sunk my

teeth into the third bite of my burger when I felt a hand on my back. I turned with a mouthful of food to meet Gavin's amused smile. I struggled to chew, trying not to choke while I hurried to swallow the enormous bite.

Gavin held up his other hand apologetically. "Sorry to interrupt. Take your time."

I washed down the food with a big gulp of my cocktail. "Sorry about that."

"No need to apologize." Gavin chuckled. "You seem totally into that burger. By all means, carry on."

"It's delicious, but not as good as Morgan's." I took another bite.

"Nowhere's as good as Morgan's." Gavin's brow wrinkled inquisitively. "So where's Elliot?"

"Oh, right, you don't know. He didn't make it. He's not coming." Saying it made me feel it all over again. Alone.

Gavin's face reacted empathetically. "Wow. That sucks. I'm sorry."

"Yeah, me too. But I'm trying not to feel sorry for myself. I can't really complain about being stuck in Grand Cayman."

Gavin sipped from the tequila Carlos had set on the bar. "There are worse places."

"I don't know what the hell I'm going to do for over a week."

Gavin grinned. "A lot more diving, I hope."

Either he was a good salesman or I was easily persuaded, or both. "I'd like that."

"Good. I can show you around, too. There's a lot more to the island."

"That would be awesome." He wouldn't have to twist my arm. Even if he was just feeling sorry for me, I'd take it.

He turned his barstool toward me and placed a foot on the leg of my stool so that his knee touched mine. I tried to ignore the ripple of excitement that the feel of his flesh sent through me and asked, "What do you have on the books these next few days?"

"Tomorrow I'm going to a barbecue at my parent's house, but I can be on the water with you any day after that. And if you don't have any plans, you're welcome to join me tomorrow, if you like."

At his parents' house? No thanks. "That's kind of you, but I wouldn't want to impose. And I need to work on my tan."

"You have plenty of time for that, and you wouldn't be imposing at all. You'd be a welcome buffer. I'd pretty much pay you to come with me." Gavin grinned.

I giggled. I'd gathered that his relationship with his father was contentious, to say the least. I could tell he meant it when he said he'd rather have me there than not. I'd be a distraction. I'd get him off the hook. "You certainly wouldn't have to pay me. But are you sure?"

"I'm positive. They love meeting new people. You should come."

He probably brought home a different girl every couple of weeks. What the hell. I wasn't doing anything else and being part of a family dynamic, even as an outsider, sounded nice. "Alright, I'd love to."

Gavin grinned. "You just made my night."

A deep voice interrupted when a heavy hand landed on Gavin's shoulder. "This lovely lady would make any man's night."

Gavin's smile spread as he looked up to the man who'd approached. "Clifton! Nice to see you. And I couldn't agree more. Meet Tessa, she's the lovely lady that joined me on the *Caribbean Dream*."

I stared up into a handsome face, lit up with a shiny white smile, and extended my hand. "Very nice to meet you, Mr. Drake." I felt silly for staring but I hadn't imagined him be so good looking, probably because the locals seemed leery of him. But he was a proper dreamboat billionaire. He wore his years well with just a hint of grey around the edges of his clean-cut black hair.

"Please, call me Clifton. How did you enjoy my boat?"

I smiled. "Thoroughly."

"As it should be. I'm glad you could keep Gavin company. My niece and nephew speak highly of you. You're welcome anytime."

Gavin motioned for him to sit. "Please, join us."

Clifton smiled at me. "I'm not interrupting?"

I shook my head. "No, not at all. Please."

"In that case, I'd love to." He took the seat on the other side of me and waved Carlos over as he asked me. "Do you drink Scotch?"

I smirked. "Only single malt if I have the choice."

Carlos didn't wait for the order. He knew his poison. I recognized the sleek, slender bottle of Macallan Reflexion. At fifteen hundred dollars a bottle, I'd never tried it. It was smooth and well worth the money when someone else was buying. "That's delicious. Thank you."

"It's my pleasure. Only the best for this fine young man and his beautiful friend, of course."

It didn't surprise me that Clifton was debonair, but how genuine he seemed did. "You're too kind."

"Nonsense." Clifton smiled before turning to Gavin. "How's business?"

Gavin's lips curled into a crooked grin. "Busier than I'd like it."

Clifton smiled at Gavin. "I don't believe that for a minute. I know you love it."

"That I cannot deny."

"You're the best at what you do." Clifton glanced my way before he turned back to Gavin. "I admire that in you."

"I could say the same for you, only it's been far more lucrative in your case. Everything you touch turns to gold."

"Not everything. But I try to hedge my bets and only go in deep on a sure thing."

I was intrigued. "So much in business is speculation. How do you know when it's a sure thing?"

"I have advisors who run all the numbers, but usually it's a gut feeling. My new project in the Florida Keys is a good example."

Gavin leaned onto his elbow on the bar, his knee pressing into mine when he did. "Oh yeah? What do you have brewing in Florida?"

Clifton sipped his Scotch before answering. "I invested in a property—an island. We're developing a resort there."

Did I hear him right? "You bought *an island* in the Keys?"

"I did. Paradise Key. And as soon as I saw it, I knew it would be a winning project. It was just a feeling. When we're finished, it will be twenty-eight acres of paradise."

Part of me cringed inside at the thought of transforming a virgin island into a luxury resort. It seemed wrong. "Why the Keys?"

Clifton shrugged. "It's America's Caribbean. And it's good to diversify."

Why would he leave the tax haven of Cayman to invest tens of millions in the US? Unless he was laundering money. It seemed as far-fetched as a plot for a Netflix series, and yet the most obvious answer. It was none of my business, and best not to press. "Makes sense."

Clifton smiled slyly at Gavin. "You shouldn't sell yourself short. You're a cunning businessman yourself. I've seen how you operate."

"Thank you for saying so. I'd do things very differently if I were free to operate on my own."

"Maybe you'd like to expand Blackbeard Divers into the Florida Keys. I happen to know of a new luxury resort in need of a dive operator."

Gavin chuckled. "Expanding into the US is probably outside my old man's comfort zone."

Clifton's expression turned serious. "Your old man's folly is that he has stayed in his comfort zone all his life."

"You hit the nail on the head there." Gavin turned up his glass to finish his whiskey. I followed suit. I needed another drink after that remark hit so close to home.

Clifton waved to call Carlos over for another round before he continued. "But your father is a good man with good intentions. I have to commend him for what he's built here. It must be noted, however, that you've improved it tenfold and brought the business into this century in the past few years. He should be grateful."

Gavin was quick to laugh. "I won't hold my breath for that one."

I laughed. "You should never hold your breath. Isn't that the number one rule in scuba diving?"

Gavin smiled and my heart beat faster when his hand rested on my back as he said sweetly, "You're such a good student."

I smiled. "Having a great instructor makes being a good student easy."

Clifton nodded in agreement. "If he weren't the best in the business, he wouldn't be diving with my niece and nephew."

"Are you guys trying to give me an ego trip? You're too kind. But knock it off." Even when humble, Gavin was still confident.

Clifton shrugged. "It's all true. But you're right, we shouldn't overinflate your ego. So, tell me, when are you taking the children diving again?"

"You know I'll make time for them. The only other thing on my schedule this week, that is a must-do, is to show Tessa a good time." Gavin rubbed my back, sending shivers up my spine.

My cheeks burned and the swirl of butterflies in my stomach made me queasy. His hand on my back had the odd simultaneous effect of stabilizing me while nearly knocking me off my stool. Even if it confused the fuck out of me, I loved that Gavin declared that I was a priority. But I didn't want to interfere with his business. I stammered to interject. "You don't have to worry about me. My schedule is wide open. And I don't expect you to babysit me all week."

"I expect you to let me show you as much of a good time as I can this week." Gavin declared with a confident stare.

I tried to act nonchalant, like I wasn't thinking the dirtiest possible implications of *a good time*. "I'll go along with whatever. You just let me know."

"Bring Tessa along to dive with the children." Clifton looked down to sign the check. "Then everyone is happy." Clifton's tone was clear that it was an imperative suggestion. He stood and offered me his hand. "I'm afraid I have to run. It was a pleasure. Enjoy your time on our lovely island."

"Thank you, I will. And thanks again for your hospitality."

"See you two soon."

After Clifton was well out of earshot, I still lowered my voice so that no one else would hear. "He's so different than I imagined."

"Yeah? How so?"

"I don't know. I guess I didn't expect him to be so nice, but that's based on random remarks."

"He has quite the reputation on the island. But most of that comes from rumors and jealousy. That happens when you're richer and smarter than anyone else around. But he's a nice guy."

"He seems like it. He certainly admires you."

"He was trying to make me look good in front of a pretty lady."

I smiled shyly. "You hardly need help in that department." His compliment made me even more confused about his intentions. Part of me wanted to push further to see, but a bigger part was afraid I was foolish to think that he was even considering it. I needed to keep myself in check and keep my heart tucked away in its icy shell. I faked a yawn. "I had a hard day on the beach. I need to get to bed." I slid off my barstool. "What time do I need to be ready for the barbecue tomorrow?"

"One?" Gavin stood and held out his hand to motion for me to go ahead. "I'm heading out, too. I'll walk with you."

His hand landed on my back again, his touch lingering while we strolled under a blanket of stars. Gavin stopped on the sidewalk and kicked off his shoes. "Come on." He waved me toward the water's edge.

I hesitated. "You want to swim?"

He took my hand in his to tug me gently toward the water. "Just get your feet wet."

I looked at him suspiciously before I slipped my toes out of my sandals and followed him to the shoreline. I paused to look up at the black sky, twinkling with a million sparkling jewels. "God it's gorgeous here. Everything about it."

Gavin took hold of my other hand and waited for my gaze to meet his before he spoke. "Everything." My legs threatened to collapse under me as he continued. "You are gorgeous, Tessa. I wanted to tell you when I met you—and I almost did on the boat but I lost my nerve. I didn't want you to feel pressured since you were basically in a captive environment." His crooked grin evoked a nervous laugh as I dropped my head.

"I was hardly a prisoner. But thank you for being considerate. And thank you for the compliment." I hoped it was dark enough that he couldn't see my blushing face when he turned my chin up to force me to meet his gaze again. My stomach dropped when his lips lowered in slow motion. The softness of his mouth parted my lips and his tongue teased mine. His fingers trailed up my cheek and into my hair as our mouths slid over one another in perfect synchrony.

It was the first time I'd kissed anyone other than Chuck in eighteen years. If we'd kissed with such passion even in the early days, I didn't remember it. I couldn't remember ever sinking into a kiss like this one.

Gavin's arm around my waist pulled my hips close and held me up when my knees felt weak. I blinked my eyes open and pulled my head back, gripping his back to steady myself in the rush of dizzying desire. His breath was heavy on my cheek as he stared into my eyes, still holding me tight. "Is that okay?"

It was more than okay. It was the most amazing thing I'd ever experienced. I was so breathless I could barely push out a single, "Yes."

His lips curled into a smile before his mouth covered mine again. My hands roamed over the ripples of his muscular back while his hand tightened into a soft fist in my hair, pulling me deeper into the kiss. The warm wave that built between my thighs spread up into my chest and the whispering huff of our heavy breath swirled with the sounds of the surf at our feet.

I wanted to rip the buttons off his shirt, strip off all my clothes and run naked into the ocean with him, but some sense of sensibility prevailed. I peeled my lips from his and drew upon all of my courage reserves to ask bluntly, "Do you want to come back to my room for a drink?"

Gavin didn't hesitate. "I'd love that."

After dreading another week alone in the room that Elliot was supposed to be in with me right now, I was glad that he wasn't there right then. Maybe the universe was looking after me, giving me exactly what I needed at the moment that I needed it.

I wanted to sprint back to the bungalow but willed myself—with deep breaths I'd learned in a hot yoga class with Elliot—to calm down and be present in the moment. We strolled hand in hand, and by the time we reached the room I was relaxed. Gavin hesitated on the porch after I'd opened the door. "Should I wait out here?"

I eyed him curiously trying to decipher whether he was just being a gentleman or whether I'd been presumptuous in thinking that this was a sure thing. I didn't remember how to read a man, but I tried to act cool. "If you want to, sure, just wait here and I'll bring us a drink. But you're welcome to come inside. Maybe you can get creative with the meager offerings of the minibar."

Gavin looked relieved at the invitation. "I'm sure you have the makings of something interesting. I'll see what I can come up with."

Something interesting was already brewing. "Have at it." I led him to the bar. "It's pretty basic."

"You have gin and you have tonic. That's all you need."

I was already headed into the bathroom for a towel to dry my sandy feet, calling over my shoulder. "I would have to agree. I love a good G&T."

"As long as your spectrum of good is broad." Gavin grinned as he cracked open the can of tonic water.

I took out my phone to connect to the sound system and wondered what kind of music people in their twenties listened to these days. I chuckled at the thought. I put on a Jason Mraz album. It was probably showing my age, but I couldn't deny who I was... a forty-one-year-old woman trying to seduce my twenty-eight-year-old scuba instructor. I was in uncharted territory. I had no idea, about any of it.

I took the drink he handed me to the sofa and tucked my feet underneath me on the couch before taking a sip. "It's perfect."

Gavin smiled as he settled next to me. "Not bad. I have to admit, even your hotel minibar is better stocked than my house bar but I do always keep a bottle of Hendrick's and tonic."

I'd discovered Hendrick's through Elliot. It was his favorite, too. He'd be impressed. I took another sip. "Tanqueray is not Hendrick's, but it will do just fine."

"This is better than fine." Gavin's hand landed on my knee.

I wasn't quite sure what to do with the surge of excitement that traveled up into my chest. I didn't need Hendricks but I could use a hardy dose of courage.

"No complaints here." I set my glass on the table to stop

myself from sucking my drink down too fast.

Gavin took a long sip before putting his glass beside mine. His palm slid up the outside of my thigh as he turned to face me. "I'm glad you decided to come on the boat. I'm lucky to have the chance to get to know you, Tessa."

How could I tell him that I felt like the lucky one without saying it? I paused to search for words but they were unnecessary when Gavin brushed my hair from my face, the backs of his fingertips trailing down my cheek. His mouth covered mine, drowning all doubt. My lips parted to let him in.

When his fingers ran into my hair as our tongues intertwined, I melted into the firm hold of his strong arms, opening myself to more than just the kiss. The desire pulsing from every pore of us both made my head swim. I swear I could almost smell it, as though our passion had unleashed some animalistic pheromone, and with it a yearning buried under a decade's worth of sexual frustration.

My palms moved over the contours of his chest while his hands slid down my back. I fumbled with the top button on his shirt with trembling hands. Gavin's lips danced over mine while I worked my way through the rest of the buttons. The tingling that translated through my fingertips when I felt the muscles of his exposed chest made me dizzy.

Gavin shook his shoulders and slinked out of his open shirt before his hands moved slowly and deliberately to cup under my ass.

I gasped momentarily when he pulled me on top of him but feeling his hardness underneath me made me groan. He pulled my chest to his as I straddled him, my breasts pressing into him as he swallowed me up in the kiss reminded me of the first time I'd made out with a guy in high school—the quarterback. The anticipation of where his hands might go next. The craving of his touch. I wanted his hands and his mouth on every part of me at once.

His fingers trailed down my sides to the hem of my dress. I shifted my hips so that he could push it over, and paused the kiss just long enough to help him slip it over my head. Gavin stopped me when I leaned in, his eyes lingering on my bare breasts. The simultaneous self-consciousness under his gaze and the rush of yearning made me feel like a teenager again.

"God, you're gorgeous, Tessa." His words dripped with appreciation while his hungry eyes feasted on my form.

My fingers traced the lines of his chest. He was the hottest man I'd ever laid eyes—and hands—on. "So are you."

His intense green eyes glittered with desire before he pulled me back into another deep kiss. His hands roamed over my breasts, lightly brushing my nipples to send shockwaves through my core. A warm flow of wetness flooded my black lace panties as my hips moved over the thick bulge under his zipper. An empty ache opened like an abyss in me that could only be filled with him.

Gavin shifted under me to move to the edge of the sofa, his broad hands cupping under my ass to lift me as he stood. I wrapped around him, clinging like a spider monkey as he carried me to the bed. My shoulders met the soft down comforter and my head fell back on the pillow as his lips trailed down my neck to my breast. I moaned when his tongue tickled my nipple and gasped when he sucked as much of my breast that would fit into his mouth. By the time he kissed his way down my stomach, I was reeling under his touch. When he rolled the black lace of my panties over my hips, the air awakened my glistening wet clit in a tingling rush. I was close to the edge of climax when his tongue traced the fold between my lips. His groans reverberated through me as he devoured my pussy in desperate gulps to quench his thirst.

I gripped at the sheets to try to hold onto the edge. As tempting as the pleasure was, I was still scared to let go. But there was no stopping the wave that crested deep in my core. All I could do was let it wash over me. Gavin held my hips as I bucked under his mouth and did not relent while I called out. "Oh my God, oh my God." As if prayers could save me from falling off the cliff into ecstasy.

I could tell by the smile in Gavin's green eyes when they locked on mine while he carried me to the heights of climax that he was enjoying it as much as I was. My body pulsed with the aftershock of the orgasm after my moans died down. Gavin kissed my inner thighs tenderly before making his way up to my lips. His mouth was wet with my taste, which had never been a turn-on for me—until now. His kiss consumed me and fueled the deep need for him to fill me.

His fingers pressed into my warm folds as I unbuttoned his shorts to free his throbbing cock, while Gavin fumbled with his wallet. "Thank goodness I still have one of these." He held up a tiny foil packet. Thank God, was right. I hadn't even been thinking about protection.

My knees spread open in anticipation as I guided him to my opening. His thick length slid in slowly, stretching me with a delicious sensation just on the edge of pain. It had been a long time since I'd had any sex at all and I'd never been with a man so well endowed. He paused when he reached the limits of my depth and my walls pulsed, clenching around him. I wrapped my legs around his hips, pulling him even deeper as I moaned. He held my gaze while he slowly retreated and smiled when I gasped as he thrust deep inside again. The slippery silkiness of his skin on mine sent shivers up my spine as his lips lowered to my ear to whisper, "You're fucking amazing, Tessa."

I held him close to my chest and buried my face in his neck to hide the tears that welled up in my eyes. The burning desire was as foreign as feeling so desired. Elliot was right. This was exactly what I needed.

As Gavin's pace quickened, sweat beaded on his chest and our bodies slid over one another in a steaming fury. He pulled out of me abruptly, staring into my eyes as he panted for breath for a moment before he swallowed my breast in a hungry frenzy. His fingers parted my lips and rubbed over my swollen clit while his teeth raked over my nipple. My hips moved of their own volition in circles under his touch as the sensation swirled up through my belly. My head fell back on the pillow and I let the tide carry me back out to sea. When my moans reached a crescendo, his mouth moved to cover my clit where his flickering tongue lifted me higher. Gavin's nails dug into my flesh to hold my writhing hips. The shrill moans that erupted when I exploded in orgasm sounded like someone else's. I'd never screamed like that during sex, even when faking it. It was hard to believe it was real.

Gavin laid beside me, smiling into my eyes as he brushed a sweaty strand of hair from my face. "You're so hot when you come."

"You're so hot when you make me come." I rolled over on top of him, inhaling his musky scent mixed with the smell of me as I kissed my way down his neck and over his sweaty chest. The salty taste of his skin made me hungry for more.

He grinned sheepishly. "Give me a minute. I want this to last."

That I could have that effect on any man at all was invigorating, but that I'd taken this fine specimen of a man so close to the edge made the tingle return between my thighs. "You tell me when you're ready."

Gavin grabbed my wrists and pinned my hands over my head as he flipped me over. His weight lowered onto me like a warm blanket. "You'll know when I'm ready." His lips grazed mine and he pulled back to watch my face as he pushed into my depths. I gasped, staring into his eyes as his mouth covered mine. He slid in and out of me with measured thrusts to control his passion. Our groans and moans mixed in a guttural symphony that filled the room. The friction of his skin and the pressure of his thrusts made my clit throb as I clenched his girth. I whimpered as the contractions spread in a penetrating wave and Gavin's lips left mine to watch my face twist into another orgasm.

I gripped him from the inside and my fingers dug into his back while he pushed harder and faster into me as I moaned. His teeth sank into my biceps and his whole body shuddered as he groaned. He pulled out and pressed his shaft into my pulsing pussy as my climax ebbed and his flowed. I'd never in my life had three orgasms in a row and my body felt so charged I might have been able to have another if I weren't so weak from the trembling.

Gavin's lips lowered onto mine with the last of his groans. Our kiss moved in a familiar rhythm, like old lovers reconnecting after a lifetime apart. The phenomenal sex wasn't as impressive as the connection that bound us when his chest lowered onto mine. Our breath mixed as we melted into a sweaty pile. I pulled away from the kiss to catch my breath. The void he left when he lifted off me took the last of my breath away.

The scary part of remembering what it was to be full was to recall the ache of emptiness I'd calloused myself not to feel. I didn't want to need a man, but I did. I needed this.

If nothing else, I had reconnected with my sexuality. For that I was grateful. Great freedom comes with the surrender to ecstasy.

Gavin returned from the bathroom wearing nothing but a big grin as he pulled back the comforter and motioned for me to join him. His arm threaded behind my neck to pull me close as I settled in beside him in the nook under his arm that seemed built for me. The weight of the warm duvet made my eyelids heavy. The last thing I remember was his breath on my hair after he kissed the top of my head.

And then... the dream. I was on a warm colorful reef swimming through a rainbow curtain of fish. So in awe, I didn't even think about the need to breathe until the ball of fish surrounding me parted and a shark pushed through— swimming straight for me. I gasped and felt the cool flood of water enter my lungs. I remembered thinking how odd it was not to choke as I exhaled the breath of water like it was air. The shark swam past and the curtain of fish closed around me again as I breathed through newfound gills.

I usually woke from the drowning dream gasping for air and grateful to be alive, but this time I woke with a smile on my face as my lungs filled with a deep breath. I exhaled in a sigh as I settled into Gavin's sleeping arms. He reminded me that I could breathe underwater.

CHAPTER 14

A rustling around the room roused me. I blinked my eyes open and my heart raced with dread, certain that Gavin was gathering his things to leave quietly and avoid the awkward morning after. I was tempted to squeeze my eyes closed but Gavin saw me awake. He smiled from the coffee machine. "Cappuccino?"

I sighed with relief. "Yes, please."

"How did you sleep?"

Better than I had in years was the real answer. "Good. And you?"

"Incredibly, I'm surprised to say. I don't usually sleep well."

His honesty spurred an openness that felt refreshing. "Neither do I."

"Well, I'm happy you feel comfortable with me." Gavin looked like a naked god with rippled abs leading to the most perfect penis ever sculpted when he handed me a steaming mug.

I pushed up onto my pillow, suddenly self-conscious of my bed hair and the makeup that must be smeared on my face. "Thank you."

Gavin sat beside me and rested his hand on the sheet over my hip. "I need to pick up fresh bread before the bakery sells out."

"Of course. I understand." I blew on the coffee before taking a sip. "Do what you need to do."

"I can wait for you to get ready so you can come along. We can get pastries for breakfast."

I sat up, surprised. "Oh. You want me to join you?"

"If you want. But I can come back for you later if you prefer. My parents aren't expecting us until after noon."

Right. His parent's barbecue. The thought of meeting his parents was less appealing now that we'd slept together. Even though it probably wasn't that unusual for him, it was outside my comfort zone. "I don't know, maybe I'll just hang out on the beach today."

"Oh no, you don't. You can't back out now. Don't make me go there alone after you got my hopes up. That's just cruel." He chuckled.

His Irish accent stirred a pulse in my groin. "Are you sure? I don't want to impose."

"Stop that nonsense right now and put on something pretty."

I might have interpreted his order as condescending or misogynistic had it not turned me on so much. He made me want to comply. I threw back the covers. "I'll shower as fast as I can."

My whole body tingled with the memory of his touch as the warm water washed away the remnants of our passion. I'd done it. I'd fucked my twenty-eight-year-old scuba instructor. It was still hard to believe. And harder to believe was that I had to go meet his parents.

Gavin admired the denim sundress that clung to my curves as I brushed my wet hair. "You look phenomenal."

I laid the brush on the counter and smiled. "Thanks. I'm ready." It was another lie I tried to convince myself of.

Gavin's relaxed demeanor quelled my anxiety and his words reassured me when we rolled to a stop in the driveway of a neat, modest one-story house. "My parents are going to love you. They might talk your ear off. If you feel like you need saving, just give me a sign."

I chuckled. "What sort of sign?"

Gavin grabbed his throat with both hands and pretended to choke. "Or something more subtle, like a wink."

"That might be just as awkward, but I'm sure it won't be necessary."

Gavin rolled his eyes. "Tell me how you feel in five minutes." He led me through the side gate into a lush tropical garden.

His father looked up from the grill and smiled, walking around the pool to greet me with a confident swagger. His charm didn't surprise me. Gavin had learned it somewhere.

Gavin kissed his mother before introducing us. Red hair tucked in an elegant twist framed her ivory skin. She looked, and acted like, the stereotypical Irish mother as she fawned over me in a barrage of questions as I followed her into the kitchen. "Lilian, meet Gavin's friend, Tessa. Lilian is James's sister."

Lilian dried her hands on a dish towel before shaking mine with a wry smile. "Don't hold that against me. Nice to meet, you, Tessa."

They put me to work right away, carrying food out to the table on the patio while Gavin tended to the barbecue with his dad. Once the table was set, we sat sipping the most delicious lemonade I'd ever tasted while the men finished cooking. Their questions continued, which might have made me uncomfortable were they not so welcoming. They treated me like family, making me miss my own.

Gavin's dad proudly set a platter of juicy steaks in the center of the table and took his seat at the head of it. Gavin sat beside me and shot me a questioning glance, checking to be sure I was okay. I smiled as he served me a steak. We chatted as we passed the side dishes around the table. I hadn't had a family meal since I'd last been in Iowa over a year ago. Chuck and I never had that, and now, we never would.

My homesick melancholy was tempered by their familiar banter. But the tense dynamic between Gavin and his father surfaced when Gavin mentioned Clifton's project in the Keys. "He bought an island that they're developing into a luxury resort."

James huffed out a dry laugh, making no attempt to conceal his disdain. "I bet they are. That's what he does. Pour money into ruining things."

He's given us a lot of business, and he's done far more to help this island than he has to hurt it, as far as I can see."

His father scoffed. "You can't see too far then."

I cringed at the condescending remark and wanted to put my hand on Gavin's knee to ease the sting but I sat still, holding my breath until he spoke.

"I know an opportunity when I see it. He wants someone to develop a dive shop at the resort. It could be good business."

His father's baritone voice declared with an unmistakable finality, "We don't do business with people like him."

I felt Gavin stiffen in his chair beside me. His eyes shifted to mine and he smiled with a resigned shrug. He knew better than to argue.

His mother spoke up in Gavin's defense. "Maybe you ought to hear him out, James."

"There ain't nothing more to hear, Catherine." He didn't need to say that she should mind her own business—it was clear as a bell in his tone.

Gavin's mom changed the subject to ask his aunt about her daughter who was pregnant with her second child as she hurried to bring out the dessert.

The contention between Gavin and his father was never revisited but it was never resolved. They barely spoke directly for the rest of the afternoon. Gavin's mother kept the conversation going though so there were no awkward silences. She was skilled at distraction and denial. I recognized it from my own coping mechanisms.

I felt for Gavin. In one sense, he was lucky to have his family close. But it seemed like he might be stifled by that proximity. It was hard to tell if it was out of respect or resignation that he kept quiet, but either way, it was clear he couldn't stand up to his father any more than anyone else could.

I was relieved when Gavin followed his aunt's lead and stood to leave when she did. He took my hand in his as we said our goodbyes. I blushed at the surprise display of affection after he'd been hands-off all afternoon.

He grinned as I slid onto the seat in his truck and he closed the door with a thud. He laughed as we backed out of the doorway. "You never had to wink. I'd call that a success."

"They were intense, but nothing I couldn't handle." I knew he could relate.

He turned onto the highway in the wrong direction to return to the resort. "Can I offer you a Hendricks and tonic under the stars?"

"How can I refuse an offer like that?" Elliot would never forgive me if I did. The thought of him made me check my phone. He'd called twice and sent me four texts, checking in. "Sorry. I have to respond to my friend. He threatened to call the police the last time I didn't answer."

I'm okay. Don't worry. I'll explain later.

I tucked my phone back into my purse. "A good gin and tonic sounds divine."

"You probably need a drink after that experience. I know I do. Thanks for coming today. You made it much more fun." He squeezed my knee and left his hand there until he had to shift gears.

We turned off the highway and rumbled to a stop at the end of a sandy lane. The headlights shone on a tiny wooden shack with white paint that had long since surrendered to the elements. It covered the grain in a thin veil and there was something beautiful about the dilapidation.

I felt like I was in a pilot episode of a Robinson Crusoe remake as Gavin led me into the tin-roofed hut on the beach. He switched on a tall floor lamp fashioned from varnished arms of mangrove roots. A mosquito net hung around the bed in the corner. The small kitchen consisted of a propane stove and an ice chest.

"I have wind and solar, but I can only make enough ice cubes for four gin and tonics at a time. So we better make them strong."

I laughed but when his words registered, I was perplexed. "You don't have electricity?"

"Nope, it's all DC, like on the boat."

"That's fascinating." He really was like Robinson Crusoe.

"I do have running water though, through a cistern. So it's one step above camping."

"I live with all the modern comforts in the middle of a big city that I love, but I'd still say you're winning."

Gavin handed me a drink. "What makes it all worthwhile is right out here." He led me out the front door and past the hammock on the porch down the two steps that spilled out onto a deserted beach.

I helped him spread out the blanket he carried. "There's nothing around. How did you find this place?"

"It's an old fishing shack from back in the turtling days. I spotted it from the boat one day and tracked down the owner of the land a few weeks after I came back from Ireland." He grinned as he continued. "A few weeks was all it took to know that I had to have my own place. It was a bonus

159

that it's about as far away from everything else as one can get."

"You're a lucky man. It's the perfect spot." I sat across from him on the blanket.

"I feel pretty damn lucky right now." Gavin's grin lit up his mischievous green eyes in the moonlight. "It's been good. It's good for now. I mean, I know I'm not going to live like this forever. But I haven't felt inspired to do the logical thing and build a house—like my father suggests on a daily basis."

He was obviously reticent to grow roots. "There's no rush. You have plenty of time."

"I feel like my time is short here. But who knows? It's hard to focus on the good when I'm fed up with my dad—and that's been a lot lately. But it's all going well here, to be honest. Sometimes I daydream about picking up and taking off, landing wherever the wind takes me, but, as you said, it's not a bad place to be stuck."

He might not know what he wanted to do, but he was in no way stuck. He could do whatever he wanted. I envied his freedom. But as much as his nomad lifestyle turned me on, it also highlighted our age gap. He hadn't grown roots. He had no commitments. The world was his oyster. I hadn't felt the walls of my carefully constructed world closing in around me until I got away. Seeing his world without walls made me realize that there could be something different out there.

We were in different places in life, but we were both still trying to figure out what to do with ourselves in this crazy world that seemed as vast as the blanket of stars overhead. He made anything seem possible. I released a deep sigh after realizing I'd been holding my breath again.

It seemed entirely appropriate that my scuba instructor was teaching me how to breathe by taking my breath away. I knew when I opened myself to the pleasure he gave me last night that I would have a hard time keeping lust in its little box and not let love in. I felt for him as he resigned to his father, and imagined how watching his mother succumb to his bullying had hardened him. As unlikely as it seemed, we connected easily. I got him, and he got me. The years and space between us dissolved like salt in the warm water that lapped the shore. I sipped my cocktail, knowing one of life's big lessons laid stretched out at my side. What it would teach me remained to be seen.

Gavin pulled me under his arm on the blanket and we laid staring up into the black sky littered with the cloud of the Milky Way stretching into oblivion overhead. The waves on the shore lulled me into a trance as Gavin pointed out the constellations. I tried to focus on the seven sisters of Pleiades but they blurred as I drifted off on his shoulder.

He shook me awake what must have been some time later. "Tessa, wake up." I blinked up at Gavin, disoriented as I tried to process his words. "Come on. We fell asleep. Let's go inside before the mosquitos carry us away."

I heard buzzing around my head as I staggered to the door. There was a reason he slept with a net over his bed.

I slipped out of my dress and into his waiting arms like I belonged there. The bare flesh of his chest on my back made my heart race but the warmth of his strong hold calmed me. His breath settled into a rhythm on my neck as he drifted back to sleep spooning me. I didn't know what the hell I was doing there, but it didn't need to make sense. It felt like home.

CHAPTER 15

I thought I might be dreaming when a warm surge of tingling woke me as Gavin's lips grazed my neck and he whispered, "Good morning, beautiful." I nuzzled my cheek into the stubble of his chin as he drew in a long breath and said what I was thinking. "You smell like heaven."

I was suddenly conscious of my morning breath, which might give the opposite impression, and tucked my chin to respond. "Good morning."

His hand slid up my belly and pulled me tight into his chest. "I had big plans to seduce you on the beach, but falling asleep under the stars was almost as good."

I giggled that he thought he would need to seduce me. "It was beautiful. Thank you for a lovely day yesterday." I sighed.

The vibration of his deep voice tickled my ear. "Thank you for making it the best day I've had in a long time."

I tried to ignore the flutter in my stomach as my gaze

wandered around the sparsely furnished room. He wasn't supposed to say all the right things. I wasn't supposed to like him so much. "Me too." I bit my lip, grateful my back was to Gavin so he couldn't see it quiver.

His fingers threaded through mine and tugged gently to roll me over to face him. He traced my lower lip with a wispy fingertip and I had to will myself not to tremble when he locked my gaze. "You're stunning."

"I don't think I've ever been called that."

"What!?" Gavin exclaimed before his voice softened again as he caressed a wave of hair along my face. "With your gorgeous hair and those bright eyes." He smoothed my brow and trailed his fingertip down the bridge of my nose. "And this perfect little button nose."

His string of compliments was so sweet and genuine I had to look away. The only thing that was perfect about me was how he made me feel.

He hooked my chin to turn my face up. "And those lips that made me want to kiss them since the moment I saw you across the bar. Everything about you is stunning."

I searched his eyes for a reason to believe that this could be real, or maybe I was looking for a reason not to believe. All doubt dissipated when his mouth found mine, moving in a slippery slow dance while his fingers buried in my hair.

Gavin stopped abruptly and winced as he said, "Dammit! I left the condoms I just bought in the truck." I stopped him when he started to wiggle away from me.

"I trust you." I don't know why, but I did.

He studied me with hesitation. "Are you sure? I mean, I know I'm clean, and I'll be careful. But I really don't mind going outside to get them."

I didn't want to wait for another minute for him to be inside me. "I'm sure." I pulled him back to my mouth and heat built in my core until it blazed through me as our tongues entangled in desperate groans.

Gavin guided my knee up onto his hip and pushed the crotch of my pink lace panties to the side. The back of his finger grazing my sex flooded me with anticipation before his broad hand cupped my ass to pull me onto his waiting hardness. He pulled back from the kiss to watch my wide eyes as he filled me with a deep thrust. The feel of his silky skin moving into my slippery warmth took my breath—so much better without the condom.

His stare held me captive while he pushed into me with long, slow strokes. Our lips crashed together in a fervor when he rolled over onto his back, pulling me onto his chest. I swiveled my shoulders to rub my breasts over his pecs. It felt like my nipples were directly connected to my clit when they grazed the carpet of ginger hair on his tanned chest.

My pelvis pressed into his with a delicious friction of lace over my swollen pleasure spot. The electric pulses of ecstasy built to a steady current that spread through me as our lips slipped over one another. When I started to moan, Gavin pulled my hips tight onto his and moved me side to side over him while his hard cock throbbed in the limits of my depth. He read my body like a book, shifting underneath me as the orgasm built to make me shudder when I finally exploded. My lips slid along his face as I moaned into his ear. Pleasure pulsed through me, my body clenching his thickness.

I was still moaning when Gavin lifted my hips to guide me off to his side and slipped out from under me. I was confused at first in an orgasmic daze when he stood on his knees but when he grabbed my hips and pulled me up to my hands and knees I knew what he was doing and I liked it. The way he manhandled me into position and rolled my panties down over my hips stirred the boiling cauldron of desire. Two fingers slid into my wetness. "God, you feel fucking amazing."

I whimpered as his fingers retreated but moaned when he replaced them with what I really wanted, what I *needed*. My pussy stretched around him while he pushed deeper than anyone had ever been. His fingers dug into the flesh of my hips to hold them steady to receive his thrusts. I gasped and groaned as he pushed harder and faster until my head spun. I was grateful when he slowed the pace and his sweaty chest lowered onto my back.

Gavin's hand slid between my breasts to my throat. Soft lips brushed my ear while his fingers tightened ever so slightly around my neck and he growled, "I love fucking you."

I had never loved anything more.

His other hand moved down my stomach, his fingers slipping between my lips. He gently teased the nub that begged for more with soft circles around the base. When he finally touched my clit, it was ripe again. His fingers moved swiftly over it while his other hand held my neck. His hips pumped while he lifted me to the point of desperate moans. "Come for me, beautiful. Come for me." He rubbed me harder until my pussy gripped him in a rhythmic pulse. He knew exactly how to make me melt. My moans filled the air that was charged with the heat between us.

He released my neck and slid out of me, groaning as he grabbed his cock, his other hand still massaging my swollen clit while he came with me. I turned to catch his thirsty eyes drinking in the sight of me like it was water at the end of a race. My breathing slowed as the final moans left my lips. He pulled me to his mouth with a firm grip on my wrists before his hands slipped around my waist to draw me closer. He paused, staring so deeply into my eyes I feared he might see me unraveling in bliss. But he echoed my thoughts in breathless words. "Woman, what you do to me."

"What *you* do to *me*." My hand drifted unconsciously to my throat. No one had ever touched me that way before. His forceful way was foreign—but hot as fuck. The sting of my skin on the tops of my hips from where his nails had dug in while he'd relentlessly pounded into me made my heart race. I would have never dreamed that I liked throat grabs and a little bit of pain until he'd shown me. He seemed to know my body better than I knew myself.

He grinned and wiggled his brows suggestively. "I hope to do a lot more of that to you."

He could do that to me every minute of every day until I left. "Well, I'm here for another week."

"That's a good start."

My breath caught as I let the thought that this might be the start of something creep in. Crazy as it seemed, it felt like it could be real as we steeped in the steam of our passion. The mystical morning light pouring in through the open wooden shudders was veiled by the curtains of white netting around the bed. It all felt like a dream.

For the first time in so long, I couldn't remember, I was light and I was free. All the reasons that it couldn't be fell away. In that moment, anything was possible. That moment was all that we had and it was all that mattered.

CHAPTER 16

Gavin parted the mosquito net and climbed off the bed, holding the curtain for me to join him. "I think a good start right now would be coffee."

He was a man after my heart. "Yes, please."

I looked around the room. I'd barely noticed it since we went straight out to the beach last night, but it was different in the light of day. It looked less like a bohemian man cave and more like a quaint beach cottage. The windows had no glass, only wooden shutters open out to the sea. The modern low-backed sofa might have seemed out of place with the other more rustic furniture, but he'd pulled it off. His fishing hut had style. "Your place is cute. I like your taste."

"Thanks, I'm glad you like it." Gavin smiled and handed me a mug. "It's not luxury, but I love it. Living off the grid isn't for everyone though."

Gavin passed me a robe off the hook beside the door as he led me to sit on the stoop of the front porch. I watched him wrap a towel around his slender waist as I held the steaming coffee under my nose to breathe in its aroma. The heat in my cheeks wasn't from the steam though. I couldn't maintain composure if I let myself think about how hot he was so I turned the conversation back to living off the grid. "I can see the appeal though. There's something to be said for simplicity."

"It's simple alright. It took some adjusting for sure, but I realized that I don't need much."

My life was full of things—things to do as much as material things I kept accumulating. Staring out at the ocean sipping coffee in a bathrobe beside a Caribbean-Irish god made all those *things* seem insignificant. *This* was the life. *That* was just pretending to live. "It's a beautiful life you've made for yourself."

"It's a beautiful life, indeed, and I'm doing my best." His smile, vibrant in the pale-yellow light, faded. "But I didn't *choose* to be back here running the family business. It was the last thing I ever wanted. But I'm making the most of it for now. It's all been a fun project."

He sounded like he was looking for a way out, ready to move on. The guilt of obligation bound him. I knew that feeling well. "You'll find the right thing when the right time comes."

Gavin grinned. "I'm ready."

The wetness that tricked from me when he said that made my heart quicken. I didn't know what he meant by his comment. I only knew it made every cell in my body scream that I was ready, too.

But ready for what? For the right thing when it was the right time? Right now, this felt like the right thing. But my confidence dissipated with my next thought—was Chuck's secretary his "right thing"? That's what men did. Gavin had said it himself—There's only the last one.

I sipped my coffee tentatively; not sure I could stomach being Gavin's next last one.

"You fancy a morning swim? I need to get to the shop at the resort shortly but I have time for a quick dip."

I looked up and down the desolate beach. "I don't have a suit."

"Your birthday suit is all you need."

Gavin stood and held out his hand, his lips curled in a mischievous grin. It was an offer I couldn't refuse. I let him pull me up then took off running after him as he shed his towel on the way to the surf. I stopped at the shore watching his tight butt, lined with dark tan lines, disappear under the surface as he ran into the waves. The water dripping from his sun-streaked hair down his face glistened in the shimmering light when he turned to yell, "What are you waiting for?"

That was a damn good question. I looked up and down the beach again to be sure we were alone before I tossed my robe onto the sand and caution into the wind. Fuck it.

The water was as warm as the air and even more inviting with a tanned hunk reaching for me. Gavin pulled me to his chest and lowered his lips to mine for a quick kiss. "*This* is why I live here. You can't find this just anywhere."

He could say that again.

"Do you swim? I mean distance."

"Not miles, but I did swim team when I was a kid." Before he was born.

"I like to swim up to a mooring ball about 500 meters up the reef. You game?"

I wasn't sure I could do it, but I couldn't say no to anything he proposed. "I'll try."

"I haven't let you drown yet." Gavin motioned with his chin for me to follow before diving under.

His easy strokes slowed when he looked back to see me lagging. My breath fell into rhythm with our comfortable pace and my body moved fluidly through the warm water. We reached the buoy before I knew it. Gavin held onto braided nylon rope that trailed off the mooring ball and smiled. "You're a fish."

"I'd forgotten how good it feels to swim." That was true of a few other things that Gavin had shown me.

"Then you should do more of it."

"I couldn't agree more."

Gavin grinned before setting off back down the reef. Once we were back in front of the hut, we waded through the gentle surf to the beach. Gavin handed me his towel and strolled naked across the sand to a bamboo enclosure beside the porch. I stepped inside and onto a teakwood grate when he held the door open.

"An open-air shower!?" My smile gaped so wide I felt giddy.

"The best kind." He turned on the water and held his hand under the stream. "Especially when you have a solar heater." He grabbed my hand and pulled me under the water that fell like rain from the large square shower head. "This shower is my favorite part of the house."

Gavin handed me a bar of soap and shampooed his hair

while I lathered up. He pulled me into his chest while he rinsed his hair, his palms gliding over my skin to rinse my body. He spun me around to wet my hair and grabbed the shampoo. "May I?"

My eyes narrowed but I couldn't stop smiling. "You want to wash my hair?"

Gavin looked up innocently. "Is that weird?"

"Maybe…"

"Maybe it's weird or maybe I can?"

"Definitely. Both. Definitely."

His lips spread in a playful smile as he massaged shampoo into my scalp. My eyes closed as my head fell back into his touch. He gently worked the suds into the waves of hair that fell onto my breasts, making my nipples crave him. They were left wanting. He pushed my hair over my shoulder to rinse it under the stream. I wanted to kiss him, but I didn't want to interrupt his task. I was enjoying it too much. When he reached behind me to turn off the water, I didn't want it to end. It must have shown.

Gavin dipped his chin to peck my lips. "Sorry I have to run. I'd love nothing more than to spend the whole day with you here."

I'd stay for the whole week if he'd let me, but I knew he had to go. It couldn't last forever.

CHAPTER 17

*G*avin held my hand as we walked down the sidewalk
into the resort. We stopped at the fork where I'd go
left and he'd go right. He gave my hand a quick
squeezed as he pecked my cheek. "I've got to run. I'm late. I'll
catch up with you later, beautiful."

"Okay, sure." I tried not to let my disappointment show. I
wasn't ready for him to go but he was already gone.

I touched my cheek where his lips had been and was tempted
to call after him. "See you at dinner?" But I talked myself out
of it for fear of sounding desperate and instead just watched
him walk away. I felt like an idiot for still staring after him
when he looked back over his shoulder. I waved awkwardly
and turned toward my room.

I took a cappuccino to the steps of the porch. What had just
happened? I'd fucked my scuba instructor, met his parents,
slept in his fishing hut, fucked him again, and somehow
fallen for him in the process.

I thought about calling Elliot more than once, but I just

couldn't. I felt too stupid. He was the last person that would judge me. But I couldn't admit to Elliot the crazy thoughts that clouded my mind and the feelings that flooded me without first admitting it to myself. And I definitely wasn't ready for that.

In lieu of his actual advice, I gave myself a stern talking to all afternoon, telling myself what I thought Elliot might say every time Gavin would pop in my head. *Get yourself together. You're just having fun, so go have fun.*

But there was nothing fun about feeling tied in knots inside. I read on the front porch but was continually distracted by thoughts of the hammock on Gavin's front porch and how I'd rather be there. As sunset approached, I grew restless and gave up on my book to set off on a walk down the beach.

The light shimmered on the water, reflecting the changing colors of the sky. This was heaven on earth. The cooling breeze on my cheeks made me smile as I imagined Boomer bounding in and out of the waves that lapped at my feet. I missed him. Other than Elliot, I didn't miss anything else about home. What I missed right now was Gavin. I couldn't even call him to see if we could meet for dinner. I'd never gotten his number.

That was probably for the best. I was too eager.

I showered and sifted through my clothes, finally deciding on a strapless white sundress embroidered with white flowers. I carefully painted my lips with a shimmering pink gloss to finish off my makeup. I liked what I saw when I rubbed my lips together and smiled in the mirror. I looked good, but part of me still wondered if it was good enough.

Carlos greeted me with a broad grin while drying a glass. "Good evening."

I smiled. "Good evening. How are you tonight?"

He put the glass on the shelf and held up his hands in a shrug. "Another day in paradise."

"You've got that right. I fall in love with this place a little more every day." I mused at my choice of words.

"Can I get you a Macallan Reflexion?"

I smiled but shook my head. "That's not included in my package and too rich for my blood. I'll stick with the house top shelf."

"For you, it's included. Mr. Drake has you covered. He told me last time you were here."

"Seriously? How much is a shot of that?" I winced after I'd asked. "Don't answer that. It's rude."

Carlos grinned. "Money is not an issue for him. Double, neat?" He seemed to enjoy giving the tycoon's money away.

Why the hell not? "Sounds fabulous."

I looked out into the blackness of the ocean in the moonless sky. The smoothest whiskey that had touched my lips wasn't as sweet as the Hendricks and tonic I wished I was drinking on a blanket on the beach.

I kept hoping Gavin would appear but resigned myself to ordering a fish plate when I finished my drink. I had to eat—even if I had to eat alone—if I was going to have another drink.

A handsome, older man sat two stools down from me just before my food arrived. He seemed to know Carlos when he ordered a gin martini before he turned to me and turned on the charm. "How are you this evening?"

I had to be polite but I didn't want to encourage him. "Great, thanks. And you?"

"Much better now. Are you here on business or pleasure?"

"All pleasure." I regretted the way that came out immediately.

"As a vacation should be. What magnificent place can we thank for lending you to us?"

I nearly rolled my eyes but managed to answer politely. "San Francisco."

"How lucky you are. I love the Bay Area."

I thought to tell him how much I loved his island, assuming he lived here, but I didn't want to show any interest. Lucky for me that I had the excuse of eating to inhibit further conversation, but it didn't stop him from chatting me up. I mostly grunted and nodded as he nattered on.

He was good looking, confident, apparently wealthy, and obviously interested. He was probably the sort of man I *should* be attracted to. But I kept looking over his shoulder hoping a disheveled scuba bum would appear. Gavin was much more than the scuba bum I'd thought him to be, though. He was a successful businessman in his own right with even greater potential according to Clifton's praise. He was impressive, indeed. And far more interesting than my persistent companion.

I shook my head when Carlos eyed my empty glass. I'd been there long enough. With a full belly and four shots of whiskey under my belt, I finally excused myself from my chatty neighbor as gracefully as possible. "This vacation life is exhausting. I better get my rest."

His smile faded in disappointment. "Maybe I'll see you again before you go."

I smiled as I slid off my stool. "Maybe so. Have a good night."

He looked like he was going to say something but I turned and headed for the exit without looking back.

I peered into my own sad eyes in the bathroom mirror after I washed the makeup off my face. I'd gotten all prettied up for nothing.

I settled under the sheets and stared up at the dark ceiling. Trying to fill the emptiness inside with deep breaths, only made me more aware of the gaping hole in the bed where I wanted Gavin to be. I'd been alone long enough to get used to it but two nights with him had reminded me how deep the ache of loneliness was.

I thought I'd worked through the helplessness and the paralyzing pain of those first weeks after Chuck left, but it came back with the vengeance of a raging river that threatened to take me down with it.

CHAPTER 18

With the dawn of a new day, there was light to draw me from my darkness, but a restless energy had me in a heightened state of alert. I needed to move my body. The spin class that Elliot had dragged me to twice a week for the past six months had worked wonders for releasing tension and stress. I could use some of that right now. I threw on shorts and a T-shirt and set out on a long walk down the beach. Swinging my arms as my feet shuffled over the wet sand at a fast pace, I pushed myself until my heart pounded and my breath was labored. The endorphin release felt like a high. Positivity started to chip away at my pessimism.

After an hour, sweat was dripping down my shoulders and off my elbows when I turned around to head back. With every step, I got a little more of my confidence back. I'd worked too hard to get over Chuck leaving me to be thrown off my game by a vacation fling. Maybe I was a fool to think it could be anything more than that, but I didn't have to be hard on myself. I'd fallen but I was back on my feet and moving forward.

I was still charged with energy when I reached my bungalow. I needed more exercise. Swimming with Gavin yesterday had reminded me of the freedom of weightlessness, before the loneliness had floored me. The calm sea had called me the whole way back.

I swam along the shoreline for several laps, the warm water washing my worries away until my arms felt like jelly. My thighs trembled as I climbed the steps to the porch but I felt strong.

I stepped into the warm shower, closing my eyes as I ran my fingers through my hair. The memory of yesterday's shower came rushing back. I could see Gavin's smile and I could feel his fingers on my scalp. Warmth washed over me with the cascade of water. Remembering Gavin's hands on me while I lathered my body made my breath hasten. He made me feel alive. Wanting him was good. Needing him was not.

I put on a fresh bikini and took my book out to the beach. I had six days to get through three books and work on my tan. I was so lost in the final chapters of *The Book Thief* that I forgot to eat. When I finally reached the ambiguous end, I was frustrated and famished. I wandered up to the restaurant and smiled at the skinny hostess I'd found annoying before. "Table for one, please." Saying it felt more natural every day.

I ordered a seafood pasta and sipped a glass of white wine, pondering the mysterious ending of the book. I wanted all the loose ends to be tied up with a nice little bow, so not knowing if it was Max who Leisel had married and lived happily after with was torture. How could the author do that to us? It was just cruel. He'd left it open as a possibility that they'd survived against all odds and ended up together, but there was nothing certain. I wanted to believe it, but that didn't make it true. It made me kind of crazy.

By the time I finished my lunch I was properly annoyed at the uncertainty in my own life. What the hell had happened to Gavin? It sure seemed like he'd ghosted me. I didn't want to believe it, but that didn't make it untrue. There was only one way to know for sure. I hung a right out of the restaurant and headed toward the dive shop.

Peeking in the open door from a distance, I spotted the leggy blonde who'd been at the dock helping a customer. A jealous pang shot through me when I remembered her brushing up against Gavin. At least he wasn't off with her right now. I walked past and stopped on the other side of the entrance for a different view. Gavin was nowhere in sight, but I couldn't see into the equipment room in the back. I knew where the back door was, though. I crept closer, pausing to listen before I got the nerve to look inside the open door. It was empty. I stepped in tentatively and turned my ear to listen. I could hear the voices from the front of the store. I recognized the supermodel's voice but couldn't understand the words she spoke in Dutch to the customer. I tiptoed back out the door. I contemplated going in as I passed the front entrance to the shop. I wanted to ask where Gavin was, but I couldn't bear talking to the Barbie doll.

I felt ridiculous looking for him anyway. He knew exactly where to find me if he wanted to. Since he'd made no effort whatsoever to do so thus far, I wasn't going to hold my breath.

I went back to the same chair I'd camped out in all week and opened a new book. On to the next story. Hopefully this one would have a happy ending.

I forced myself to keep reading but reining in my wandering mind proved difficult. The e-reader screen couldn't hold my eyes that kept searching the figures on the beach, hoping to catch sight of Gavin. As the sun started to sink toward the horizon, I flagged down a waitress passing by on the beach and ordered a Cayman Sunset. It went down easy and I was ready for another one before the actual sunset. I read and reread the same chapter three times by the time I finished the second drink, and there was still no sign of Gavin.

The white wine and strong cocktails amplified my annoyance. I had just enough of a buzz to be pissed off, which made me want another drink. I knew it wasn't the smart or healthy thing to do, but I was beyond giving a fuck. I shook out my towel and headed back to my room.

I sat in one of the Adirondack chairs on the porch with a Tanqueray and tonic. The sky over the deep blue ocean exploded in orange and red. Once again, I was wishing I had someone to share it with. I texted Elliot.

How's it going?

Dammit. He was supposed to be here. If he'd come, I wouldn't have slept with Gavin and I wouldn't be so fucking miserable right now. Luckily Elliot saved me from my self-inflicted torment and called.

"Hey, Sweet T, how's island life?"

"Oh, it's beautiful. The sunset is incredible right now. I wish you were here."

"Me, too. Believe me." Elliot sounded stressed.

I winced at how whiny I must've sounded. "Yeah, how's work?"

"Better but still a mess. But I don't want to talk about work. Tell me about your vacation. What have you been up to? You never even got to tell me about the yacht! And you haven't answered my texts from yesterday."

Where did I begin? "The yacht was amazing. Like *you cannot believe* amazing. I felt like I was in a film."

"Was it like that *365 Days* film?"

My face scrunched in confusion. "What's that?"

"Oh, never mind. It's a bad movie with great sex on a yacht. The lead is a really hot Dom. Anyway, were there any sparks with the hot young lad on your boat?"

My cheeks blushed and my lips parted in a smile that surprised me. "Not on the boat, no."

"It sounds like there's more to that story. Go on." I could hear Elliot smiling.

I didn't know how to say it without sounding ridiculous because I felt so stupid. "Well, he was really sweet after a little mishap on our first dive and I started to think that maybe you were right, that I needed a fling. But he didn't make a move."

"Wait, what mishap?"

I recounted the shark knocking my mask off story and finished with the fabulous dinner in the master cabin. "The next day we went for a couple more dives with the kids. Gavin is great with them. He's just great at what he does."

"*That's* what I want to hear more about. I mean I'm glad you're okay and he kept you safe, but I want the goods. I take it you've seen him since."

I could picture Elliot's face and felt all warm and fuzzy inside that at least he was sharing the moment from afar. I sipped my cocktail down to the ice. "Yeah, in a moment of weakness, after I found out you weren't coming, I kind of took him home with me."

"You did not!"

I pulled my feet in close to my butt in the oversized chair, grinning. "I did."

The line was silent for a second before he asked, "So, how was it?"

"It was good—really good. Pretty fabulous." The smile that spread over my face made joy rise up into my chest as I gushed the details. "It was the best sex I've ever had. I mean, *ever*. And then the next day we went to his parent's house for a barbecue and ended up spending the night at his little cottage on the beach. He lives like Robinson Crusoe in a revamped fishing hut."

"Of course he does."

I grinned. "He has a bamboo shower on the beach."

"That sounds sexy."

"It was *so* sexy. We had a dreamy morning before he dropped me off yesterday. And I haven't heard a word from him since." I looked down at the ice cubes in the glass that was as empty as I felt.

"What!? What do you mean? Did you text him?"

"I can't! I don't have his number."

"How do you *not* have his number? You've gone on a trip and slept together."

"I guess I haven't been on my phone much and never thought about it when we were together. I kept hoping he'd show up last night and all day today. But, nope, he's nowhere to be found." I felt the smile melt off my face as I deflated. I got up to mix another cocktail. "I guess this is what it feels like to be ghosted."

"It was only yesterday that you saw him. You might be jumping to conclusions there. Who knows why he hasn't called? Wait—he can't even call. Just chill, Sweet T. I doubt he's a dog." Elliot chuckled. "But then again, what do I know? I don't know this guy from Adam. Maybe he's a one-and-done kinda guy. They're out there, Tess. It's ugly, but not always. Try to relax and take it as it comes."

Feeling like your heart might be ripped out of your chest and stomped on the ground in front of you was hard to take. I didn't know how to enjoy the intimacy without feeling something. "I'm trying." I sipped the fresh G&T.

"Worst case scenario, it was a fun few days. It might be even better if you don't see him again. Who knows? Just let it unfold."

The thought of not seeing Gavin again made my stomach sink, but I could see Elliot's point. "Yeah, it's all pretty silly I suppose. I mean, this is not who I am. I'm not a cougar."

Elliot laughed out loud. "No, you most certainly are not." He chuckled heartily. "God, Tessa, you're not old enough to be a cougar."

"I'm too old to be sleeping with men in their twenties."

"He's almost in his thirties. And you're barely in your forties. Besides, you're not looking for a husband. You should be

187

looking for a good time. And it sounds like you've already had that, so I'd say you're winning."

Then why did I feel like the biggest loser on earth? I loved how Elliot could always turn me toward the positive in any shitty situation, though. He'd had plenty of practice.

"Hey, I think being a cougar is winning. I'm not ashamed." It was a gin-fueled lie I loved to tell myself. Emboldened by booze, I almost believed it.

"You shouldn't be ashamed, but you are *not* a cougar. Not even close."

"Oh, I think I'm close. I'm at least *almost* a cougar chasing after this perfect specimen of a much younger man."

"No, you're not." I could picture him shaking his head as he shut me down.

I giggled and slurred a little when I said, "I can be a cougar if I want to."

"You can be whatever you want, dear." Elliot chuckled. "Are you drunk?"

Hearing his smile made me giggle. "A little. I've had a couple of gin and tonics." I wouldn't mention the wine with lunch or the two strong frozen drinks on the beach. I was too busy gushing over Gavin. "Oh, that's another great thing about Gavin. He loves Hendricks. It made me think of you."

"It sounds like everything makes you think of Gavin. You seem smitten."

"I am not." I was indignant in my denial of the obvious.

"Relax, I'm happy for you, Tess. Even if this turns out to be nothing, it's been something."

I wished I was rubbing my foot on his on my coffee table right now, like I'd done in so many of our wine sessions on my couch. "It's a lot more than I bargained for."

"It's good for you! You're excited about something other than work. That's amazing! Enjoy it, love. Even if nothing else comes of it, enjoy the high. I told you all you needed was some good D."

"I think you might be right."

"If there's anything I know about, it's good D. I know I'm right." He took a deep breath. "But listen, love, I've got to run. I'm still trying to wrap up a few things for work."

"Oh, of course. Sorry, I'm rambling. Thanks for putting up with me."

"Don't be silly. You know you're my girl. Now, go get some dinner. I'll check in with you later."

"Sounds good. Thanks for everything."

"Shut the fuck up and go eat."

"Alright." I was smiling long after I'd hung up the phone I clutched at my chest.

Elliot was right. I needed food to absorb the booze. And I needed to relax. I ordered a fish sandwich and a Perrier from room service and searched for the boat sex movie Elliot had mentioned on Netflix.

He wasn't kidding that it was bad, but the guy was so hot I couldn't turn it off. The ridiculous storyline was irrelevant. I understood what Elliot meant about him being a Dom. He was far more hardcore, but there was something in the forceful way he handled the woman that reminded me of Gavin.

I climbed into bed when they were on the yacht. Even if I didn't identify with the characters, the heat of the sex they had all over that boat lit a fire inside me. My hands were drawn to my tingling nipples. I watched the hot couple on the screen but I thought of Gavin in his bed draped in mosquito nets while I touched myself. Memories of him made coming easy.

It was leaving that would be hard.

CHAPTER 19

Squinting into the sunlight as I opened the curtains, my head throbbed. I shouldn't have had that last gin and tonic. The ocean stretched out in a transparent sheet to the horizon, a waveless reflection of the blue sky overhead, easing the ache behind my eyes. I couldn't complain about anything waking with that view. I couldn't complain about anything anyway. Elliot's pep talk had helped put things back into perspective. This thing with Gavin, whatever it was, had been a good thing. Even if I was scared of the feelings that he'd awakened, feeling anything at all was an improvement. Especially the orgasms.

Remembering the intensity of the climax I'd given myself last night almost embarrassed me. I'd much rather have Gavin take me there, but it was good to know I could reach such heights of pleasure by myself. Being with him had rekindled a long-forgotten desire.

Inspired by the tranquil expanse of the sea while I sipped my coffee, I decided to go for a long swim before breakfast.

After a long shower, I returned to my familiar spot on the beach and got lost in my new book. The Rom-Com was light reading and the promise of the predictable happy ending put me in a good mood even if it was contrived and make-believe. I was going to enjoy the rest of the week with or without Gavin, but I couldn't help hoping he'd show up.

I got up to go for a walk late in the afternoon, restless after hours of looking for Gavin periodically while I read. I walked along the shore, wishing for a breeze in the broiling summer heat. After twenty minutes, I turned back, parched. I'd been avoiding alcohol, but it was time for a frozen cocktail. On my way back to the bar, I saw Gavin standing out front of the dive shop that sat back in the shade of palm trees off the beach in the distance. I looked down and veered back toward the water.

After hoping to see him for the past three days, my first instinct was to avoid him. I was perplexed at my reaction while my heart pounded in my chest. I picked up my pace and headed back toward my beach chair, but his voice carried in the windless humid air.

"Tessa. Hey! Tessa!"

I pretended not to hear and kept moving, but he called louder.

I stopped, taking a deep breath to find the nerve to face him. He jogged toward me, waving when I finally looked his way.

He smiled like nothing had happened. As though it was totally normal to ditch me after we'd slept together twice. For him, it probably was. Bile boiled in my belly as he approached with a nonchalant smile. "Hi! I was just looking for you."

Yeah, sure he was. I didn't even try to temper my bitchiness. "Really? Why now?"

Gavin looked confused and spoke slowly like he was explaining to a child. "Because I'm here now. I got back a couple of hours ago."

My eyes narrowed. "Back from where?"

"Clifton kidnapped me." He grinned, but his smile faded as he hurried to continue when I held my scowl. "He took me for a spin on the yacht and a day and a half later, here we are."

Knowing the nature of their business relationship, his explanation was plausible. I wanted to be mad, but I got it. He couldn't say no. I'd had that problem since we met. "Was it a good trip?"

"Nothing compared to the trip we had on that boat." His jade eyes pierced me with a sparkling grin. "But yes, it was good. Very productive, in fact." He held my gaze and took my hand in his. "I'm sorry I couldn't call you. I can't believe I don't have your number."

My heart fluttered. "I know, crazy, right?"

"I don't know how that happened, to be honest. But, yeah, I'm sorry to disappear like that. I told Ingrid to let you know where I'd gone if you came by the shop."

I kicked myself for not going in to ask for him yesterday. I could have spared myself the angst and the hangover. "It's okay. I understand."

Gavin glanced up the beach toward the restaurant. "Are you hungry?"

"Famished."

"Me too. I didn't have lunch. Let's get some dinner."

I looked down at my sundress and sandy toes. "I'm not dressed for dinner."

"You look beautiful." He smiled as his eyes roamed up my body appreciatively.

"I'd have to change first. Or we could order room service." I hadn't meant to suggest that. I wasn't aware of having even thought it. It just came out.

The look in Gavin's wide eyes turned from surprised to devious, and made my breath catch in my throat when he spoke. "That sounds perfect." His fingers laced through mine. "Shall we?"

It sounded like the perfect kind of trouble. The wise move would be to keep my distance, but when he was in front of me all I wanted was to get closer.

Gavin ordered appetizers and cradled the phone on his shoulder while he asked, "You want some wine?"

I looked up from dusting the sand off my feet. "Is there ever a time the answer to that question is 'no'?"

He winked. "Not that I can think of."

He added a bottle of white wine to the order and grabbed two bottles of Perrier from the fridge "Wanna sit outside?"

"I need the A/C." I'd been baking in the sun for two days straight.

"Yeah, it's sweltering. The best place to be on these calm days is underwater."

"Or under the A/C." I grinned as I sat and tucked my feet underneath me on the sofa.

"Good point." He sat close and crossed his foot over his knee. "But I'd love to get you back underwater. How about we go diving tomorrow? I'm taking Evan and Eleanor for a dive and then snorkeling at Stingray City."

I'd read about it. "Oh, I'd love to see that."

Gavin's face lit up. "You do a lot more than *see* that. It's an experience. I'll try to time it between the cruise ship groups so we won't have hoards of tourists."

"I'll try and keep up with the kids so you don't have to look after me."

"I like looking after you." His hand moved to my knee and squeezed. "But you don't need it."

I needed it more than I wanted to admit.

We nibbled at the appetizers while sipping wine, staring out at the flat calm ocean that mirrored a cloudless sky. I got up to bring the bottle to fill our glasses. "Was the trip with Clifton productive?"

"There was a lot of talk. Clifton loves to talk. It probably won't ever amount to anything. But he's my best client. I have to indulge him when he asks, which isn't often."

"I know exactly what you mean." I'd done my share of ass-kissing.

"I know you do. That's one of the many things I love about you."

His saying that added to the list of things I loved about him. He was more than just a sexy younger man with a perfect body. With every glimpse into who he was, I liked him more. He might be a player, but he was a charming one. And he made me feel more like myself than I had in years. "I love your confidence. I'll try not to disappoint."

"If you're coming, you can't disappoint me."

I took a deep breath. "That's good. As long as your expectations are low."

"I try not to have those. They're bad news."

Wasn't that the truth?

Night fell as we finished the food and nearly all the wine. I switched on a couple of lamps to light the dark room. The conversation was easy but Gavin seemed fidgety.

"What's wrong? Do you have something you need to do? If so, no worries."

"No. I mean, yes, I have plenty of catching up to do. But that's not why I was wondering if I should stay." His eyes lifted to meet mine.

Holding his gaze wasn't easy. "Why would you want to leave?"

"I don't." His hand slid up my thigh just enough to send me reeling as he continued. "But I can't be responsible for what happens if I don't."

"Who wants to be responsible? That's the first thing anyone asks when something goes wrong—'who's responsible?'"

"Exactly!" His neck craned and nodded in a decent Kramer impression. "Best *Seinfeld* line ever."

I blinked at him, pleasantly amused but shocked that he'd gotten the reference. "How do you know *Seinfeld*?"

Gavin's full lips curled into a grin. "You mean the greatest show ever made? It traversed the high seas to land on our little island five years after it hit the rest of the world, like pretty much everything does, or *did* before the internet."

He got *Seinfeld*. That gave him a lot of cred in my book. "Ah, I'm impressed. And don't worry, I won't hold you responsible." I was a grown-ass woman. I knew exactly what I was getting into. All the reasons that I shouldn't were shushed as my body screamed for him.

Gavin's fingers burrowed into the hair at the nape of my neck and twisted as he pulled my lips to his. I fell limp into the deep kiss, allowing him in, and hung there while he swallowed me up until I was gasping for air. My hands moved up his back when I pulled away to look into his eyes. After a long moment's gaze, our mouths crashed together again, devouring one another ravenously.

His fingers trailed up my chest to rest on my neck, sending a sharp jolt to my groin. A low moan escaped my lips to vibrate into his mouth.

He worked my dress over my head as I rolled his T-shirt up his back. He pulled away to eye my bikini.

"God, you're so fucking sexy. I've been thinking about you since the moment I kissed you goodbye—nonstop."

If that was true, it would be a great relief that it wasn't just me. But the fewer the expectations, the better. Besides, the past and the future were irrelevant when the present was so perfect. There were no words that could justify not kissing him again.

I threw a leg over to climb on top to straddle him. Hands slid furiously over flesh and our lips locked in a slippery exchange while I unbuttoned his shorts to free the hardness that pressed into his zipper. When my fingertips brushed the silky skin of his throbbing head, I ached for him inside.

Gavin's hand slipped behind my ass to move the crotch of my bikini to the side before he guided me down onto his waiting length. He stretched me tight as he pulled me onto him, my bikini rubbing between my lips creating a delicious friction that made me groan. His mouth moved down my cheek and neck to take my breast in a gulp. When his teeth raked over my nipple I moaned and when they clamped down around it, I squealed. His firm biceps flexed into my sides while he lifted me up and slammed me back down onto his cock. A current of bliss pulsed through me as my fingers dug into his scalp. When my moans increased, he released my nipple to cover my lips and swallow my cries.

I fell limp in his arms, still trembling inside while he kissed me. My feet hooked behind his back when he shifted forward to stand. He carried me around to set me on the edge of the sofa back, easing out of me slowly before he pushed my bikini bottoms down to the floor. I licked my lips as he grasped his shaft, craving his throbbing cock. He watched my face as he pushed hard into me and grinned when I gasped. I clenched him from the inside where he reached a place no one had ever discovered.

His thrusts carried me to the crest of another wave even more powerful than the last. He didn't wait for my moans to quieten before sliding out, leaving me gripping at emptiness when he manhandled my hips off the sofa back and spun me around. His broad hand on my back pushed my chest into the sofa and dug into my skin as he held me in place to fill me with his hardness once more. The friction of the fabric on my nipples with his forceful thrusts made my whole body light up in an electric pleasure storm. He reached around my pelvis to part my lips. His fingertips moved over my charged clit with savage intent while he pumped in and out of me with equal fervor.

One orgasm bled into another almost seamlessly with no time to recover in between.

I could barely lift my chest when the tremors inside finally receded. Gavin slipped out of my pussy so drenched that my juices trickled down my thigh. To think I'd had to use lube with Chuck for years was astounding. I was so hot for this man I was literally dripping with desire. That had never happened to me before. None of it. Ever.

I was so drunk with delight I could barely stagger on my feet when Gavin led me by the hand over to the bed. He cradled my head in his hand as he lowered me to the pillow. His gaze locked mine and I laid mesmerized and paralyzed while his palms slid down to my ankles. My eyes shot open when he pushed my feet up over my head and entered to the limits of my depth. He stared with animalistic intent as he pumped harder and faster, his face contorting when he finally decided to let go and let his climax come.

He retreated from my warmth only to slap his shaft down onto my sex. Watching his mouth twist in the almost pained expression of ecstasy while he pressed himself onto my throbbing clit sent me into another tailspin of rapture. My moans echoed his groans as he released onto my breasts and belly.

He knew how to send me over the edge. The aftershock of

orgasm was so intense I could barely feel anything at all, left me a whimpering mess.

Gavin brought a washcloth and gently wiped his fluids from my skin. Part of me wanted to keep that part of him there.

He smoothed a sweat-soaked strand of hair from my forehead and pinned me under his stare. "That was fucking amazing." His lips brushed mine before he laid on his side, his body stretched along mine.

It was more than amazing. It was transcendental. His breath on my neck sent shivers up my spine. My lips curled in an uncontrollable smile. "You're pretty good at that."

"Only when inspired."

I didn't believe that for a minute, but I loved hearing it. Gavin's chin nuzzled into my neck. Soon our breath was in sync and my eyelids grew heavy while his fingertips grazed my belly.

I wasn't sure if he'd nodded off as well when I woke and raised up to look at the clock beside me.

He smiled when he saw me awake and planted a soft kiss. "I wish I could stay but I haven't been home since I saw you last. I need to go check on the house."

"Of course." I didn't want to let him go, but I knew I had to while I still could.

I stared up at the ceiling, my body pulsing with longing long after he'd gone. Missing him was nothing new but it wasn't something I wanted to get used to. No one had ever made me feel the way Gavin did. My rational brain said it was just good sex that I was confusing with love. I tried to reel in my emotions but they ran.

He hadn't ditched me like I'd thought. And maybe he wasn't the player I suspected him to be. But he was always leaving. Or I was.

I scrambled to brick up the wall I'd built around my heart. I couldn't let him in. But it was futile. He was already there.

CHAPTER 20

*R*ays of the morning sun caught the blonde in Gavin's hair as he stood smiling on the dock beside the dive boat. "Good morning, beautiful."

My face flushed as much at the sight of him as from his compliment. "Good morning. Do I need to get anything from the shop?"

"Nope, I've got you all taken care of."

How I wished that were true. I tried to ignore that last thought. "It looks like a good day for diving."

"Conditions are supposed to be perfect."

"That's great news." I looked around but saw only the boat captain in the flybridge. "Where are the kids?"

"They'll be here shortly. Let's wait in the shade on the boat." He held my hand to help me aboard and stood with his hand on the bulkhead behind me so that his face was so close I could feel his breath. "I missed you last night."

His comment flooded my body with the longing for his touch that had kept me from sleep last night. I fought the urge to duck under his arm and run away. I wanted to stay so badly that I needed to go. "I know you had to get home."

"I did. But then once I was there I regretted not staying with you. Especially since I have a dinner meeting with Clifton so I can't hang out tonight either."

I was disappointed, but a little relieved. "That's okay. I'm the one on vacation, not you. You gotta do what you gotta do."

"Unfortunately, I do. But if I finish up in time, maybe I can see you after?"

His hopeful grin made me smile just as wide, but no expectations was a safer bet than hoping I'd see him. "Knowing Clifton, you'll have a long talk with several whiskeys. Let's see how it goes."

"Tessa! You came!" Eleanor jumped onto the boat and made a beeline for me.

I hugged her as she threw her arms around my waist and smiled at Evan who was climbing quietly onto the boat behind his sister. "I wouldn't miss a chance to dive with you two again."

Eleanor pulled away and shot a glaring glance toward her brother. "Evan lost a compass on our last dive."

"Oh, I'm sorry to hear that." My heart ached for Evan with his red face staring toward the ground. "Accidents happen."

Gavin chimed in quickly. "I lose stuff all the time. But sometimes I find things—very nice things." His arm slipped around my waist and pulled me into his side.

I took a deep breath, conscious of my steady smile while I pretended that his cheesy flirtation wasn't melting my heart.

Evan's face brightened with piqued interest. "What's the coolest thing you ever found diving?"

Gavin stroked his chin. "Hmm, that's a tough one. Either the megalodon tooth or the vintage dive watch."

Evan's eyes grew wide in wonder. "What kind of watch? Was it from Jacques Cousteau?"

I snickered that it wasn't the giant shark tooth that impressed him. Gavin chuckled and shook his head. "Not that cool, but almost."

"If you found Jacques Cousteau's watch you'd just lose it." Eleanor chided with her hand on her hip.

"I would not!" Evan glowered with a trembling lower lip.

My mouth gaped at Eleanor's bitchiness and my heart ached for Evan. It was a good thing I didn't have kids. I couldn't handle that.

Gavin's scolding reply was far more polite than I would have been. "You're a sweet girl with a kind heart so I know you don't mean to be mean, but making someone else feel bad is not nice. Maybe you can help *me* remember things better by checking the tanks that I rigged up for you two to be sure that nothing is missing."

Eleanor's face lit up and she started toward the tanks but paused to smile at her brother. "Evan, you can help. You're good at that stuff."

I leaned into Gavin when his arm pulled me closer as we watched the siblings fiddle with the gear and smiled up at him. "You're pretty good at that stuff."

His eyes danced above a sly smile. "I recall similar words commending me on other skills last night."

I lifted my brows at his flirtation within earshot of the kids and lowered my voice. "Both are true."

"Good." Gavin slapped my butt softly. "We need to get off the dock. Sit tight here, I'll be back once we're underway."

The four of us went to the bow for the ride out to the reef. You could see every blade of seagrass below the glassy surface. Gavin's heavy arm rested on my shoulders, pulling me close. Conditions were perfect.

Gavin held my hand as he led us along the shallow reef where the creatures seemed to line up to meet us. Four sea turtles and millions of colorful fish comprised the procession over the coral reef and starfish-littered sand. I smiled so hard that my mask leaked. Gavin took hold of my elbow and signaled for me to clear the water. I didn't need his help but having him look after me felt good. The kids both dove like pros and were bubbling with comments as soon as we surfaced.

"Did you see that turtle swimming with Evan? He liked you." Eleanor giggled at her brother.

Evan beamed. "I'm going to call him Tiny because he was the smallest one of the lot."

Gavin rustled Evan's hair. "He's small because he's young, like you. Did you know that sea turtles can live to be a hundred, maybe more?"

"Wow, that's old." Evan looked pensive as he turned to me. "How old are you?"

My cheeks blazed red. Even if it sounded that way, I knew he didn't mean to equate me with a centenarian turtle. I cleared my throat and forced a smile. "Nowhere near a hundred. I'm forty-one."

"Oh. And how about you?" His inquisitive eyes fixed on Gavin.

"Old enough to order you around. Go break down the gear. We'll be at Stingray City in three minutes."

Both kids hurried excitedly toward the tanks.

I eyed Gavin. "Why didn't you answer him?"

"Because we don't have time for silly discussion about irrelevant matters."

I suspected it was because both kids were old enough to do basic math and we both preferred to avoid that difference.

Two boats were leaving the snorkel site when we pulled up to the mooring ball. "Perfect timing. We have the place to ourselves." Gavin pulled a bag of fish pieces out of the cooler. "Let's go play with the rays."

The boat captain shook a submerged chum block off the stern, drawing dozens of hungry stingrays.

"Can they sting you?" Eleanor looked concerned at the swarm under the ladder we were supposed to descend. I was wondering the same.

"Only if you step on them. You don't have to be scared. They're like puppy dogs. You can even pet them. Just be careful not to touch the barb on their tail."

"Cool!" Evan already had his mask on and was eagerly donning his fins.

Gavin nodded and asked me quietly, "You ready?"

"I guess so." I wanted to ask about the crocodile hunter who'd been impaled through the heart with one of those barbs, but I thought it better not to scare the kids.

The excited rays swam around us curiously at a distance until Gavin pulled out the fish. Then they moved in. I gasped in my snorkel when I first felt their slippery skin on mine as they clustered around us. Gavin tried to hand me a piece of fish but I shook my head to decline and kept my hands tucked under my arms. I didn't want to encourage them to get any closer than they already were.

The kids' fearlessness calmed my nerves though and soon I asked Gavin for a morsel to feed the rays. Of course, it would be the largest of the pack that came for it. I squealed into my snorkel when he snatched it from my hand. He swam away quickly but turned fast, practically climbing on my back looking for a second helping.

Gavin took hold of my elbow to steady me when I coughed at the water I'd sucked into my snorkel during the commotion. He gave me the okay sign with a question mark in his eyes. I nodded as I coughed and gave him the okay sign. I was okay as long as I could breathe.

The same big ray returned and put his belly against my chest where my heart pounded. The ray remained motionless while I ran my fingers over his flat body, tentatively at first but with growing confidence. For several surreal seconds, I felt like the luckiest girl alive.

~

Once we were back on the dock, Gavin patiently directed the kids to take all the gear off the boat and rinse it. I loved that he was teaching them.

"I have a couple of hours. Do you want to go to Hell?"

I tilted my head, perplexed. "I'd rather not."

"Haven't you heard of Hell? It's a field of algae-covered rocks that somehow became a tourist attraction."

"Oh right, I read about that. I have to say that visiting Hell wasn't at the top of my list, but if you think it's worth it."

"I've been very clear that it's a field of algae-covered rocks. I guess the real attraction is being able to say that you've been to Hell and back."

I already had that covered. But I'd go to Hell with Gavin if he wanted. "Then, by all means, let's go to Hell. Just make sure you bring me back."

The wind that swirled through the Land Rover blew his golden ginger hair around his grinning face. "It will be a short visit, I promise."

I didn't want any visit with him to be short. But he wasn't kidding when he downplayed the tourist trap. It was, as promised, a field of rocks blackened by algae. Thirty seconds was long enough to take it in, but it seemed obligatory to admire it for a few minutes.

Gavin led me through the surrounding stalls selling all sorts of island kitsch to a colorful slat board post office.

"You can send a postcard from Hell!"

It was silly but sounded kind of cool. "Why the hell not?"

I inscribed one to Elliot. *It was hell being here without you.* A memento to be sure he'd never forget standing me up. I wrote a second to myself. *"Proof that you can go to Hell and back."*

My heart sank as we neared the resort. I didn't want to say goodbye. But I'd better get used to it. Sunday was coming fast—too fast.

The part of me that missed him already wanted to spend every waking moment with Gavin until then. The part of me that was scared shitless of wanting him too much reasoned that it was probably better not to spend too much time with him anyway.

I tried to distract myself with my book, but even the Rom-Com proved too heavy for my taste. I finally gave up and headed to the bar for another dinner alone.

Carlos's smile made it hard to feel sorry for myself. "Macallan?"

I knew he meant the Reflexion at Clifton's expense. "I really shouldn't. I don't want to abuse his generosity."

"You really should." Carlos poured me a double. "Did you have a nice day?"

"I had a great day! I went diving, then snorkeled Stingray City, and sent myself a postcard from Hell."

Carlos grinned. "I'm glad you had fun."

I'd had a blast, but coming down off that high left me lonely. All the fun I could have here would still end in me sitting at the bar alone. I'd lost what little appetite I had by the time my food arrived but I forced my dinner down. I declined when Carlos tried to insist I have another whiskey. Drinking to forget hadn't worked out so well for me so far.

I clutched the duvet under my chin in the bed that felt empty around me. How long would I be wishing Gavin were there? A week? A month? A year didn't seem far-fetched. The only sure answer was—too long. But I'd gotten used to sleeping alone once, and that was after seventeen years of sharing a bed. This time it shouldn't be so bad, but I suspected it might be even worse. Either way, I'd get through it. That was for sure.

I chuckled at the thought of receiving the postcard from myself a week from now. *Proof that you can go to Hell and back.* It was more like proof that heaven and hell were the same place. But in this case, Hell wasn't a field of algae-covered rocks, it was a broken heart.

CHAPTER 21

*T*he notification's ding of my phone sounded on the nightstand. I groaned, groggy and annoyed that I hadn't silenced it last night. I blinked to focus on the clock. 09:34. I'd slept for nearly eleven hours. That hadn't happened since—maybe ever. The sun and water yesterday had tired me out but I suspected that the protective hibernation was my way to avoid thinking about Gavin.

I stretched through a long yawn before forcing myself out of bed. While the coffee machine made my cappuccino, I unplugged my phone to see what had woken me. Emails. Spam no doubt. I clicked on the icon and spotted Marjorie's email at the top of the list. The subject line made me hold my breath. *A little issue with Brumley.*

Not even two weeks away and there's a "little issue" so big that Marjorie would email me about it while I was on the vacation she insisted I take. I knew I never should have left. Fuck. I clicked to open the email but it lagged. I punched the subject line with my thumb angrily. I scanned Marjorie's words when it finally opened. She was vague but it was obvious that our biggest account wasn't happy. She didn't want to worry me because it was all under control, she said, but she wanted to let me know that they may need me on a call later today.

What the fuck? Brumley was solid. What could have gone wrong?

It was only seven a.m. in San Francisco and Marjorie's email had come in a half-hour ago. She was clearly already working. Fuck it. She'd woken me up. I rang her cell.

I didn't even try to feign pleasantries when she answered on the second ring. "Marjorie."

"Hi, Tessa. I'm terribly sorry to bother you. How is Grand Cayman?"

I was in no mood for small talk. "I'll tell you all about it next week. I'm sure you know why I'm calling. So tell me what's going on, please."

"There might be an issue with the Brumley account. Brad got mixed feedback yesterday afternoon." Her voice fell off with no further explanation.

I paced the floor with the phone on speaker. "What's the issue?"

She hesitated before answering. "They're looking at another firm."

My palms got clammy and blood rushed to my face. They'd been with us—with *me*—for ten years. "I'll book the next flight."

Marjorie spoke softly and slowly like she always did when trying to smooth over a situation. That's probably why she'd been with me since before Brumley. "I was afraid to tell you because I knew you'd overreact. Brad assures me he has it under control. I just thought you should know."

I attempted to mirror her calm, poorly. "Damn right I should know. Thank you. But I need to be there. Brad cannot handle this on his own."

She continued to try to soothe my nerves. "Nothing is happening today, or tomorrow. There's no reason for you to come back early, only to deal with it next week. It can wait till Monday, Tessa. We may need you on a Zoom call later though. How's your connection there?"

"It's fast. You booked a top-notch resort. Thank you for that, too." I should thank her for forcing me to go on vacation. I'd needed it more than I ever imagined. But I wasn't exactly grateful now that the business was in peril. If we lost Brumley we'd have to lay off a quarter of our staff. "I'll talk to Brad first. I'll get back to you later this morning."

"Okay. Try not to worry. I'm sure it will all work out."

I rolled my eyes. She had to say something, but nothing anyone could say would stop my worry. "I'll try. Sorry to bother you so early."

I dialed Brad straight away, disregarding the hour. If he was worth what we paid him, he wouldn't have slept much last night and should be up trying to solve this problem by now anyway. He sounded wide awake when he answered immediately.

This was no time to mince words but I tried to be polite even though inside I was screaming. "Sorry for the early call, but Marjorie emailed me."

"Right. Yes, well, it's been interesting."

Interesting? Was that the best he had? "What the hell, Brad? Two weeks away and we're on the verge of losing Brumley? I'm sure you're aware they're over twenty percent of our business. How did this happen?"

His sharp breath whistled in his nostrils before he exhaled his response. "New management trying to make budget cuts, as far as I can tell."

The insult hit me like a blade in the gut. We weren't cheap, but we'd helped them make millions over the years. Everything we'd ever done for them had been successful. And I'd worked tirelessly to foster the relationship. I took a deep breath to try to replace my anger with reason. "Have you spoken to Warren?"

"I tried him yesterday afternoon but haven't heard back."

I couldn't let Brad fuck this up. "I'll call him now. I'll try to set up a meeting for tomorrow, assuming I can get a flight out of here today." A glanced at the time on the top of the screen. Almost ten-thirty. Fuck! I had to hurry.

I was so focused on trying to see that tiny numbers that it took a second to register Brad's next comment that came through the speakerphone. "Chuck called yesterday, too."

I stared at the screen like the calls and been switched somehow and a stranger spoke words that made no sense. After a long second, I finally replied. "Chuck!? Who the fuck brought Chuck into this? He's never worked with Brumley. He's useless. He'll only make matters worse. Keep him out of this."

"He contacted me yesterday afternoon. I don't know who told him. I agree, he shouldn't intervene. That's why I was thinking maybe a video call with you today and a meeting in person Monday was the best plan."

It might be too late by then. It was far better to prevent a train wreck than to clean up after one. And letting Chuck anywhere near this mess was a cow on the tracks. No fucking way he was going to fuck this up.

"I'll let you know if I can get out today. Meanwhile, I'll call Warren after eight your time. Tell Chuck I'm working on it and that I'll contact him personally if we need him to step in." I should tell him myself, but I didn't trust myself to maintain composure.

I pulled out my laptop and found a flight leaving at 4:20. I could be at the airport by three if I hustled. I booked it and sent the confirmation to Marjorie and Brad, then sent them both a text.

I leave at 4:20 via Houston, arriving at midnight. Itinerary is in your inbox.

I tried Warren twice before leaving a message with his secretary requesting a Friday meeting. I looked around the room at all that I had to pack after ten days of making myself at home. I threw my suitcase on the bed and started to load it when I remembered I should eat. I called room service for an omelet breakfast.

It was only when I took a break to eat that I thought about Gavin. Shit. I should call him. At least we'd finally traded digits. But I took the coward's way out and sent a text.

I'm leaving this afternoon. Work emergency. Sorry.

I read and reread it at least ten times after I sent it. It was callous, but I didn't know how to express what I didn't even know I felt. I'd been falling for Gavin—hard—but it seemed like a childish fantasy I'd been entertaining now that I couldn't think about anything other than the Brumley account. What I had with Gavin was never going to be more than the fun fling it had always been. It was always about to be over. That didn't stop me wanting it not to be. Leaving early might spare me further heartache. Maybe that was the silver lining in this fucked up situation. The universe acts in mysterious ways.

I put the phone down and went back to packing. I showered after my bag was ready and was rubbing moisturizer on my face when I heard a knock at the door.

CHAPTER 22

My heart pounding in my chest made it hard to breathe when I opened the door to meet Gavin's worried emerald eyes. "What's happening? Is everything okay?"

"No. It's not okay. And I have to fix it."

Gavin looked over my shoulder and back at me with a desperate look in his eyes. "Can I come in?"

"Of course, please." I stepped aside and followed him to the sofa.

Gavin put his hand on my knee and searched my eyes. "What is it? What happened?"

I took a deep breath and tried to be concise. I didn't have it in me to have to explain. "A problem with a major account. Losing them could cripple the business for years."

Gavin's normally rosy face was pale. "I'm sorry to hear that. But you have to leave today?"

I checked my clock for the time. "Yes. My flight leaves in less than three hours."

His jaw clenched. "And that's it? You're gone?" he said anxiously before pressing his lips together.

I rubbed the top of his knee. "I'm leaving two and half days early, but I was always leaving." It was the cold hard truth that neither of us wanted to hear.

Gavin's voice had reduced to little more than a whisper. "I know. But I thought we had a few more days. I was looking forward to it."

I winced at his dejected tone. "So was I. I wish I didn't have to go. But I do. I'm hoping to remedy this tomorrow." I had to shift the focus back to my problem to avoid even acknowledging "us."

He didn't seem to appreciate my avoidance as evidenced by his snippy reply. "You gotta do what you gotta do."

"I'm really sorry, Gavin. I don't have any other option right now."

"Life is full of innumerable options at any given moment. But we're creatures of habit. You have to go fix things because that's what you've always done."

I smiled sympathetically and shrugged. "It's what I do."

"Don't be too busy fixing external things that you don't fix what's most important." His palm rested on my chest.

Nausea washed over me and I felt a little faint. I couldn't mend a broken heart that fractured more with every thought of him. I looked over my shoulder anxiously at the clock. "I will try to fix it all. But I *have* to go."

Gavin looked at me in disbelief. "I didn't want it to end like this. I didn't want it to end at all."

I didn't either, but it was always ending before it even began. There was no other feasible outcome. I sighed with a pained look. "I know. I feel the same. But we knew what we were getting into, right?"

"I had no idea what I was getting into with you. Whatever I might have thought in the beginning was out the window once I realized how fucking amazing you are. So, no."

I grabbed his hand. "I didn't expect any of this either. I've had an incredible time. But I have to get back to real life."

Gavin's fist clenched. "This felt real to me."

I couldn't admit that it was more real than anything I'd ever felt. "You know what I mean."

He huffed before changing the subject. "Can I drive you?"

I was tempted by his offer but it would only make it more difficult. "Thanks, but I have a taxi coming in a few minutes."

"Of course you do. I'll leave you to it then." Gavin stood and strode toward the door like he couldn't leave fast enough.

I shuffled to catch up before he opened the door and took his hand. "I'll call to check in after things settle down back home."

He was upset, but his green eyes were kind as he squeezed my hand. "I hope you will. You're a special woman, Tessa, and I wish you all the best in your *real* life."

I felt guilty for the sting he'd obviously felt from my words. But there was nothing I could say that wouldn't make things worse. "Thank you."

His lips brushed mine for a tease of a kiss and then he was gone.

The familiar pressure in my chest that came from missing him returned as soon as I closed the door. I couldn't let myself feel it right then, though. There was no time and that was probably a good thing.

CHAPTER 23

$\mathcal{W}$arren's email confirming tomorrow's meeting came through just before the plane took off and I could finally exhale. I'd have felt like an idiot for going home early for nothing. But I needed to get home, if not to save the business then to save myself.

I enjoyed priority boarding and settled into the cushy third-row window seat. The flight attendant offered me a drink while we waited to take off. Oh, the perks of first-class.

"What's your top-shelf gin?"

"Bombay Sapphire."

Elliot would scoff, but he'd take the free drink. "A Bombay and tonic then, please."

I'd prefer Hendricks because it reminded me of Gavin, but it was better that it wasn't an option. I pulled out my laptop and reviewed every campaign we'd done for Brumley in the last ten years. I spent the whole flight compiling a spreadsheet. They'd spent a lot of money with us, but we'd made them far more. I just had to find a way to convince Warren we were worth it tomorrow.

It was one-thirty local time—after four a.m. in Cayman— when I finally got home. I didn't want to wake Gavin with a text any more than I wanted to awaken the feelings for him I'd been trying to forget for the whole trip home. I'd deal with that tomorrow. Boomer nearly knocked me over when I pushed my way in the doorway with my suitcase. He had been trained not to jump for over five years but he was more excited than I'd ever seen him. I muscled my luggage inside and set it down before patting my chest to tell Boomer it was okay to jump up on me again. I scratched behind his ears and held my breath while he licked my face before pulling my head back to giggle. "I missed you too, buddy. Don't worry, Mama's home."

Boomer tried his best to trip me as I crossed the living room to open the blinds. The lights of the city made me almost as happy to be home as his excitement did. He didn't leave my side while I thumbed through the stack of mail Elliot had left for me on the countertop, mostly junk.

Fuck, Elliot. I hadn't even told him I was coming home early. It was too late to text. It would have to wait until morning like everything else.

Boomer followed me to the bathroom and squeezed himself between me and the sink while I washed my face and brushed my teeth. He whined beside the bed after I settled under the duvet. He didn't seem interested in his own bed in the corner, and I didn't want to sleep alone any more than he did. I patted the covers beside me. "Come on, buddy. I know you've been lonely."

I counted to time my breath, inhale for a count of five and

exhale for a count of ten. I closed my eyes and tried to visualize a perfect outcome for the meeting tomorrow. I tried not to let the gravity of the importance of the meeting weigh in. Less than perfect wouldn't be good enough. I didn't mind the pressure though. It was good to feel needed.

Boomer took up half the bed, pushing his back into me to remind me I was back where I belonged.

The bed felt empty even with Boomer beside me when I woke at six-thirty. The meeting with Warren wasn't until three so there was no reason to be up so early. I tried in vain to find sleep again. Damn this jet lag.

I shuffled over the cool tile floor of the kitchen to make a pot of coffee. I hadn't planned on going to the office but I was tempted since I was up. I decided against it after thinking it through. I didn't want to see anyone there until this was settled. They had to be as crazy with worry as I was. It might make me a nervous wreck. That wouldn't do anyone any good. I had plenty of catching up to distract myself while I waited.

I squinted out the bay window in the living room to try to make out the city obscured in the thick morning fog.

"Let me have a cup of coffee first, big guy." I pulled my laptop out of my carry-on and scanned the list of unread emails in my inbox while I got my caffeine fix.

We had time for a long walk so I let Boomer pull me for several blocks. I rehearsed the argument I'd prepared for Warren in my head as Boomer led me out of our small neighborhood streets to a main artery. Luckily primal instinct kicked in when I heard the blaring car horn.

I stopped hard just before entering an intersection. An angry driver stared through the windshield, as relieved he didn't kill me as I was.

I reprimanded myself out loud as we continued down the busy street. "What the fuck is wrong with you? Pay attention." I'd relaxed so much on vacation I'd lost my edge.

I was on high alert for the rest of the walk, which made me keenly aware of the absurd amount of traffic we had to navigate. I had never been particularly bothered by it before but my tolerance seemed lower to the crowds and the noise. "Too bad we're not walking Seven Mile Beach, buddy."

I led Boomer back home on the quietest route possible. This was going to take some getting used to again.

I poured myself another coffee and snuggled under a blanket on the couch to weed through the trove of emails I'd ignored for nearly two weeks.

I was so consumed with work that I didn't think to text Gavin and Elliot until I was getting ready for the meeting. I stared at the text to Gavin before sending it. It seemed distant, but there was a lot of distance between us now.

I made it home safe and am dealing with the fallout now. Wish me luck.

I hurried to text Elliot.

No need to check on Boomer tonight. I came home early. I'll explain later.

I wasn't the least bit surprised when the phone rang a minute later, but a brief flash of hope, mixed with dread, that it might be Gavin clenched my throat before I saw Elliot's name on the screen. I answered on speaker while I painted my lashes in mascara. "Hey."

"Hey. What happened? Where are you?"

"I'm home. There's a cluster fuck at work. I have a meeting in forty-five minutes so I can't talk long. I'll explain later."

"Is everything okay?"

"It will be." I hoped. "Meet you for a drink after?"

"Sure, I have a dinner date but I can do happy hour at Louie's if that works for you."

"Okay, see you there at five."

CHAPTER 24

*W*arren stood and walked around his desk to welcome me with a smile.

"So nice to see you, Mrs. Bright."

His formality surprised me. "It's Tessa, you know that. But now it's Tessa Taylor. Chuck and I are divorced."

Warren's smile straightened. "I'm sorry to hear that."

"Don't be. It's a good thing. But rest assured, the business is continuing as usual. This will not affect how we handle your account, if you decide to stay with us."

Warren cleared his throat. "I don't like how this was handled on our end. I didn't mean to blindside you with the news. But since my father retired, the board brought in a new VP who's been cleaning house to reduce costs. David told me that he tried to reach you but couldn't get through."

"I was on vacation. The timing was not good, to say the least. But I'm here now." I pulled my laptop from my bag and opened it on his desk. "I prepared a spreadsheet of the last ten campaigns we've run for you, with the costs for each and the results we achieved." Warren listened intently and nodded as I ran through each of the campaigns. "While I don't have hard numbers on the earnings generated, I think it's clear from the interaction metrics that they were all extremely successful campaigns."

"We've always been happy with your work. To be honest, David had heard the news of your divorce and when he was unable to reach you to discuss the cost of the next campaign, he worried that you were leaving the firm. Since you've always been the one handling our account... when the analyst recommended shopping around for a more cost-effective option, it seemed like a prudent move."

"I'm not going anywhere. We are as dedicated to your account as we've ever been. I hope you will consider these numbers and reconsider the idea of leaving."

Warren nodded decisively. "I don't need to reconsider. I appreciate your dedication. Let's proceed as we always have. I'll deal with the new VP."

I smiled, somewhat stunned. I hadn't expected it to be so easy. "We appreciate your loyalty." I stood and shook his hand. "You won't be disappointed."

I had plenty of time to walk across town to meet Elliot. Louie's was our favorite after-work spot, right in the heart of the Financial District with an old-school dive bar feel that was hard to find among the growing chicness of the city. Elliot was already waiting at our favorite table by the window. I eyed the cocktail sitting in front of my empty spot, tall and clear with a mint garnish when he stood to give me a hug. "Ah what are we having today? Is that a mojito?"

"A jalapeño mojito, to be exact. The perfect blend of sweet and spicy, like the Cuban men I know." Elliot grinned as he released his embrace and held up his glass for a toast.

I smiled and sat across from him. "I'll drink to that, I guess." He was incorrigible.

"Well, fill me in. What the hell happened to make you come home early?"

"A combination of bad timing and new management made our biggest account shop around for another firm. Luckily, I just convinced them to stay, so it was a tragedy narrowly averted."

Elliot's concerned brow relaxed. "I suppose that's a good reason for cutting your vacation short. And a good reason to celebrate! Cheers!"

The mojito had a spicy kick that I loved. "God that's delicious."

"Right? And dangerous." Elliot had already downed half his drink. "I can only have one more, so don't try to twist my arm."

I chuckled. He was the arm twister. "Right, you have a date. Anyone interesting?"

"Very." Elliot lifted a brow. "Sergei. He's Bosnian. We're meeting some of his friends tonight, and heading up to Sonoma for two nights tomorrow."

"Wow, that sounds serious."

"You know me, I don't do serious. But we're having tons of fun. Speaking of fun, how'd it end with your Irish islander?"

I sipped the spicy concoction in my glass before I shrugged. "I think he was a little pissed off that I had to leave so abruptly, to be honest. But it's all for the best."

"I don't know about that. But I do know that meeting him was good for you. You look like a new woman."

My brow wrinkled. "What's that supposed to mean?"

"It means it's been a long time since I've seen you so happy."

"I'm *happy* to be home. But you and Marjorie were right, I needed this vacation. It helped me disconnect from work and reconnect with myself."

"Don't forget the D! That's what I'm talking about. Reconnecting with the D was good for you." Elliot slurped down the last of his mojito with a grin.

My cheeks flamed. "The sex was amazing. I needed that, too."

"We all need that, Sweet T. Are you planning to see him again?"

"Well, I'm not planning another trip to Grand Cayman, so, no."

Elliot shook his head with narrow eyes. "I think you're going to miss him."

A pang in my gut reminded me that I already did before I pushed it out of my mind again. "I'm sure you're right. But it is what it is."

"What's that exactly?"

"Over." I finished my drink and flagged down the waiter for another round.

Elliot lifted sympathetic eyes. "That's too bad. Maybe you should keep the option open."

"There's no option. He's there and I'm here. And he's twenty-eight for God's sake."

His mouth twisted into a wry grin. "That's never stopped me."

"Let's be honest, very little stops you."

"This is true. But seriously, you shouldn't be so hung up on the age thing. You look like you're thirty. Get those young ones while you still can."

I chuckled. "You're determined to make me a cougar yet."

"You're a long way from cougar, love. Don't be so sexist. You wouldn't think twice about a man your age dating a woman Gavin's age would you?"

I rolled my eyes. "Chuck didn't seem to have an issue with it. His secretary is even younger."

Elliot grimaced. "Ew. Don't bring him into this."

"Agreed." I took a long sip of mojito to wash down the bitter taste his name had left in my mouth.

"So what are your weekend plans while I'm in wine country?"

"I plan to pretend I'm still on vacation and do absolutely nothing."

"That's a plan I can get behind." Elliot glanced at his watch.

"I'm sorry to run, but Sergei awaits. Let's do dinner after I get back."

I stood to kiss him goodbye. "Sounds great. Have a blast in Sonoma. I know you will."

"You know me well." Elliot kissed me on the cheek. "Enjoy your staycation."

I planned to stay and finish my cocktail but I became aware of the largely male crowd as soon as Elliot left. I wasn't in the mood for people. I took one last sip and headed for the door. Avoiding the bus for the same reason, I called an Uber, but the rush hour traffic was equally annoying. There was no escaping people.

CHAPTER 25

arjorie jumped to her feet with a broad smile as I approached her desk Monday morning. "Welcome back!" She came around to hug me.

I stiffened and patted her back awkwardly, surprised by her unusual display of affection. "Thank you. It's good to be back."

I started into my office but she hurried ahead of me to open the door. I realized why when I spotted the streamers and balloons around the room and a giant "Welcome Home" sign on the wall. "What in the world? You guys shouldn't have."

"We wanted you to know how much you were missed—and how much you are appreciated. You saved the day, Tessa. Everyone here knows it."

I was touched by her sincerity, which prompted the same from me. "Just doing my job like everyone else. But thanks for noticing. And thank you for the vacation. I needed it."

"I'm happy to hear that. I hope you'll tell me all about it after you've had time to catch up."

"You bet." I smiled as she turned to leave. I wouldn't be telling anyone but Elliot *all* about it.

It felt good to be appreciated, but I was surprised at how little I *felt* in general. Marjorie's exuberance was warranted. It was a big deal what I'd accomplished. Of course, I was happy that it worked out, but I didn't *feel* happy. But I did what I always do when I start to think about my feelings... returned to my work.

~

Marjorie buzzed me on her way out to lunch. "Chuck wants to see you this afternoon to discuss the Brumley account."

I huffed out a laugh. "Chuck has nothing to do with the Brumley account. Tell him I'm busy."

The line was silent for a second before she finally said, "Understood."

I shouldn't have been surprised at his audacity when he barged into my office unannounced two hours later.

"I hope you enjoyed your extended vacation." His disdain made it apparent he didn't think that I deserved it.

"I did, thanks. Very much." I stared expectantly for him to get to the point of his unwelcome intrusion.

"I don't appreciate you having Brad call me off the Brumley situation. I had already reached out to Warren. You made me look like an idiot."

I bit my tongue not to say that he did that all on his own.

"Brumley has always been my account. I have the relationship with Warren, not you. I rushed back to take care of it myself because it was an emergency. You realize how dire the consequences for the firm would be if they left, don't you?"

"Of course I do. It's *my* firm too. And I'm perfectly capable of client relations, even if it's an account you've always worked on. It's *our* account."

I'd insulted his fragile little ego. I gritted my teeth before I took a deep breath to relax my jaw. "I didn't say you weren't capable. Your assistance was not necessary."

My calm seemed to agitate him more. "If we're going to continue to work together, there has to be a certain degree of trust—and respect."

His comment flew all over me and banished my calm. "*You* want to talk to *me* about trust and respect?"

"You've got to leave the past in the past and move on if this is ever going to work. We're partners. We should treat each other as equals."

I was seething but couldn't give him the satisfaction of blowing up. "Let's leave it here, Chuck. I don't want to insult you further." I leveled my eyes on his. "But let's be clear about one thing—we don't work together. You have your accounts and I have mine. They both contribute to the bottom line. I cut my vacation short to come back and do what I had to do to save my account. But you reap the benefits of that because they comprise twenty percent of *our* bottom line. So, you're welcome." I finished with "motherfucker" in my head so loud I thought he might have heard it.

Fuck that cocksucker.

I left work early to go try out an indoor pool I'd researched over the weekend. Swimming had helped free my mind while working my body in Grand Cayman. I needed that. While it wasn't the ocean, it was my only option. I passed by a sporting goods shop on the way to buy goggles and a one-piece sport suit.

Once I got past the strong chlorine fumes and the constriction of the lane ropes which insisted I swim a straight line, I found a rhythm in my strokes. Moving my body and focusing on my breath felt good, but it wasn't the same as the Caribbean. Swimming in circles didn't have the freeing effect as the endless shoreline of Grand Cayman.

Thoughts of Gavin crept in while I dined alone on the couch, but I'd gotten used to dismissing them as quickly as they came. His terse reply to my text Friday was a simple: *Glad to hear it. Call me when you can.*

He'd acted like he didn't believe me when I said I'd call him once things settled down here. Now I understood why.

CHAPTER 26

*T*hankfully I had dinner with Elliot to look forward to Tuesday. Just being in the same building with Chuck irritated me.

I waited at Kai's sushi bar with a carafe of sake. I smiled up at Elliot when he slipped his arm around me for a hug before taking his seat on the stool beside me. "God am I glad to see you."

"Aw, thanks, love. Me, too. How've you been?"

"Surviving. But tell me about Sonoma."

Elliot grinned. "It was Sonoma. How can you go wrong, especially with a hot Bosnian? What's this about surviving? Troubles at work still?"

"Not really, but yes. Chuck is a douche. I can't stand the sight of him. It's hard to imagine how this is going to work. But it is what it is."

"You need to stop with that."

"With what?"

"The whole 'it is what it is' thing." His impression was mocking. "Why do you relegate yourself to accepting things that you can change? That's not how it's supposed to work. I know you've read that hokey serenity prayer."

"I'm open to suggestions."

Elliot rolled his eyes. "No, you're not. But okay. Take the money and run!"

"That's probably exactly what Chuck is hoping I'll do." The thought of letting him win made my blood boil.

"Who cares!? You'll be laughing all the way to the bank and you'll be free, Tessa. You really can't put a price tag on that. But two million is a good start."

"I can't just walk away. I've worked too hard to build this business."

"And you'll build another one if you want to."

"There's a noncompete clause, so that's not so easy."

"Then do something different. I'm sure you can figure something else out."

I couldn't imagine doing something different than what I'd always done. And I didn't want to let Chuck win. "I just have to get back into the groove and settle into the new normal. It will be okay."

"You don't *have* to do anything. You have options. You can live off the interest of two million in a hut on the beach." He wiggled his brow so that I knew which hut on the beach he was referencing. "But I'll shut up about it. You've already heard my two cents."

I chuckled at the thought of his silly suggestion, but Elliot had a point. If I rented my house, I could afford to live anywhere if I wanted a fresh start somewhere the noncompete clause didn't apply. Somewhere with less traffic and fewer people, and no Chuck. "I appreciate the suggestion."

"Anytime, Sweet T. Here's another great suggestion: Be my date for a dinner party at my boss's house up in Marin Friday night. It's a big thing and I'm dreading it."

I chuckled. "Wow, how could I refuse such a promising good time?"

"It will be fun, and there will be lots of single straight men."

I leered at him. "I'm not looking for a date."

"Honey, you don't need to look. They'll find you. You just need to be open."

He'd told me the same about Gavin and it had nearly gotten my heart broken. "I'm as open as I want to be right now."

"All right, I'll mind my own business. Don't be open. Shoot them down before they get close. But please come. It will be so much better with you there."

Now that, I couldn't refuse. As much as he'd been there for me, I had to show up if Elliot was asking for support. "Of course I'll go. Meet me at the office after work Friday?"

I stopped by the liquor store for a bottle of Hendricks on the way home. I'd been craving it for days. I thumbed through the stack of mail I grabbed from the mailbox on my way in as Boomer bounced around at my feet. The postcard from Hell staring back at me took my breath. The tacky devil statue guarding over the field of black stones took me back to my short trip to Hell with Gavin. It had felt more like Heaven.

I reminisced about all the things I missed about Grand Cayman while sipping my nightcap. I could smell the ocean and see the moon overhead when I closed my eyes. My body lit up like a Christmas tree at the memory of Gavin on the blanket beside me.

Part of me would give anything to be back there. But the rest of me knew that could never happen.

CHAPTER 27

*E*lliot texted that he was running late Friday afternoon so we agreed to meet at the train station.

He smiled when I found him waiting on the platform and kissed my cheek. "How's the rest of your week been?"

I sighed. "It's been pretty awful, to be honest."

"Aw. I'm sorry. What happened?"

"Nothing. Aside from wishing daily that Chuck would get hit by a bus, work itself is going well. I just don't feel like being there."

"You and me both, on both accounts. And now we get to go hang out with all my coworkers all evening. Yay." Elliot rolled his eyes after his dry remark.

"We can hang out by the open bar and make fun of people."

Elliot grinned and patted my knee. "That's why I brought you."

"You know I came for the open bar."

"That makes two of us."

We made a beeline for the bar after greeting the host. Elliot seemed like a different person around his boss. I wondered if any of them knew the Elliot that I loved. I looked around the enormous room decorated with so many sculptures and paintings it looked like a gallery. "Wow, what a house."

Elliot lowered his voice. "Great to see all my work is making *someone* rich." He smiled at a handsome bearded man who approached the bar. "Hey, Peter, how's it going?"

"Going well, Elliot. How about you?"

"Just peachy." Elliot turned back toward me and waited until Peter had gotten his drink and was out of earshot. "I know you're not looking, but he's also recently divorced."

"Just what I need. Someone else who's equally fucked up."

Elliot shrugged as he sipped his drink with a smile. "Well, at least you'd have something in common."

I jabbed him with my elbow. "Thanks."

My phone sounded inside my clutch purse. I nearly dropped it when I saw the name on the screen. I felt the blood drain from my face.

Elliot craned his neck to see why I was stunned. His eyes grew wide when he spotted Gavin's name. He punched my shoulder softly. "Answer it."

I silenced the ringer. "No way. I can't talk to him now. I'll call him back later."

"Liar."

"Stop it. Get me another drink."

My phone buzzed as I slipped it back into my purse. A text message from Gavin.

I'm having an existential crisis. It's an emergency. Please call back.

I snickered at his mock melodrama. *I can't talk right now. What's the crisis?*

I believe the right to choose should be fundamental and paramount. But there's a surly waiter insisting that I have the pork surprise and I'm not sure what to do.

I blinked at the phone like the message was in alien characters when Elliot returned with our drinks.

"What now?"

I tried to tell him but my mind was tangled in knots trying to make sense of what I'd read. I turned the screen toward Elliot.

"What's that supposed to mean?"

"I told him about Sam Wu. I think he might be there."

I jumped when the phone buzzed in my hands, ringing.

"You better answer it, Tessa. I'm never speaking to you again if you don't."

"Liar."

"Okay, well, answer it anyway!" He pushed the phone toward my face.

I fumbled to press the green button. "Hello?"

"This waiter is adamant. He also insists I need a beautiful woman from Pacific Heights to join me for dinner." His accent made my knees weak.

"What are you talking about? Are you at Sam Wu?"

"I had to see for myself what all that talk of surrender was about."

I tried to inhale but couldn't until Elliot snapped me out of my silence with an urgent whisper. "Is he here?"

I nodded with panic in my eyes and my heart pounding in my chest.

"Go! Answer him!"

Jesus, was this really happening? I stammered. "I'm at a dinner party in Marin. It will take me forty-five minutes to get there."

The relief in his voice was evident. "I can wait all night if I have to."

I blinked in disbelief after I hung up. Elliot was exuberant. "Oh my God, Tess! How romantic is this guy?"

I shook my head, dumbfounded. "He's insane."

"It seems like he is crazy in love."

Love? "I don't know what he's thinking, but I don't think it's love."

"Stop thinking and get in an Uber right now." Gavin pulled out his phone. "My treat. He'll be here in four minutes."

I carefully set my drink on the bar so as not to drop it. My hands felt numb. "This is nuts."

"Go with it, hun. Come on, let's get your coat."

"Do I look okay?" The dress I'd worn to work was good enough for a dinner party but seemed lacking for a romantic rendezvous.

"You look gorgeous." Elliot directed me into the car like I was a drunk at the end of the party. "There you go." He patted my shoulder. "Go with your heart, Sweet T."

I'd left my heart back in Grand Cayman. Maybe Gavin brought it with him.

CHAPTER 28

*M*y hands were shaking when I gripped the back of the seat and leaned forward to speak to the driver. "Please look for the fastest route. I'm late to meet someone."

"I always do. I don't get paid by the hour, lady."

I cringed and shrank back into my seat. I must've sounded like the epitome of privilege. "Okay, thanks."

My mind raced as quickly as the driver did, weaving in and out of traffic on the Golden Gate Bridge like Mario Andretti. I didn't know what Gavin was thinking, or what I was thinking for that matter. I only knew I had to go. We were going alright—at warp speed. I was tempted to tell the driver that he didn't need to get us killed but I didn't dare complain. I wasn't sure if it was the harrowing journey or the prospect of seeing Gavin that made me nearly hyperventilate. I gave the driver a ten-dollar tip and slid out of the back seat onto shaky legs.

"Here goes nothing," I said to no one in particular. 'Here goes everything' would have been more accurate.

I spotted Gavin at a table against the wall before he noticed me so I saw his face change when he did. His lips turned up in a broad smile and his eyes lit up like deep emerald gems that caught the light. My heart skipped a beat. He was even sexier than I remembered, which seemed impossible since he was godlike in my mind.

It felt like I was moving in slow motion toward him. He stood with expectant eyes and took my hands as I approached. "Hello, beautiful."

"Fancy meeting you here." I stared into those eyes that had gotten me from the start.

"Funny what happens when you follow your heart."

My throat closed and I thought I might faint, or cry, or cry before fainting. Gavin had indeed brought my heart with him and he held it in his hands. "Your heart brought you to Sam Wu?"

"My heart brought me to you."

He cradled my face and lowered his lips to mine. I might have collapsed if he hadn't slipped one hand around my waist to draw me close. His scent took me back to the island and made me wish we were there in his cottage on the beach and far from this real life. I was so lost in the kiss I couldn't say how long we'd been there when a gruff voice interrupted our shameless PDA.

"You finish your kissy kissy? Food is getting cold." The waiter reached around us to drop the steaming plates on the table.

I chuckled and took the seat Gavin motioned toward. "That's the charm of the place."

"You know this is my kind of service. Makes me feel like home."

"Yeah, the wait staff trained at the same school as Morgan's."

I let Gavin serve me food but I didn't think I could eat. I pushed the food around on my plate to help it cool. "What prompted this surprise trip?"

Gavin shrugged and grinned. "I was just in the neighborhood."

"Ah, are you here on some sort of business?" It would make more sense if he happened to be in town for another reason.

Gavin's mouth twisted into a confused scowl. "No! I came here for you, woman."

I tried to breathe but the air caught like baby hiccups all the way in as I stared into his unwavering gaze.

Gavin reached across the table for my hand. "I never should have let you leave without telling you how I felt. I was afraid you wouldn't take me seriously. I still am."

"Traveling nearly three thousand miles is pretty convincing. Go on."

"It sounds terribly cliché but I've never felt the way you made me feel with anyone. And you get me. You saw through my defenses from the start and made it easy to be myself with you. I couldn't tell you any of that, though. I mean, you're way out of my league."

I chuckled at that. I thought he was way out of mine.

Gavin's voice trembled as he continued. "But I should have told you."

I was touched but I kept the cynical shell cinched tight around my heart. "Told me what exactly?"

"That I didn't want you to go. That I couldn't picture tomorrow without you. That I knew it was impossible but I wanted you to stay." Gavin's deep breath was as shaky as mine felt. "It seemed ridiculous to hope that you'd leave your life behind and stay with me, but that's what I wanted. Then I looked at my own life, and I wasn't sure I even wanted it. When something I was sure I *did* want was slipping away, I realized I would happily leave it all behind to have the chance to be with you, Tessa."

What was he saying? Had he bought a one-way ticket to San Francisco? Maybe he was crazier than I thought. "I wouldn't ask you to give up your life either."

"You don't have to ask me. I'm ready for something different. That's part of why I had to come see you—to tell you about an opportunity."

I cocked my head. "What's that?"

"Clifton's project in the Florida Keys."

"Oh, the resort? Does he want you to run the dive operation?"

"He practically wants me to *give* me the dive operation. I mean, I'll pay back the initial investment in profit sharing for the first five years—if I decide to do it."

He'd be crazy not to. "Why would you pass that up?"

"For a better offer."

Heat rose to my face. "I can't offer you anything that would compare with that opportunity. You should do it."

"I probably should. But I'd rather be anywhere with you." His jaw clenched, highlighting its sharp angles to make my stomach flip over itself as he continued. "I know you're established here. This is your home. If this is where I have to be to be with you, then I'll move. I hear there's great diving in the kelp forests."

I needn't have worried about my heart in his hands. He laid his own brazenly at my feet. But the cynical part of me that thought I wasn't worthy of his love wouldn't let me believe it might be real. "You hate city life. You said so."

"I hate living without you. If you love it here, I'm sure I will, too. Where you are is where I want to be."

I nearly choked on my words but they flowed like a fountain. "I don't know where I want to be. I've been miserable the whole week I've been back. I hate the traffic and all the people and the weather. Not to mention my job. I really hate that."

Gavin's hand covered mine on the table. "Maybe you're ready for a change. Come with me."

That he was serious was finally sinking in, but I continued to argue out of stubbornness as much as a protective instinct. "And do what?"

"Work from there. Do something new. Or work with me." His grin melted me. "You're smart and resourceful. You'll figure something out, something brilliant no doubt."

Despite his youth, Gavin was confident enough to recognize my strength. More. He revered it. That might have been his sexiest trait. I struggled to pluck a response from my swirling thoughts. "I don't know what I want to do with my life. I'm having a real-life existential crisis."

Gavin was quick with a witty reply, another of his sexy traits. "Real life *is* an existential crisis."

Chuckling helped calm me down. "Waxing philosophical, are we?"

"One of my favorite pastimes." He leaned onto his elbows on the table to get closer. "Listen, beautiful, I don't know what I'm supposed to be doing with my life either, but that's not the question."

My brow wrinkled quizzically but my breath quickened. "What is the question then?"

"The question is: do you want to do it with me? Because wherever and whatever it is—I want to do it with you."

There it was in plain English. Nothing to interpret or second guess. A clear declaration and a clear question.

My heart pounding in my chest reminded me to answer from there. "I didn't want to leave you either. But it seemed so impossible that what we had was real that I barely let myself imagine it."

"I thought it might be impossible, too, but that doubt is what limits us. Anything we dare to imagine, and even what we're afraid to, is possible."

"You really are a philosopher at heart."

"You ought to know. You've had my heart since you left." His Irish accent when he said "heart" made mine flutter almost as much as his mirroring my own thoughts did.

We'd been holding one another's hearts without knowing it. Now that I knew I had his, I didn't want to give it back.

A world of infinite possibilities was a far more appealing alternative to my pigeonholed existence, but it was crazy. "We barely know each other. It might never work."

"I know how you make me feel. In my experience, this is the sort of thing that comes along once in a lifetime. I can't imagine life without you. I don't want to." He stared so intently into my eyes that I felt him trying to read my thoughts. "If you feel the same way, we should give it a chance. We can decide *where* we'll do that later. But for now, just say yes."

I felt like I was standing on the back of the dive boat, afraid to jump. I either had to take the plunge or let the opportunity pass me by. "If you're okay with that level of uncertainty, then yes, I think we should give it a chance." I'd be crazy not to.

"That's all the certainty I need."

His eyes held mine, peering so deeply I thought I might splinter. After several hypnotic seconds, I broke his gaze to look down at the plates we'd barely touched. The only thing I was hungry for sat across from me. "Should we get out of here?"

"Definitely." Gavin glanced up to look for the offensive waiter. "I'm almost afraid to ask for the check."

"I'm sure he'll be thrilled to see us go."

Gavin's hand on my back felt like it belonged there as we made our way out to the sidewalk. "I have a nice room on Union Square."

"That sounds lovely. But I have a dog that needs a walk in my nice apartment in Pacific Heights. Do you mind if we go to my place instead?"

Gavin's eyes were serious but his smile was playful. "I told you, woman, I will follow you anywhere."

My heart swelled in my chest and the hint of possession when he called me "woman" made my panties wet. I wanted to kiss him when he said, "And you have a dog? I'd love to meet him—or her."

If he didn't like dogs, it would never work. "Him. Boomer. I didn't tell you about Boomer?"

Gavin shook his head. "I'd remember Boomer."

I ordered a ride on my phone and grinned. "Boomer is unforgettable. The car is just around the corner so you'll see for yourself soon enough."

Gavin's arm slipped around my waist to pull me into his chest. His lips brushed the tip of my nose, sending a pulse into my core when he whispered. "Not soon enough."

CHAPTER 29

*I*t was all I could do not to climb on Gavin's lap on the way home. All the longing I'd bottled up while pushing him from my mind for the past week came rushing out in a swift stream that I'd willingly let carry me away.

Boomer kept my passion in check when he ambushed us at the door. "Hey, buddy." I scratched behind his ears to try to calm him but he wiggled free of my hold and jumped up to land his paws on my chest. I stumbled backward before I got my footing. "He knows better than to jump but he reverted to bad habits while I was away. I think it was separation anxiety." I scratched under Boomer's jaw before I pushed him down.

"I can relate to that." Gavin smiled as he stroked the tuft of hair on top of Boomer's head while the dog sniffed his legs. "Missing you made me want to jump all over you when I saw you again, too."

"Very funny." I smirked. Boomer's tail wagged so hard his

whole body shook while he looked up at Gavin. "He likes you. He's so excited he can barely contain himself."

Gavin scratched up and down Boomer's back. "Aw, I like you too, buddy." Gavin grinned up at me. "You know dogs are a good judge of character."

"So I hear." I chuckled. "I'd offer you a drink but it would be cruel not to walk him first."

"Of course, let's take this beast for a stroll."

Boomer bounced like an oversized and clumsy rabbit while I pulled the leash off the hook by the door. "Jeez, Boom. You're acting like a puppy. Chill." I wrestled him to clip the leash to his collar.

Gavin took my hand as we strolled several blocks, stopping every few feet for Boomer to sniff the remnant scents of those who'd walked before him. "What a great neighborhood."

"I know. We were so lucky to get in when we did. I'd never pay what it costs to buy here now, even if I had the money. This city has gotten so crazy expensive it hardly seems worth it. Working seventy hours a week to pay your mortgage."

"The American dream."

"More like a nightmare." I was surprised by my own disillusion. I'd bought into that dream for two decades but it seemed so pointless now.

"Well, Pacific Heights doesn't seem like a bad place to be stuck."

I loved that he'd remembered me telling him the same about his island home. "Is anywhere a good place to be stuck though? I mean, the nicest cell in the joint is still prison at the end of the day."

"Who's waxing philosophical now?" Gavin squeezed my hand and grinned as he tugged to stop me from starting up the walk to my house. "You're only stuck if you choose to be. Here's a secret"—he lowered his voice to whisper in my ear—"the cells aren't locked."

It was true. I'd chosen my path. I'd trapped myself in an open cage. Gavin offered me a glimpse of the door. That's why I was so afraid to fall for him. "Escape is scarier than captivity."

"And *that* is the trap."

I fiddled with the key in the lock. "You're not wrong."

Gavin stroked my hair. "Oh, I know. I keep flying back to the damn cage."

"You don't have to. It's a choice." I swung the door open and held out my hand for him to pass.

He paused to meet my gaze. "I *chose* to come here for you."

I hung Boomer's leash and suddenly felt nervous to be alone with Gavin after we'd bared our souls. Still fully clothed, I felt more naked than I'd ever been with him.

"Can I make you drink? I bought a bottle of Hendricks."

Gavin stepped closer to take my hands. "I'd rather have a tour of the rest of the apartment first."

The heat in me melted my nervousness away. "There's not much more to see."

"I'm looking at everything I ever need to see." Gavin's hungry gaze traveled down my front before he grabbed me by the wrists and pulled me hard against him. "God, I've missed you."

The heat between us radiated up through me in a rush when he pulled me toward the open door of the bedroom. We barely made it through the doorway before Gavin's mouth was over mine. His palms slid over my hips to lift my skirt. The throbbing between my thighs took my breath.

I tugged his shirt up his back and he pulled away from the kiss long enough to let me slip it off. He reached around my neck to carefully lower my zipper and trailed his fingers down my arms to my hands, causing goosebumps to rise in the wake of his touch. His fingers laced through mine and squeezed hard to hold me in the kiss. I sighed into his mouth as an electrifying surge of yearning consumed me—a want deeper than I'd ever known.

I hurried to unbutton his jeans while he slipped my dress up my back. I gasped as my lips left his and our eyes locked before he pulled my dress over my head. Gavin's lips turned up in a smile as his eyes moved over me. He pushed a chestnut wave of hair gently from my face, leaving his fingertips on my cheek in the slightest whisper of a touch. "You're so fucking gorgeous."

My hands moved over the firm contours of his chest and abs. "You're the sexiest man I've ever known." A ginger blond lock fell into his jade eyes when he stumbled as he tried to step out of his jeans that I pushed over his hips. He looked like an underwear model.

His admiring eyes found mine. "I knew you were gorgeous the minute I saw you. But you're so much more than that."

I fumbled with the waistband of his boxers to reach his

hardness and started to drop to my knees when Gavin's hands caught under my arms to pull me back up to him.

"Slow down, beautiful. Let's take our time." He cupped my face in his hands and gently lowered his lips to mine. His palms moved over me in a slow study of my every curve while he nibbled gently at my lower lip. He guided me to the bed and lowered me softly to the pillow, his lips trailing down my stomach. His teeth tugged at the waist of my panties while he looked up with hungry eyes. I couldn't wait for him to devour me but I knew he wouldn't give me what I wanted too soon.

He kissed my inner thighs like they were kissing him back as he gently pushed my panties aside to slide two fingers into my warmth. I gasped while his other hand moved back up my belly to squeeze my breast with its hardened nipple pressing into the black lace of my bra.

He hit one pleasure spot after another as fingers explored me with deliberate thrusts that reached all sides. He already knew my body so well, yet he seemed to want to discover every last inch of me again. My body pulsed in response, gripping his fingers tight as the fingertips of his other hand rubbed over my nipple, squeezing it through the lace when I started to moan. He kissed up my thigh until his mouth hovered over my throbbing mound. The heat of his breath ignited the yearning in me that only he could.

Gavin's emerald gaze held me in its trance while his fingers pressed into a spot behind my pubic bone. My eyes widened and I gasped as the pressure of his touch stirred an electric storm deep inside me. Gavin grinned deviously before biting into my lace-covered sex. His teeth raking over my clit through my panties while he gently twisted my nipple sent ripples of pleasure through me.

I grasped around his fingers that prodded into that magic spot deep in my core while the wave of contractions took over. I writhed under him, gripping at the sheets and gasping for air between the string of moans. His touch lightened as my orgasm abated. Gavin smiled into my eyes from between my legs.

"You have the prettiest pussy. I can't get enough of it." Moving the lace of my panties to expose my clit that craved his touch, he ran his tongue inside one of my lips and back down the other in slow circles that felt like he was French kissing it. The tip of his tongue teased my clit until it was firm, and then flicked harder and faster until my hips bucked under him.

My fingers burrowed into Gavin's hair while his arms around my thighs held me captive under his mouth. His eyes held mine while his groans vibrated through me and I moaned until the trembling stilled.

I tried to catch my breath but Gavin slowly rolling my panties over my hips took it away again. He worked a hand underneath me to unhook my bra, slipping it off to admire my breasts.

"I've never been so obsessed with a woman's body. It's all I can see when I close my eyes at night." His lips covered my breast, his tongue tickling my nipple as he sucked it softly.

All those nights that he'd flooded my thoughts, I'd been in his too. I breathed heavy into his neck as his weight settled onto me. "I haven't stopped thinking about your body, and what you do to mine, since the first time we touched."

He ran his fingers into my hair as his thick erection pressed into my thigh. "What you do to my body is astounding."

The anticipation of him inside me was a dull ache that made me clutch his girth when he entered my wetness. My breath caught as I stretched taut around him until he reached my limit. He fit perfectly.

Watching my face react to him inside me made his mouth twist into a smile before it covered mine. His kiss consumed me in a wet fever as he slid in and out of me in measured thrusts, taking his time to find the spots in me that only he had discovered.

Gavin paused when he was as deep as he could get and then pushed a little deeper. I clenched around him and wished he could stay there forever. He lifted from the kiss to stare into my eyes while he pulsed under my grasp.

I felt his heart pounding through his chest as I breathed in the breath that he breathed out. My moans were echoed in his when a swell of sensation traveled through me in a torrent. I tightened around him in fast flicks of contraction that culminated in a summit higher than I'd ever reached. Gavin's eyes locked on mine as I came, holding me at my peak until his throbbing inside me reached its limit and he pulled out to slide over my slippery clit while he released into the scant space between us.

Life with Gavin might be one long string of orgasms. I wouldn't complain.

After we caught our breath, I went to clean myself up and returned with a glass of water.

"We should hydrate." I took a long gulp before handing him the glass. He downed the water and handed it back to me.

"Thank you, beautiful." He held the covers back for me to settle in beside him.

I snuggled into his side. "I hate for you to waste all that money on a nice room on Union Square, but I hope you're staying the night."

"I'm not going anywhere, beautiful." He turned to kiss my cheek. "Don't worry about the room. Clifton booked it for me."

"Oh yeah? How come?"

"Well, I'm flying to the Keys tomorrow to meet him."

I raised up onto his chest to look him in the eye. "Tomorrow?"

"Yeah, about that…"

I stared expectantly for the rest of the sentence.

"Do you want to come with me?" He smiled with hopeful eyes.

I looked at him like he was crazy. "To the Keys—tomorrow?"

His fingers ran through my hair and down my back. "I know it's short notice. But it's the weekend. I'd have you back in time for work Monday."

I shook my head no but I wanted to say yes. "I can't leave again. I just got back. Boomer would disown me."

Gavin flashed a crooked grin. "Then bring him with us."

"That's complicated. I don't have the paperwork or a crate that he would need to fly."

"You don't need any of that on a private jet."

"Seriously?" It shouldn't have surprised me but it was so absurd that it did.

He strummed my spine. "So is that a yes?"

There was no good reason not to, and a million and one reasons to go. I nodded slowly, still stunned. "I suppose it is."

"I suppose you just made me the happiest man in the City by the Bay." Gavin hugged me into his chest for a soft kiss. "The only thing is…we have to be there by lunchtime."

"Lunch? On the east coast? What time do we take off?"

"Six o'clock."

"That's in five hours! I need to pack." I wiggled free from his embrace and started toward my closet.

"Pack? Bring some shorts, T-shirts, and one of your hot little bikinis."

"I'm a girl. It's never that simple."

"You're a woman, and there's nothing simple about you."

CHAPTER 30

*A*fter three hours sleep, we Ubered to Gavin's hotel to grab his bag on the way to the airport. Boomer sat between us in the oversized SUV, resting his head on Gavin's knee. Gavin rubbed Boomer's neck gently. "I think he likes me."

"I think he loves you." That made two of us.

I stopped and stared up at the jet that was much larger than I imagined in the light of dawn. I looked back over my shoulder to Gavin while I followed Boomer up the steps. "I feel like a movie star."

The cabin was every bit as nice as the interior of Clifton's yacht. A table for two was set between two captain's chairs near the front. A long sofa lined the opposite wall on the other side of a bulkhead followed by another four captain's chairs and another sofa. It was huge. "Fuck me."

"That can probably be arranged."

I rolled my eyes. "This is over the top."

"Would you expect anything less?"

We took our seats and buckled up. "It kind of makes you wonder what the resort is like."

"I'm very curious to see what they've done to that island in the Keys. If it turns my stomach, there's nothing to consider. And that is a distinct possibility."

"I'm sure it's gorgeous. But I know what you mean. Working for something you don't feel good about is no fun."

"Yeah, I think I'm done with that."

I wished I could say the same.

A flight attendant appeared from the front of the plane, extremely chipper considering the early hour. "Good morning." Boomer jumped to his feet but thankfully didn't jump on the slight woman. "Well, hello there." She patted Boomer's head as he stared up with his tongue dangling from his mouth. She glanced at our laps. "Great, you're all buckled in. He doesn't need a seatbelt, but try to keep him still during take-off. We should be moving any minute. I'll serve you breakfast once we're in the air. Let me know if you need anything in the meantime."

Gavin grinned up at her. "We've got everything we need."

The take-off was so smooth even Boomer was calm and soon we were above the clouds. We devoured the delectable French toast and fresh fruit breakfast and made ourselves comfortable on the sofa.

I settled under Gavin's arm and kicked off my shoes to tuck my feet up under me on the couch. Boomer jumped up and inched closer until he was against my legs. I rested my hand over Gavin's belly. "So how far along are you in negotiations with Clifton?"

"Far enough that he's offered me pretty much everything. But nothing is written. I didn't want to get serious until I know if it's something I'd even want to do."

"When would he want you to start?"

"They open in a month. So, now."

He might be leaving again. He said he wouldn't go without me, but what if he should? If it was the perfect opportunity, I wouldn't want to hold him back. I couldn't say that, so I said the first dumb thing that came to mind. "Wow. That's nuts."

"Yeah. We'll see. It's only one of the infinite possibilities." Gavin hugged me in tight to his side.

I rested my head on his shoulder. Infinite possibilities all just a choice away.

We dozed on and off until the flight attendant asked us to take our seats for landing at the minuscule Marathon airport.

A man in a white linen shirt and tailored indigo shorts waited when we deplaned. "Welcome to the Keys." He shook each of our hands and eyed Boomer curiously like he hadn't been expecting him. "Follow me."

He led us to the car—another huge SUV. Thank God there was space for Boomer. "We'll be there in about twenty-five minutes, depending on traffic. Enjoy the ride."

Enjoying the trip wasn't difficult. From what I could tell, the Keys were comprised of tiny strips of land connected by bridges—the Atlantic Ocean on the left and the Florida Bay which became the Gulf of Mexico on the right. The water was the same crystal blue I'd never seen before Grand

Cayman. Crossing the Seven Mile Bridge put the Golden Gate to shame.

"From Seven Mile Beach to Seven Mile Bridge." Gavin chuckled at the parallel between Grand Cayman and the Keys. Though similar in many ways, the Keys seemed more virgin.

Mangrove trees lined the stretch of road south of the bridge which became more remote with every mile. It seemed so undeveloped. There was still something wild and rustic about it. The thought of a five-star resort amidst the wilderness made my stomach churn. I knew exactly what Gavin meant. It would be hard to get on board with that even if it was the lap of luxury.

CHAPTER 31

I was lost in the scenery when the car slowed to turn into a large, virtually empty parking lot. We rolled to a stop in front of the lone building on the property, a small white cottage with indigo blue trim and a tasteful sign over the entrance that read Paradise Key Resort. I turned to Gavin, confused. "I thought you said the resort was opening in a month? Where's the hotel?"

The driver smiled at me in the rearview mirror and answered. "It's out there, on the island." He pointed toward the water where a speck of green was visible in the distance. "*That's* Paradise Key. *This* is where guests will take the boat out."

"Ah, this is just the parking lot." I turned to Gavin. "I didn't realize it was water access only." Talk about remote.

"Neither did I. Pretty cool though, right?"

"Very cool for those who want to get away from it all, for sure."

A long concrete dock stretched out into the crystalline water. The elaborately carved sign over the dock said it well. Welcome to Paradise.

When the driver was out of earshot retrieving our bags from the back of the car, I said, "I don't know anything about land prices in the Keys, but I bet this is a million-dollar parking lot."

Gavin nodded. "With the cost of the dock, easily double."

I could only imagine how much the whole project had cost. "It's mind-blowing."

The driver insisted on carrying our small bags out to the boat on the end of the dock. The navy-blue hull and shiny varnished wood trim gave the boat a classic feel. The captain offered me his hand to help me onboard. Boomer stood whining on the dock. "Come on, boy, you can jump that far." He was hesitant but finally made the leap after I patted my thighs.

The captain petted Boomer's back. "You're our first canine visitor." He looked up with a grin. "Make yourselves comfortable. It's only a mile and a half, so we'll be there before you know it."

We looked over the side as the boat sped over the glass-like water. "Does this remind you of home?"

Gavin put his arm around my back and pulled me into him. "This might be better than home."

Boomer had found his sea legs by the time we pulled up alongside the wooden dock. He jumped off as the attendant who met us at the boat got our bags.

I started down the dock but stopped in my tracks to take in

the view. To the right of the dock was a long stretch of sandy beach lined with palm trees large and small. You could tell which ones had come with the island and which had been added. To the left was a two-story white wooden house with dark blue shutters. I recognized Clifton approaching the dock from the beach.

He met us halfway down the long dock, stopping to pet Boomer on the head before he kissed my cheek. "I'm thrilled you could join us, Tessa. I'm sure Gavin is even more pleased." He landed a firm hand on Gavin's shoulder and smiled like a proud father. "Welcome to Paradise."

"You aren't kidding. This place looks amazing."

"I hope you like it so much you want to stay." He patted Gavin's shoulder before starting down the dock. "Lunch is waiting. Shall we?"

Clifton gestured toward the ornate wooden staircase inside the entrance that wound up to the second floor. "The dining room is upstairs, but let me show you the bar and billiard room first." He led us past a hostess station through an equally ornate carved wooden doorway.

A sitting area lined with bookshelves already stocked with books to the left sat behind two antique-looking pool tables. A long wooden bar stretched along the back wall to another sitting area with large leather sofas and chairs. A canoe hung on the wall at the other end. Across from the bar, windows opened to the porch that overlooked the beach and bay, flanked by several pairs of leather chairs with a small table between them, each with a unique lamp. The detail to design was spectacular.

Gavin slid his hand over the wooden bar. "Hemingway would have loved this place."

Clifton's face lit up in an appreciative grin. "That's exactly what I was going for."

I could picture the white-bearded author lounging on one of the leather sofas in the library with a glass of rum and a cigar. I loved that they both liked Hemingway enough to make the connection.

Clifton led us up the grand staircase to the dining room filled with several empty tables. A waitress showed us to the table that was set for us on the terrace. She smiled down at Boomer. "I'll bring him some water."

I smiled back at her. "Thank you."

The waitress poured three glasses of white wine from the chiller stand beside the table before graciously backing away. Clifton rubbed his hands together excitedly. "I hope you're in the mood for lobster."

I smiled as I spread my napkin in my lap. "Always."

Gavin snickered. "Always in the mood, are you?"

I shot Gavin a wide-eyed glare but I couldn't help but smile. "For lobster—always."

Clifton either didn't seem to notice or politely ignored Gavin's suggestive comment. "Conch chowder is a local favorite," he said as the waitress served three bowls of soup.

I blew on a steaming spoonful. "It smells amazing." The rich flavors of the tomato broth laden with chunks of seafood exploded in my mouth. "And tastes even better."

Clifton smiled warmly. "I'm glad you like it. So tell me, Tessa, what do you do in San Francisco?"

"I own a marketing and design firm. Actually, I'm half owner.

I have a partner." A bitter taste threatened to invade my happy palate.

"Interesting." Clifton sat back in his chair to allow the waitress to serve our entrees.

I changed the subject. Work was the last thing I wanted to think about right then. "It's quite amazing what you've done here. Logistically this must have been a challenge to build with no road."

"That's an understatement. But building was a walk in the park compared to the permit process."

Gavin nodded. "Judging by how much of the undeveloped land I saw on the way here, I imagine the building restrictions are strict."

"It took three years. 'Long is the way and hard, that out of Hell leads up to Light.'"

I recognized the Milton quote. "Paradise Lost. How apropos."

Clifton's smile widened. "Paradise Found is more like it. If we weren't an eco-resort, it never would have happened."

I was busy savoring the lobster in a Thai chili sauce with mango but my ears perked up. "Eco-resort?"

"Yes, everything was designed to have minimal environmental impact. We have solar power for all our hot water and wind generators for half our power. Wherever possible we used green materials. All organic waste is composted. We make our own fresh water with a desalination plant and our sewage treatment plant makes greywater we can use for the gardens in the dry season."

I blinked in disbelief. Not only was it done in exquisitely

good taste, but it was also sustainable. "An eco-resort for the Tesla crowd."

"Your understanding of marketing is astute."

My cheeks flushed at such high praise from a business tycoon. "Thank you."

"We use a firm out of Chicago. So far they seem good but we'll see how they perform. I'd be happy to give you the contract if they falter."

I was flattered at his generous offer but it seemed odd considering he'd never seen our work. "That's very kind."

"Provided of course that we're happy with your proposal, but I don't think you'd have a problem with that, especially after having experienced Paradise Key."

"For your sake, I hope you're happy with the Chicago firm and they help make your opening a success. Marketing this place would be easy, though, to be honest." Money was certainly no object on the advertising front, I imagined.

"We're already booked for the first two months. That's why I have to get this dive business sorted."

Gavin sipped his white wine before responding. "Wow, that's great. What's your capacity?"

"Eighty, but that's at four guests per bungalow so it could be as little as forty even when we're full."

"That's a lot of divers." Gavin placed his napkin on his plate.

Clifton grinned. "That's why we have a big boat."

Gavin grinned excitedly. "I can't wait to see it."

"We can go now if you're ready. Unless you want dessert?"

Gavin patted his belly. "No, I'm stuffed. How about you, beautiful?"

His compliment made my breath quicken. "Me too. I'm ready when you are."

"That's what I love about you." Gavin's wry expression made me chuckle.

His hand drifted to my back as we followed Clifton toward the stairs. "I'll show you to your house. Your bags are already there."

Fern-lined brick pathways snaked through the property. An assortment of one and two-story white wooden cottages in the same style as the restaurant were scattered through the lush vegetation. The path stretched under the shade of the palms to the end of the long stretch of sandy beach and beyond. After passing a stand of mangroves, we arrived at a smaller beach. Clifton led us up the steps to the smaller of the two houses that flanked the ends of the small shoreline. I was no longer surprised by the tasteful decor I'd come to expect, but I was as impressed as ever. It looked like a magazine spread. The enormous open floor plan kitchen-living-dining area downstairs was flooded with light from windows on all sides.

We followed Clifton out the French doors to the porch beyond the living room. Steps went down to a rectangular pool with a jacuzzi on one end. "The pool is small but there's a larger communal pool on the property."

Beside the jacuzzi was a shower nearly hidden in the vegetation. I squeezed Gavin's hand. "Look, there's an outdoor shower. Just like home."

"Maybe even better than home."

"I hope that's how you feel about the house because this is where you'll live if you decide to accept my offer."

Seriously?

"This is not what I was expecting when you said housing on-site would be included."

"The staff housing is on the other end of the island, past the restaurant. This house was built for me, but I realized as soon as the walls were up that I needed more space so I built a bigger house at the other end of the beach. I thought you'd be happier here than in staff housing—as long as you don't mind being my neighbor."

"I'd be honored." Gavin raised his eyebrows at me in a *'Can you believe this?'* expression.

"Lucky for you this one comes with its own pool and hot tub."

Clifton turned to me. "Every cottage has its own pool and jacuzzi—and outdoor shower—none quite as nice as yours though." I liked thinking of it as mine even if only for a couple of days. I smiled as he continued, "I'll let you show yourself to the bedroom upstairs. Make yourself at home. I'll have Gavin back within the hour."

"Thank you, but, please, take your time. Boomer will keep me company."

I wandered up to the bedroom and could only smile at the stunning beauty. A king-size wooden poster bed with a canopy of gauze sat in the center of the expansive room. A terrace looked out over the water on each end of the room. If this wasn't paradise, it didn't exist.

I spotted our bags on a luggage stand and debated whether I

should change into a swimsuit. I couldn't decide if I wanted to read in the hammock on the porch or go for a swim. The answer was neither. I was itching to explore the rest of the island.

I put on my excited mommy voice and animated Boomer. "Let's go for a walk." He jumped up to dance a circle on his hind legs.

Boomer sniffed his way along the edge of the path through the lush tropical gardens. The guest cottages were secluded amidst the greenery with an abundance of space between them. We soon reached the shore opposite the sandy beach. Only two small single-level cottages were built on the water with a mangrove stand between them.

Boomer bounded into the water at the shadow of a large ray flitting past a few feet offshore.

Boomer's tongue swung as he frolicked in the shallow water. I let my mind wander while I watched him play. It was hard to believe Gavin had the opportunity to live here. It was right up his Robinson Crusoe alley. I was scared he might want to stay but even more afraid he wouldn't. It would be too much pressure on the relationship from the start to pass this by and to try to make it work in San Francisco. Even though he'd probably stay in the open cage of the city… Gavin was an island boy at heart.

I eyed the idyllic cottage on the beach, a simple hut compared with the house that would be Gavin's. In another life, I could see myself there. Real life was a little more complicated than tropical paradise fantasies.

It was better not to consider hypothetical situations at this stage. Gavin would know soon enough if it was a real deal.

"Come on, boy." Boomer rushed to my side and shook himself proudly. I laughed as I jumped back to escape the spray of droplets from his fur. "Lucky for you there's an outdoor shower."

By the time I got Boomer rinsed and half-dried, an hour had passed. I pulled my kindle out and was headed to the porch to read when Gavin returned.

He was grinning ear to ear. "Can you believe this place?"

"No, I really can't. It's incredible. But tell me, how did it go? Did you guys get into details?"

"Yeah, we covered pretty much everything."

"And… Is it a good deal?"

"Fuck, it's an awesome deal. I mean, unbelievable in the literal sense. The boat is spectacular and the shop is stocked with brand new gear. It's ready to go!"

"So he's offering to sell the business to you or make you a partner?"

"It would be mine but with profit sharing. He offered me the whole operation for twenty percent of the profits. The boat and gear would be mine after I pay them off with an extra thirty percent of the profits for however many years that would take. I'd have to run the numbers to project. After that, the twenty percent would cover the rent of the building and this lovely cottage."

"So you get a turnkey business with zero initial investment?" It sounded too good to be true. "What's the catch?"

"I keep thinking there must be one, too, but if there is, I can't see it. It seems like he just wants me to do it."

"And you get to live here? That's a dream, Gavin. I'm happy for you."

"I haven't accepted yet." The way the light danced off his eyes as his gaze held mine made my chest constrict.

"You'd be crazy not to accept."

Gavin stepped in and pulled me close, looking into my eyes with a boyish grin. "I'd be crazy to accept if you won't come with me. We don't have to decide that now though. Let's go for a swim."

"Great idea. I'll change into my suit. I've been dying to get to the beach." A week back in San Francisco had made me miss the sand and the sun.

Gavin's mouth twisted mischievously. "I was thinking more along the lines of skinny dipping in the pool."

The thick perimeter of tall bamboo plants obscured us from view on all sides. What the hell? "Sounds divine."

"We don't have to meet Clifton until seven so we have a few hours."

I knew what he had in mind and I liked where he was going with it.

We kissed our way from the pool to the hot tub and back to the pool before we were horny and waterlogged. Gavin led me by the hand upstairs and laid me gently on the bed, reminiscent of his tender handling of me last night. My head spun while he kissed every part of me, taking me twice to the brink before I fell over the cliff of ecstasy. He found the right spot with every part of him and the waves of climax came twice more while he whispered sweet words I tried not to remember. Trying not to think about how much I'd miss him when he was gone again made me think only that as we laid panting for breath in the middle of the gigantic bed.

Luckily there was no time to go too far down that dead end. I'd lost track of time but Gavin was paying attention. "We should get showered and ready for dinner." He looked out the windows toward the bay. "The sun is getting low."

CHAPTER 32

*C*lifton was waiting at a table on the porch of the bar. "I'm having a cocktail. I hope you'll join me." He held out his hands for us to sit at the table.

I smiled as I took my seat. "Hemingway wouldn't have it any other way."

Gavin smiled up at the waitress who approached the table. "Hemingway might not approve, but I'd love a gin and tonic."

"Any gin in particular?"

"Hendricks if you have it."

"And for you?" She smiled my way.

"The same please, with extra lime."

Clifton asked, "What do you think of the project?"

I was surprised to look up from my drink to find the question directed at me. "I think you've done an incredible job. This is quite the undertaking."

"It's been years in the making, but it's finally finished—almost."

"Cheers to that." Gavin raised his glass.

"The only thing lacking to make it complete is you and your business."

"Thank you for putting it that way. I'll run some numbers and think it over. I appreciate your very generous offer."

"I'm happy to offer you the opportunity if you're looking to break out on your own. Don't feel pressured, though. I know your family and your life are back on our island and it's not an easy decision to leave. I have bids from two local operators to buy the business. I'm not offering them what I'm offering you, of course. But that's because I'd rather have you here."

Gavin nodded appreciatively. "That means a lot."

The way Gavin gingerly skirted any remark indicating his intentions impressed me. He was evading commitment to keep all options open. Smart man.

I interjected with a question that had occurred to me on the walk around the island earlier, as much out of genuine curiosity as to redirect the conversation to take Gavin out of the hot seat. "How many boats do you have to bring guests from the shore?"

"Two for now."

"What happens when you have the whole place booked for an event? You have fifty to eighty guests arriving and leaving at virtually the same time. That won't be enough."

"We have the dive boat that we can charter in those cases. But I like the way you think."

I chuckled. "It's what my brain does—logistics. I'm glad you appreciate it. Some people find it annoying, especially when it's unsolicited and none of my business."

"On the contrary, I find it fascinating—and potentially useful. Do you have experience in event planning?"

My brow wrinkled at the odd question. "Not formally, no. Other than a few team-building retreats we've done for our staff over the years. Why?"

"Because we're looking for someone. We have our first wedding booked for December and the local wedding planners we've interviewed have a different vision than what we're looking for."

"Ah, I understand."

"I think you do. I also believe your marketing prowess is exactly what we need to promote the event side of the business. Actually, the wedding in December is the owner of the Chicago firm that's doing our marketing."

"Really? They should be able to help you with that part of it then. That's just another campaign."

"I suppose they will. We'll see how it works out. But if I had someone on-site that could manage the logistics and the marketing for the events, it would be even better. That person would be quite valuable to the resort." He grinned. "I know you have your own business on the west coast, but if there was a way to lure you from it, I'd try."

His confidence in me might be misplaced but it made me feel good. It was nice to be appreciated. "Thank you for that."

"No need to thank me until you accept."

Clifton's unwavering gaze made me realize that he was

serious. For a second, it seemed like a real possibility. But there were no fairy tales in real life. "I wish I could. It sounds like a dream. But I have so much invested in my company that I'm not in a position to drop everything to follow a dream." I'd welded every junction in my carefully constructed cage myself. Open door or not, I couldn't just fly away.

"A life without chasing your dreams isn't really living, the way I see it."

"Isn't that the truth?" Gavin glanced my way as he answered Clifton.

"You're quite persuasive." I smiled at Clifton before turning to Gavin. "Both of you. But good luck trying to refuse his charm."

Clifton interjected before Gavin could respond. "I hope you're not looking to refuse, but I'll stop trying to recruit you two. Let's go upstairs. You must see the sunset from there before you go."

The waitress served us the finest Cabernet Sauvignon that had ever crossed my lips. As the sun approached the horizon, the lower half of the sky illuminated in rich warm bands.

Clifton swirled his wine, then held it up to inspect the "legs" dripping down the inside of the deep glass. He smiled through the glass in the orange-hued light. "They say when the sun touches the sea you can sometimes see the green flash. I think I saw it once, but I wondered afterward if I'd hallucinated it after wanting to see it so badly."

"Amazing. We have the rare spectacular sunset in San Francisco but we normally can't see the sun at all."

Gavin stared with playful eyes. "I suppose it makes you appreciate it that much more, a rare glimpse of beauty."

I peeled my eyes from his to follow the sun on its final descent to the sea. The fiery ball seemed to touch the water and spread out like it was melting on impact for the first long seconds before it sank into the water before our eyes. The sky changed from blood orange to purple in a spectacular display as we dined. Even the green flash couldn't have made it more perfect.

Clifton regaled us with stories of the history of the Keys while we enjoyed filet mignon cooked to medium-rare perfection in a gorgonzola sauce.

His eyes lit up like the evening sky with the passion for the tales he told. The Keys might have been the last of the American frontiers, complete with Indian attacks not long before the civil war.

Gavin was enthralled. "That's fascinating. It sounds like you've done a lot of reading."

Clifton nodded. "The Keys were the southernmost remnants of the wild wild west. The history is what made me fall in love with the place. There's still something wild and raw about it, such a juxtaposition to Miami a mere two hours away."

"There's a lot to fall in love with." Gavin glanced my way and winked almost imperceptibly. "How are you doing there, gorgeous?"

My eyelids felt heavy from the red wine and lack of sleep. "Starting to fade a little, but I'm good."

Gavin reached to squeeze my hand on the table. "I'm

exhausted, too." He turned back to Clifton. "I hope you don't mind if we turn in early."

"Of course, you've had a long day. I hope *you* don't mind if I stay here for a brandy." Clifton grinned as he stood to kiss my cheek goodbye.

I grinned after kissing him back. "Make Hemingway proud."

"Let's get you home." Gavin held me close to his side as we strolled home in the humid night air. I rested my head on his side and inhaled his musky scent mixed with the earthy ocean smells as he kissed my hair.

He led me by the hand up to the bedroom. I slipped out of my dress and settled onto Gavin's chest under the feathery duvet.

Gavin stroked my hair as he asked, "What did you think about Clifton's job offer?"

I chuckled sleepily. "I think he's as crazy as you are."

He kissed my cheek. "I might be crazy but I'm crazy for you."

I bit my lower lip and breathed him in. I'd never been head over heels for anyone before Gavin, but I didn't want him to make big mistake on my account. "You'd have to be crazy not to take this offer. This is your big chance."

"You're my big chance. Anything without you just won't do."

I lifted my head to look him in the eye. "Don't be ridiculous. You have a sure thing here. I can always come visit."

"You sound like you have your mind made up about not coming here with me. And if that's the case, I will happily forge a new path in the City by the Bay. I'm not going anywhere without you. Unless you've changed your mind about us? Because I'm sure. You're the one, Tessa, and I'm not going to let you get away again."

My heart melted but my skeptical inner voice told me it was too good to be true. "I thought you didn't believe in 'the one'? Didn't you tell Carlos that there's only 'the last one'?"

Gavin's eyes narrowed and a slight grin softened his serious look. "Were you eavesdropping the night I met you?"

I grinned shyly. "Maybe."

"Listen, woman, you *are* the last one. Not the last one as in the one before. The last one as in none will follow."

The only words that came were those that filled my thoughts. "I hope so."

He lifted his head to kiss my temple. "I know so. Goodnight, beautiful."

"Goodnight, handsome." My fingertips fanned over his chest hair while he traced a line down my back.

If home is where your heart is, mine was there, in his arms.

CHAPTER 33

The yellow light of sunrise streamed through the east-facing terrace, giving the room a golden glow that made it feel like I was still in a dream. I slid out from under Gavin's arm and was surprised to find Boomer still asleep on the sofa downstairs. I patted his side. "Hey, buddy. You wanna go outside?" Boomer's ears perked up and he jumped to his feet.

He led me along the path past the mangroves to the long stretch of beach and then raced ahead of me to zigzag along the water's edge. He circled back to repeat his circuit three times before I reached the pier. The sight of the boat at the end of the dock made me melancholy at the thought of leaving.

Gavin had worked his way under my skin. I believed him when he insisted that I was "the one" because I felt exactly the same.

I knew this opportunity was his dream come true. But he felt like mine. I couldn't let him go, but I couldn't let him stay. I was as twisted up inside as I'd been on Grand Cayman a week and a half ago. Worse. Then, it felt like a fling and there was no other option. Now, it felt like true love and I had a choice.

Boomer romped in and out of the crystal water ahead of me as we headed south, back down the beach with the backdrop of the peach and pink painted sky. The fresh ocean breeze filled me with a sense of freedom as I recalled the dream I'd awakened to on the morning of my divorce—the dream that had given me hope for the dawn of a new day.

This island, this life, this opportunity was not only Gavin's dream come true. It was mine, manifest.

The perfect man. The perfect job. In Paradise. This fairly tale could be my real life.

I kept telling myself I couldn't just up and leave my real life, but what I had with Gavin felt more real than anything I'd be leaving behind in San Francisco. Other than Elliot, there wasn't a single thing I'd truly miss.

I didn't love the city as much as I'd told myself I did all those years I'd been stuck there doing little more than working. Chuck had ruined work for me, so I didn't even have that anymore. Never having to see him again in my life was the cherry on top.

I would trade it all to wake up in Gavin's arms every day. I'd much rather do that here, with daily strolls on the beach and swims in the ocean, than there. The life I'd stubbornly clung to seemed insignificant compared the possibilities in front of me—infinite possibilities just a choice away.

Holding onto the past was the only thing stopping me from chasing my dreams. I was ready to let go.

~

Gavin was making coffee when I returned. "I was just going to come find you." He handed me a mug with a smile.

I smelled the brew and smiled. "I'm pretty sure *I* just found me."

He looked up inquisitively. "Existential crisis resolved?"

"Yep. I'm right where I'm supposed to be."

Gavin's playful expression turned curious. "Is that so?"

I took a deep breath to prepare me for the plunge I wasn't sure I was ready for but I was sure I had to take. I knew it in my soul. "Yes. I want to be wherever you are."

Gavin set his mug on the counter and took hold of my hands before he raised his eyes to mine. Tears brimmed up into the deep green fields that called me to roam. "I've known since you left a hole in my heart when you left Grand Cayman that with you, is right where I'm supposed to be."

I held his gaze. "I think we're both supposed to be right here, on this island."

Gavin blinked like he wasn't sure if he'd heard me correctly. "You want to stay?"

"Everything else in my life is uncertain. You're my sure thing." My gut feeling couldn't be denied. I let out my breath in a sigh, relieved to get it off my chest. "I've lived in my comfort zone for too long. It's time for a change. I'm ready." I'd leave everything I'd ever known to be by his side.

"I will go wherever you want because beside you is where I want to be. But I think we can make a nice life here. If you come here with me, Tessa, I promise I will never let you regret it." He paused to waggle his brow, squeezing my hand. "I'll be your Johnny if you'll be my June."

My cheeks flamed as I grinned at his reference. He was my other half. Just like Johnny and June. "If we keep chasing our dreams, we'll have nothing to regret."

If you can't wait to see how dreamy Tessa and Gavin's new life in Paradise Key will be, be sure to check out Christmas in Paradise! Elliot comes for the holidays too. (Yep, meant to do that!)

—Spoiler Alert!! —The wedding that Tessa organizes involves a favorite character from the already complete Happier Ever After Series which you can start now!

And if you do GoodReads, please be sure to review! I love interacting with readers there and I read every. single. one.

Be the first to know about new releases, freebies, and exclusive content one my newsletter at MacyButler.com

ACKNOWLEDGMENTS

As with the others before it, this book would not have come to be without the love and support of my two amazing teenage sons.

Thanks to my editor, Margot Mostert, whose patience with me seems endless.

And my BFF, Keri Peyton, for all the listening and talking about my characters like they're our friends.

I am eternally grateful to the plethora of fellow authors who continue to offer advice and support. I'm constantly in awe at how some people want to lift up others around them. One day, I will pay it forward.

ABOUT THE AUTHOR

Macy is a foul-mouthed tennis addict whose sweet side comes out with her two teenage sons. Strong, smart heroines inspire her as much as hard-bodied heroes with hearts of gold.

When she's not on the tennis court or locked in her writing cave, you'll find Macy on the beach with a sunset cocktail or out on the boat near their home in the Florida Keys.

Connect with Macy, and get exclusive content and special offers at www.macybutler.com

- [f] facebook.com/macybutlerauthor
- [O] instagram.com/macysracyreads
- [a] amazon.com/author/macybutler
- [BB] bookbub.com/authors/macy-butler

ALSO BY MACY BUTLER

Happier Ever After series

Unholy Trinity- a steamy romantic suspense duet

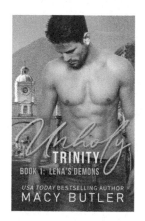

Made in United States
Orlando, FL
03 November 2021

10175109R10167